THE
PERFECT
DAUGHTER

KERRY WILKINSON

Bookouture

Published by Bookouture in 2021

An imprint of Storyfire Ltd.
Carmelite House
50 Victoria Embankment
London EC4Y 0DZ

www.bookouture.com

ISBN: 978-1-80019-729-9
eBook ISBN: 978-1-80019-728-2

PROLOGUE

There was a time in my teenage years when I remembered everything. I didn't bother revising for my exams because I was one of *those* kids. The smart-arses. The little sods who somehow got by, despite spending around forty per cent of class time trying to ping a rubber band or hair tie off the head of whoever was sitting at the front. By the summer, I'd be doing an exam in the stifling gym, and able to recall with perfect clarity something that Mr Rodgers had waffled on about five months previously.

That was only the start. I could remember the directions to get to places, even if I'd only been there once – and long before Google Maps turned everyone into a cheat. I'd know the birthdays of all my friends and family, plus I could reel off song lyrics for entire albums, even if they'd only just come out. Memory was my superpower.

And now…

Now, I can barely remember the day of the week. I spent last year thinking I was forty-two when I was, in fact, forty-one. Last week, I went to IKEA and forgot where I parked the car. I went to the security office and said it had been nicked, only to find out I'd parked two rows away from where I'd been searching. Even then, I walked past it twice before the officer pointed to my car and asked if it was mine.

Today's aberration is that, once again, I didn't pick up the bags for life before heading into the supermarket. Every time I get to the checkout and have to pay seven pence for a new bag, it kills a tiny bit of my soul.

It doesn't help that today's plastic bags are thinner than Polly from three doors down after she had the gastric band fitted. As I heave my shopping into the back of the car, placing them on top of the unused bags for life, it feels as if I'm running a dangerous grocery gauntlet. Nothing says sophisticated, mature adult like chasing an escaping tub of Caramel Chew Chew Ben & Jerry's across a car park.

I'm not sure what it is that catches my attention. Maybe there is some sort of noise, or perhaps it's one of those corner-of-the-eye movements that later feel as if they were never really in view. But something makes me glance across to the recycling banks in the corner of the car park. They are a pair of scratched, metal monstrosities; the type of things that always have clothes or shoes littered around the base. Nobody ever remembers them being installed, as if they've eternally occupied the same spot.

It's one of those December days when it doesn't feel as if the sun has fully risen. The murk makes it hard to see, but I can make out two lads by the bins. One is broad and tall. He looms over the other like a bloated giraffe next to a gangly, bulimic goat. They're at that awkward mid-teen time where it's not easy to guess an age. Some have shot up to six-foot-plus by their fourteenth birthday, while an unlucky few still talk with a high-pitched squeak at seventeen. Some in their twenties continue to be peppered with spots, but there are also fifteen-year-olds with stubbly beards.

You see everything as a private tutor.

The slap happens so fast that it is like I hear it before I see it. There's a crack and the larger boy's hand whips across the other's face. The smaller boy reels sideways and bounces off the side of the recycling bin. I've taken a few steps towards them before I realise

I've moved. Pure autopilot. I recognise the taller boy now I'm a little closer. I should have known him from the height alone. Josh is in the year below Katie at school. He's fifteen or sixteen but already the size and shape of a fully-grown man.

'Hey!'

I shout across and both boys turn towards me. I don't recognise the smaller of the two but he's half hunched, anticipating another blow. Josh has a hand paused in mid-air. The smaller boy catches my eye momentarily but he isn't stupid enough to hang around. He only needs a second – and he takes it, turning and dashing past the bins into the trees beyond. By the time Josh realises what's happened, he's left spinning on the spot, looking between me and his escaping adversary.

I'm only a few steps from the recycling banks now, almost lost in the shadows of the surrounding trees in the corner of the car park.

'What's going on?' I ask.

Josh squints down, trying to place me. He's one of those local kids that I know solely through reputation. It's hard to miss a boy who's already over six foot. I'd guess many in the area know him by sight alone.

'None of yer business,' he replies.

'You can't go around hitting people.'

'It's nothing to do with you.'

A shiver passes through me and though there's a chill to the air, I'm not sure it's that. It feels like I've missed something that was in plain sight.

Josh has turned towards the woods, in the direction the other boy scuttled – and I'm left standing awkwardly, unsure into what I've just interjected myself, or what else I could possibly say.

I head back towards my car, where the door is still open and my shopping sits untouched in the boot. I push everything towards the back, wedging the bag with the yoghurts into the arch so that it can't escape, and then close the hatch.

I'm about to get into the driver's seat when I notice the woman loading shopping into the 4x4 a few spaces down from mine. The thing with places like Prowley is that everyone grows old together. Sharon Tanner was in my class at school three decades ago. We've never been friends, and probably not even at the level where we might nod to one another on the street. I would guess we've seen each other once a week or so for all those years – but barely swapped a word.

Sharon is strapping a toddler into a child seat on the passenger side of her vehicle. I can hear her muttering something, though it's too quiet to make out anything specific. She's in a Sports Direct special, some sort of cheap pink-and-green tracksuit, even though I doubt she's seen a track in her life.

I shouldn't judge.

After fastening in her child, Sharon steps back from the car and starts to turn towards her shopping, which is on the tarmac at the back of her vehicle. She stops when she sees me staring and returns the look with a mix of confusion and defiance.

'What?' she says.

I nod towards Josh, who is ambling across the car park towards us. His hands are in his pockets and his head dipped.

'I saw Josh,' I say, hesitating over the words.

Sharon turns to take in her son and then looks back to me. 'So?'

'He, um… I saw him hitting another boy over there.'

I motion towards the recycling bins across the car park. By this time, Josh has reached his mother's 4x4. He leans on the back window and stares at something on his phone. It's hard to tell through the gloom but it looks like he rolls his eyes.

There's a silence, punctuated only by the sound of a revving engine from the far side of the car park. These are probably the most words I've said to Sharon since we left school all those years ago.

I see some sort of annoyance in the narrowing of her eyes but it's hard to tell who it might be for.

'That true?'

Her reply is spiky, and, though she doesn't turn her head, it's somehow clear she is talking to Josh. She continues to watch me as Josh shrugs a silent response. There's no way his mother could have seen it but she still knows.

'Get in the car,' she snaps – and, perhaps surprisingly, her son immediately does as he's told.

There is a gap of a few seconds and then Sharon picks up a shopping bag from the floor. She pushes it into the back of her car and then wedges in three more bags before closing the boot.

I've not moved, though it's hard to know why. I have no idea what to say next, if there's anything to say at all.

Sharon walks to the driver's side door and then stops to turn to me.

'Jennifer Owen,' she says, almost as a hiss.

My old maiden name. I have an urge to tell her it's 'Hughes' now, even though Bryan and I are separated.

'You should mind your own business,' she adds quickly.

'I wasn't trying to get involved. I *saw* him hitting another kid, he—'

Sharon offers a shrug that matches her son's. 'So? It's nothing to do with you. Besides, it's not like Katie's perfect.'

I'm not sure exactly why it happens but the mention of Katie's name feels like a slap in itself. Perhaps it's because I have no idea why Sharon would know my daughter's name.

My arms seem to have folded themselves across my front. 'What do you mean by that?' I reply.

I get a snarling smirk as a response. The type of expression that says so much more than any words could do. I feel momentarily lost until Sharon speaks again.

'How about you look after your own kids and I'll look after mine,' she says.

If I have anything to say, then it's caught at the back of my throat. By the time I might get anything out, it's too late because

Sharon's already in her car and she closes the door with a slamming *thunk*.

It's only as she reverses out of the space that I realise we have an audience. There are seven or eight people dotted around the nearby spaces watching everything that's just happened. I feel myself shrinking as I glance to the tarmac to avoid any stares and then cross back to my own car. I fumble the handle, trying to get inside and away from the accusatory stares. People might pretend otherwise but everyone loves a good public argument. There's nothing quite like free, live entertainment to cheer everyone up a couple of weeks before Christmas.

I reverse out of the space and drive past the petrol station. I'm not sure why I feel so shaken by a few cross words but it's hard to escape the sense that Sharon was right about one thing.

Perhaps I should mind my own business.

ONE

Another day and the combination of potholes and rain from the past week or so has created pulsing rivers along the edges of the dark country lanes that surround Prowley. I weave across the barely visible central line in an attempt to stay out of the deepest trenches but there's no avoiding the worst of it. Spiky jolts of pain fire along my back and neck as the car lurches into an unseen crevice and bounces back up onto the main surface.

The council never seems to do anything about the craters that appear in the local roads – and it doesn't help that there are huge slurries of mud to avoid as well. Those come from one of the multitude of local tractors that seem to hold up traffic whenever I'm in a rush and trying to get somewhere.

Gosh, the middle-class perils we have to endure.

One of those newish Christmas songs that will be forgotten by next year is on the radio. The end is interrupted by the DJ, who tells everyone that it's seven o'clock, which means it's time for the evening news. There's some sort of political upheaval going on but that could be the news for any day out of the last few years. There's always something.

I pass the 'Thank you for driving safely' sign and ease around the next bend. I'm now out of Prowley and there's a good few miles of overgrown hedges and narrow country roads before I reach anything close to mass civilisation. There are only a handful of farms and remote houses this far out of town – but that doesn't stop me having to swerve around a wheelie bin that's been left too far away from the verge and not brought in by the homeowner. I spot it at the last second and curse under my breath as I slosh through a mini lake on the other side of the road. It's a good job nobody was driving the other way.

Driving along these roads is pure muscle memory. I've been doing it for so long that I know instinctively when to start slowing for the next bend. I ease onto the brake and take the turn onto Green Road, which will take me almost to the college.

I'm starting to accelerate when my phone dings with a text. I glance down to the well next to the handbrake where the phone's screen is momentarily illuminated before fading to dark again. I didn't see who'd messaged me but it's likely Katie. I'm late picking her up from football practice – and she won't be happy. I was busy bunkering down on the sofa with a Fruit & Nut when I remembered I was supposed to be collecting her. It doesn't help that it's so cold and wet. She'll be fuming.

The engine roars as I press harder on the accelerator. A mist of light rain appears across the windscreen – and I'm probably at least ten minutes from the college. Katie has every right to be annoyed.

I take the next bend and then my phone pings a second time. Everything happens in the same instant. I glance down to my phone, where the screen has flashed white with a name I can't quite make out. I reach for it but, in that precise moment, there is a crunching thump from the front of the car. It's reflex as I slam on the brakes. The car slides sideways and there's a point in which a hedge is directly in front of me. I'm not sure what I do – it's certainly nothing conscious – but I must twist the steering wheel back the other way as the car swerves onto the correct side of the road. It slides a little further on the slick surface and then rolls to a stop.

It's only when I next exhale that I realise I must've been holding my breath the entire time. The tightness bristles in my chest as the windscreen wipers continue to flash back and forth with a gentle squeak. I stare ahead as the beam from the car's headlights disappear into the grim blackness of the night.

There's nothing out there.

I'm frozen; my hands squeezing the steering wheel, foot pressed on the brake. It takes me a few seconds to remember to put the car in neutral. Even then, the car rocks backwards a little until I wrench up on the handbrake.

A third beep of my phone has me yelping with surprise. I look down to the well again – and Katie's name is clear this time – but I ignore her and stare out into the darkness.

I must have hit a bin.

People keep leaving them out on the edge of their properties and, this far away from town, there is no pavement. They rest on the grass verge, or the side of the road itself, often until the next day.

Stupid, lazy, *stupid* people.

I press the red triangle in the centre of the console and the orange hazard lights start to flash at the front and back of the car. In the muddle of the last minute or so, I try to get out of the car without taking off my seat belt. The cord slices into my breastbone as I open the door and strain against it before realising why I can't move. Everything is a jumble. I unclip the belt and then grab my phone.

Out of the car and the rain is harder than I realised. More of a rippling head-basher than a mist. I pull up the hood of my jacket and then crouch to check the front of the car. The moon is blurred by the grim clouds but my car is silver and there's enough light from my phone to see any darkened scuffs. I'm expecting some sort of deep dent, perhaps even a broken headlight but, as best I can tell, the only mark on the front is a soft graze. It's nothing new: the mark came courtesy of a pillar in a multistorey when I was trying to reverse out of a space. Those pesky unmoving pillars.

I run a hand across the wing but come away with nothing but a wet palm. Aside from the scratched indentation that was already there, it doesn't feel as if there's anything else.

That's one thing, at least. There's still another four months until the car is paid off. There are already enough bills to pay with Christmas around the corner – plus spending hours on the phone with an insurance company is as appealing as watching anything presented by Piers Morgan's smug plasticine face.

I take a step away from the car and stare back towards the way I've come. It's only now I've stopped that I remember Bryan lives somewhere around here. The woman with whom my ex-husband is now shacked up has one of these houses out in the sticks. I'd recognise it in the daytime but some of the entrances to people's driveways are hidden by the hedges. At night, it's hard to tell where anything is.

Must've been that bin.

Must've been.

I move back towards my car and then figure I should check I haven't spun the bin further into the road. It was bad enough that I clipped it but it could cause serious damage to someone else if it's now in the middle of the lane, especially at night.

There's a large puddle at the edge of the road, so I edge around that before continuing back down the street. A stream is flowing across the tarmac at one point, pouring from a field on one side across to the gully on the other. There's always flooding around this area through the autumn and winter; always some reporter on the local news standing in a field with water up to his knees talking about how wet it is.

I walk for thirty seconds or so but there's no sign of a bin in the road. I stop and turn back towards my car along the lane, its hazard lights winking into the darkness.

The only sound is the pitter-patter of rain on ground and, for the second time in as many days, a shiver goes through me. There is no one here and I feel alone and exposed out here in the open. I wonder if I perhaps clipped a parked car's mirror, except there's no sign of anything. Aside from my own vehicle, the road is clear in both directions.

I've already taken a step back towards the car when I see it.

It's down in the gully, where the hedge meets the sodden grass before it becomes the road. I think it's a crumpled bin bag at first. I almost carry on walking but there's something about the shape that sets the hairs on my arms standing.

Her hair is splayed wildly; her knee bent at an abnormal angle to the way it should be.

It's the Sports Direct special that gives it away. That cheap pink-and-green tracksuit.

Sharon Tanner lies unmoving in the gutter, her body crumpled by my car.

TWO

I take a step off the road onto the sodden bank. The ground is squishy and almost grabs my foot.

'Sharon?'

The word disappears into the night, swallowed by the crescendo-ing rain. There's no answer and she doesn't move to acknowledge there's anyone here.

'Sharon?'

I almost take another step towards her but then back away onto the road. There's nothing I can do for her now. I only know basic first aid and, even if I knew more, I think she needs more than rolling into a recovery position.

I have to stab the three nines into my phone because the rain is interfering with the touchscreen. My thumb hovers over the green call button and I'm so close to pressing it before the trembling, creeping thought whispers its way into my mind.

What if Sharon is… dead?

Despite the rain and cold – not to mention any pain from the injuries – she hasn't twitched since I spotted her. Her arm is folded unnaturally under the rest of her body. It's probably broken and there are gloopy spatterings of something dark across her face. Mud, or… blood.

It was only yesterday that we were arguing in the car park. We'd been shopping at the same time, going about our lives… and, now, here she is in the gutter.

I know what I should do. Anybody would. Everybody does.

Except…

If I called to report this, I'd likely end up on some sort of death by dangerous driving charge. I could be done for manslaughter. Does it count as manslaughter if someone's in a car?

'Sharon?'

There's a large part of me that wills her to get up and shake it off, as if this is all fine. There's another that doesn't want that because, if she does pull herself up the bank, she'll tell everyone it was me.

'Sharon?'

She doesn't move and it's too dark to see if she's breathing.

I know I should go to her. I know, I know, I know…

I clear the phone app from the screen and switch on the flashlight again, before crouching to take in the ground next to the road. It doesn't look like I left any sort of footprint in the sodden grass. There is no one else here; no street lights or CCTV cameras.

Nothing…

I don't check the rear-view mirror as I ease my car back onto the road. My hands are wet and clammy; my face singed from the rain. I know I should stop and go back. I should call an ambulance. There's lots I *should* do… but what then? There were people who saw Sharon and me arguing in the car park yesterday – including her son. People will say I hit her on purpose.

Is she dead?

If so, it might not just be death by dangerous driving, or manslaughter. Is it… *murder?*

It feels like a blink but, as I pull into the car park at the back of Katie's college, I know I must have been driving for between five and ten minutes. The word 'murder' swims through my thoughts but I don't get a chance to think any of it through because the passenger door opens and Katie flops onto the seat with a squelch. She twists herself around and drops a bag onto the back seat, before turning back to the front.

'I don't want to talk about it,' she says, unprompted.

I can't stop picturing Sharon in the verge; her hair splayed, leg shattered. It takes a moment for me to realise Katie can't be talking about that.

'About what?' I manage.

'Football. What else?'

'Oh.'

'Didn't you get my texts? I've been waiting.'

'I, um…'

'You said you'd be on time. Everyone else has already gone.'

'I was driving – and didn't your coach wait with you?'

'He doesn't count.'

Katie unlocks her phone screen and angles it towards the window so that I can't see what she's looking at, even if I wanted to.

'Are we going?' she asks.

In years gone by, I might have scolded her for the tone – but Katie is seventeen going on eighteen and isn't usually like this. I'd be annoyed if someone had promised to pick me up and then left me standing in the rain.

I start to pull away but the car bunny-hops forward and stalls to a stop. I can sense Katie's sideways stare as I re-turn the key, only to stall a second time.

'Are you okay?' Katie asks.

'I think the engine's wet,' I reply, with no idea if that's an actual reason for why a car might stall.

'I failed my test for less than that.'

Her words prickle but I clench my teeth and manage not to rise to it. If it wasn't for what has just happened back along Green Road, we'd likely be in the middle of an argument.

At the third time of asking, I manage to pull away properly. I check all my mirrors and then indicate to get back onto the main road, even though there are no cars in sight.

The speed limit is sixty but I'm only doing a little over forty. From unconsciously getting from the scene to the college, I'm now hyper-aware of everything around me. I watch studiously for bends or bumps in the road. I might usually take the straighter line when navigating these country lanes but, even though the markings are faded and obscured by the rain, I stick religiously to my own side of the road.

Katie is tapping something into her phone, with the white of the screen catching in my peripheral vision. I almost tell her off for focusing on her phone but I'm not sure I'd be able to get those hypocritical words out of my mouth.

If only I hadn't have glanced down to my phone.

If only, if only…

'Are you all right?' Katie asks.

'Um…'

'You're twitching,' she adds.

It's only as she mentions it that I realise she's right because my hand is jerking on the steering wheel. I once saw a girl at school have a fit and have never quite forgotten the way her body convulsed as she was on the floor. My instinct was to help her but I didn't know what to do. In the end, a teacher came along and supported her head. That's what it feels like now as I watch my fingers spasm for no reason.

I scratch my head and then my leg, before needlessly resting it on the gearstick.

'Low blood sugar,' I say. 'Forgot to eat tea.'

Katie doesn't respond, though I sense an eye roll.

'Why are we going this way?' she asks.

'What way?'

'The long way home.'

I can hardly tell her that I have no desire to drive back on the same roads I've just been on.

'Someone said there was roadworks the other way.'

There might be another eye roll but I'm watching the road, not Katie. Either way, it is followed by a couple of yawns, before she focuses back on her phone.

When I return my hand to the steering wheel, it is no longer flinching. I continue to drive under the speed limit, not daring to shift my foot. The road is twisty but there are only a handful of junctions until we get home.

Blink.

Sharon's in the gutter.

Blink.

There's a road in front of me.

Blink.

She's face down, hair splayed.

Blink.

There's a road in front of me.

As I slow for the junction, there's a burbling in my stomach and that horribly familiar acidic taste of bile at the back of my throat. I have to gulp it away. Not now.

It's as I stop at the T that a spinning blue fills the lane. There are no sirens – not out here at night – but an ambulance slows and takes the turn with its lights blurring. I'm paralysed as a second set of whirring lights burn through the night, with a police car following shortly behind.

'Wonder what's going on,' Katie says, looking up from her phone.

Any words I might have been able to say are caught in my throat.

She pauses, before looking back to her phone. 'Probably nothing,' she adds.

THREE

I almost stall the car once more as I pull into the garage. I catch the biting point at the last moment and manage to stop properly without Katie noticing anything. She reaches into the back seat and grabs her bag before letting herself out of the car. I'm not sure whether there's any point at which she stops looking at her phone. Today's teenagers are the greatest multitaskers this world has ever seen. I unclip my belt but she's already on her way to the connecting door into the house without a word.

It's only when she's gone that I realise there's a damp patch on the seat from her wet kit. In another time, this would be one more thing over which to argue. I'd have called her out for getting into the car when she was so wet, then she'd have pointed out that I was late. Then I'd have said it didn't matter because she was wet anyway from the training – and that she could have found something to sit on to stop the car getting wet. Then she'd have said that I must have known it was raining, so why didn't I pick up a blanket to help her out.

The argument that hasn't happened feels so close that it's almost as if it has.

Something creeps along the back of my neck and I picture Sharon in the gutter. Again. All those fights with Katie and Bryan now feel so pointlessly stupid. Why did I ever pick squabbles over things that were so meaningless? I would make a big deal over a pair of shoes being left on stairs – but that's nothing compared to what I've done. If a person gets angry over a pair of shoes, then what does it mean when that same person has seriously injured someone?

Or *killed* them?

I blink the thought away. It's too late to go back now. The moment I decided to leave was the moment going back became impossible.

An ambulance was on its way towards Sharon, which means somebody else must have found her. Does the ambulance mean she's alive?

I'm not a monster. I want her to be okay. It's just... *I* want to be okay as well.

In the light of the garage, I check the front of the car once more. It's extraordinary considering what happened but the only mark on the bumper is the small multistorey scuff that I'm certain was probably there already. I check the other side of the car, plus the back, just in case, but there's nothing except a few patches of mud and spray. If I were to go through a car wash, there wouldn't even be that. It's almost as if I didn't hit anything, or anyone... except I know that I did. I heard the thump. I saw Sharon's body.

I lock the car and head into the house, putting my wet jacket over the radiator. There's no sign of Katie downstairs but there's the vague sound of the shower blasting from above. Now I'm away from the car, I finally check my phone properly. I had three texts while I was driving. Two were from Katie – 'Where are you?' and 'Are you coming?' – with a third from the local MOT centre. It's time to get my car checked over again and it was a reminder that I should call to book in.

That was the message I received when I reached for my phone. The one that distracted me in the fraction of a moment it took to glance away from the road.

I find the font on my phone too much of a strain for my eyes, so head into the living room and hunt around for the iPad. I've never really got to grips with using a touchscreen instead of a keyboard and fumble over typing 'What to do if you hit someone when driving?' into the search bar. The results throw up the obvious stuff that I already failed to do, such as stopping and calling the emergency services – but it's the next bit that makes it feel as if the air has escaped the room. Failure to stop at the scene of an accident can get a person six months in prison and an unlimited fine.

I keep reading but it doesn't get better. A dangerous driving charge can get a person up to fourteen years in prison.

I find myself struggling to swallow as I read the final line. They changed the laws a couple of years ago and *death* by dangerous driving can now be life imprisonment.

Life.

I tap away from that screen and click onto the first news story.

A former postman from Ipswich was sentenced to nine years in prison yesterday after being convicted of causing death by dangerous driving.

Anthony Smith, 51, was doing 52mph in a 30 zone while sending a text message when he hit Cassandra Harper, 23, who was on a zebra crossing.

Smith left the scene of the collision but was later reported to police by his wife.

Smith was also disqualified from driving for six years.

There's more but I can't read on. The disqualification seems ridiculous considering the driver is going to be in prison anyway. Why wasn't it a life ban from driving, anyway? The news story is from before the penalties changed but he still got nine years. I'm horrified – this man killed a twenty-three-year-old woman because he was speeding and using his phone. It feels like it should have been a longer sentence, except...

Now this is me as well.

In the past, I've been one of those people who have sneered from afar. A couple of years ago, there was a video of people barging through supermarket doors at the start of Black Friday. The crowd rampaged towards a stack of on-sale televisions, with the bigger, stronger blokes grabbing as many as they could carry before dashing off towards the tills.

That was almost the normal part.

After those first few, the people behind started fighting over what was left. Punches were thrown; people fell to the ground and were trampled upon. Within a minute or so, the display had been emptied and there was a slew of groggy bodies picking themselves up from the floor. Someone had their arm broken.

I laughed incredulously when I first saw the video. How could people go so crazy over getting a bit of money off from an already cheap, unbranded TV? Why did people need two? Or three? It was senseless.

But that's the thing: human beings often *are* senseless. There is nobody alive who hasn't done something and immediately thought, 'Why did I do that?' Many situations don't give people time to make informed, reasoned decisions. Something will happen in an instant and, once we react, we have to live with that singular moment in time.

Easy to sneer when it's someone else.

Life in prison.

Life.

I think I'm a good person and genuinely believe most people who know me would agree. I have two charity direct debits. I've volunteered at the local food bank for the past three Easters. I give money to homeless people when I'm in the city. I'm part of the neighbourhood watch scheme. I pay my taxes.

But one stupid mistake – just one – and it's life in prison.

Life.

I suppose there's a fairness in that it's a life for a life – but it's not only me in this. What about Katie? She's nearly an adult but she has exams to take that will guide the rest of her future. What happens to her if I admit what happened? It isn't only about me. It's not only *my* life that would fall apart, it's Katie's too.

That's what I tell myself, as I try not to think about Sharon and her family.

Then I'm angry. Why was Sharon in the road? It was dark and raining – plus the middle of nowhere. What was she thinking? It can't all be my fault. It's *not* all my fault.

I load Facebook but don't need to scroll to see that word is already out. Polly from three doors down has updated her status.

Polly Appleton: *Warning: Part of Green Road is closed. The police just turned me around out there. Had to come the long way home. Doesn't look like it'll be open anytime soon.*

The replies are already coming in underneath.

Jean Burrard: *What happened?*

Polly Appleton: *Something about a hit-and-run.*

Jean Burrard: *OMG! Hope the person hit isn't anyone we know. Who'd drive off?*

Polly Appleton: *Dunno. Seems serious though. Heard the person might be dead.*

FOUR

I shriek as the doorbell sounds. How could the police have got to me so quickly? Was there CCTV after all? Was there some sort of witness hidden in the shadows who saw what I did?

I hurry to the window and push the net curtain to one side, trying to get an angle on whoever's outside. The glare proves to be too great, although there is no sign of the inevitable police car in front of the house.

When I open the door, it's probably the first time I've ever been grateful to see Katie's boyfriend, Richard. It's not as if we have some sort of feud going – I'm not one of *those* mothers – but it isn't hard to see that he's punching well above his weight with my daughter. Well, seemingly not hard *for me* to see that. Katie clearly doesn't agree given that they're still together. He is nineteen years old, without a proper job or career path – and isn't in any kind of training. I have no clue what he actually does with himself.

Richard nods towards me but doesn't quite make eye contact as I step aside to let him in. It's no surprise that he's wearing all black: I have rarely seen him in anything else. I suppose he could be a ninja, though it seems unlikely given the way he trips over the doorstep as he moves into the house.

'Hi, um, Mrs Hughes,' he says with a stammer. 'Is Katie in…?'

He is already angling towards the stairs, knowing the answer to his question.

Before I can say anything, Katie appears at the top of the stairs. She's out of her football kit and now in some sort of cross between a tracksuit and pyjamas. Either way, it looks comfy and makes it seem clear that she isn't going out again.

She nods towards her room, ignoring me: 'You coming?'

Richard doesn't need asking twice. He mumbles something I don't catch and then hurries past me, tripping on the bottom step, before righting himself and heading up the stairs. Moments later and Katie closes her bedroom door with a solid clunk.

I wait for a few seconds, watching upwards, although I'm not sure why. When I was Katie's age, my mother would have never allowed me to have a boyfriend in my room. If she'd have had her way, I would have been married before I was allowed to hold hands with a boy. I blink the memory away.

Back in the living room and there are more replies to Polly's status.

Jean Burrard: *OMG!!!!! Dead?*

Alison Smart: *I heard it might be Sharon Tanner. She lives out that way. I've seen her walking along Green Road before. I am praying for her safety. Peace and love.*

Jean Burrard: *I've seen her out there with Frank in his push-chair. There's no pavement outside her house. I've been saying for years that it's dangerous. I hope you're wrong.*

The chills are back. When I saw Sharon in the car park yesterday, she was strapping a toddler into a child seat. I don't know the kid's name – but I assume this is the Frank they're talking about. I didn't know Sharon lived that far out of town – but then we're not friends. Why would I know?

I can't stop looking at the word pushchair.

She can't have been out with her little boy in this weather. She just *can't* have been. I saw her in the verge but there was no sign of a buggy.

I close the tabs and put down the iPad. I've been holding my breath again and my chest burns. I've already left an adult for dead. It's unforgivable... but a child as well...? It can't be true. I would have seen the stroller on the side of the road... wouldn't I?

There's a noise from the hallway and then Katie is in the doorway. Her hair's wet and she's wearing the glasses she only needs for reading. Since she got them about a year ago, it's been impossible not to see my teenage self in her more than ever. I was stuck with an NHS special of thick, transparent rims when I was her age. Katie would never settle for something like that – kids today, and so on. Hers are thick and black – which gives her a bookish charm I only believed I had. Yes, it's a cliché that glasses make people look smarter, but clichés are only there because there's a truth somewhere.

'Can I borrow the iPad?' she asks.

'Oh, um, I was using it...'

Her gaze darts towards the abandoned device on the seat next to me.

'For coursework,' she adds. 'You did buy it as a family thing...'

She's right, of course. When Bryan was still around, it was bought as a device for anyone to use. The cost was justified as something to help Katie with her revision when she was doing her GCSEs. Instead of that, she was keener on getting a laptop. Hard to blame her but that meant the iPad quickly ended up as a general device that I used more than anyone else. Strictly speaking, it's still a *family* device.

'What's wrong with your laptop?' I ask.

'I'm typing on that. It's easier to find things on the iPad without having to switch tabs.'

It sounds close enough to truth that I'm prepared to go with it.

'How are you concentrating on your coursework with Richard here?'

Katie eyes me defiantly for a moment but doesn't react. 'He's job-hunting, so he's got his own thing to do,' she says.

I've already blinked with contemptuous surprise before I know what I've done.

'The labouring with his uncle is too much,' Katie adds. 'It's too cold at this time of year. His uncle's pulling apart those flats above the post office but Richard wants something better.'

It's the thing I've been hinting at for months, although 'hinting' might be the wrong word. I've openly told Katie that her boyfriend should be doing something more than flitting between cash-in-hand work for his extended family.

'Oh,' I say – and it's impossible to miss the barely there smirk on my daughter's face. 'Is he going to put back in for his exams?' I add.

'I don't think so.'

That's a clear 'no' – and much more of what I would expect.

There seems little else to say, so I pass her the iPad. She turns to leave but it's only then that I remember what was almost the last thing Sharon said to me. It feels more pertinent now than it did yesterday.

It's not like Katie's perfect.

'Is there anything else going on?' I ask.

Katie half turns back, watching me over the top of her glasses. 'Like what?'

'I'm not sure.'

Her eyes narrow a fraction. Suspicion is a natural teenage response, I guess. 'Everything's fine.'

She takes a step towards the stairs and, when I don't add anything, she pads her way back up, before there's the sound of a closing bedroom door.

Since Bryan left, the living room has felt nothing but empty. We picked out the leather furniture together back when we thought it would be forever. Everything in the room is something that we had a joint hand in choosing, whether it's the neutral magnolia wallpaper with dark pinstripes (me) or the oversized TV unit that can hold up to two hundred DVDs (him). None of the items have moved but the room feels so desolate now. Katie spends almost all her time at home in her room – and any other moments in the kitchen or bathroom. This was an enclave for Bryan and myself – but now it's only me.

I can't be in this room, not right now, so I move into the kitchen and turn on the radio. I've never quite been able to get myself into Radio Four, largely because that's what Mum used to have on in the mornings. To listen to it would be a concession that I'm an old woman. Five Live is busy with a football commentary, so I change the station to the local BBC network. The presenter is waffling on to some caller about whether veganism is a threat to local farmers. It's nonsense, of course, but it's comforting to have some sort of voice in the background.

I'm not sure what I spend the next half hour doing. I think I clean a bit, though it's all a blur. I scrub and I scrub because it erases that image of Sharon in the gutter.

Except it doesn't.

I only tune back in to where I am when the radio cuts to the news. There's something about a local councillor who is under pressure to quit and then a story about a fire from a few days ago. When the presenter reaches the travel news, I find myself tensing once more. He says that Green Road has been closed by the police and likely won't reopen until the morning. There's a pause as he takes a breath – but then he moves on swiftly to a list of roadworks.

I don't know what to do.

Children look up to adults and believe they know everything – but the truth is that adulthood is a lifelong bluff. Nobody knows what they're doing. It's all guesswork until the inevitable time when the truth of our uselessness is exposed.

Deep down, I know I should hand myself in. It might not be too late. I could tell the police that I thought I hit a bin – which isn't even a lie. I saw on Facebook that someone had been hit by a car and I want to make sure that it was nothing to do with me. I don't have to say that I saw Sharon in the ditch. There's a lot of truth in everything I could say – and an omission isn't a specific lie.

Except that people *saw* us arguing in the supermarket car park. None of those people were close enough to know what it was about but that wouldn't matter. It could so easily go from being the accident it was to some sort of attempted murder. Or *actual* murder.

Life in prison…

Life.

I fill the kettle and switch it on, then I find myself wondering if I can drink tea at a time like this. That leads onto a stream of thoughts as to what I *can* do now. Can I bring myself to eat? To sleep? To drive? Can I laugh at some nonsense on television? It feels as if so little matters any more. There's Katie and then… I don't know. Myself, I suppose.

A couple of minutes must pass because the next thing I know is that the kettle plips off. I stare at it but can't bring myself to make a drink.

It's when my phone pings with a message that I realise I've brought it into the kitchen with me. There's a text waiting for me from a 07 number that isn't stored in my phone. The only people who generally message me are parents enquiring – or booking – private tuition for their children, or Katie. It's not as if I have a burgeoning social life.

I assume it's going to be from a parent who has got hold of my number and is looking to book my tutoring time. The next four or five months leading up to various exams are far busier for me than the first half of the school term. This is when parents start getting a sniff of how things might end up going and begin to panic.

That's not who the text is from.

I read the message over and over, trying to make some sense of it. Wondering if there might be a meaning other than the obvious one.

There isn't. There's only one meaning.

Anon: *I know what you did*

FIVE

My hand is shaking, like it had on the steering wheel. I look behind, towards the empty hallway, as I take a few steps into the living room. There's no one there – nor anybody visible in the darkened back garden.

How could someone know?

There were no other cars parked on Green Road. No street lights. Nobody was watching.

My hands are trembling so violently that it takes a good minute to type out a reply.

Me: *Who are you?*

I grab a glass from the cupboard and fill it with water from the tap, before downing it in one.

No reply. Not yet.

I screech even louder when the doorbell sounds again.

I whisper 'get a grip' under my breath, as if saying it out loud will make any difference, then head back into the hall. I don't bother checking through the window this time, though immediately think I should, because this time it *is* the police.

Sort of.

Gary from over the road is a sergeant, although I'm not completely certain what that entails. When we first viewed this house, he was washing his car on the street and I asked him what the area was like. He said it was quiet and that he was a police officer. Something about that made me feel safer in the moment, although it's hard to remember why. Prowley is hardly a hotbed of crime. This is the sort of place where young people hanging around in the park can – and will – get angry letters sent to the local paper.

Gary's not in his uniform. He's tall and lean, wearing jeans and a cosy-looking woolly jumper.

'Didn't interrupt anything, did I?' he asks, with a smile.

'I was just making a tea.'

He nods along, though I suppose there's nothing to add to this stunning revelation. He glances sideways and, just for a moment, I think he's eyeing the garage, with my car beyond. A little voice tells me that he knows and, as I feel my hand shaking, I hold it behind my back, and clench my fist.

'Can I help?' I add.

He winces slightly, uncomfortable or embarrassed. I see this a lot with parents talking about their children's results at school. It's hard to admit that a child with your genes might need extra help. I already know what's coming before he opens his mouth.

He *doesn't* know.

'It's Leah,' Gary says. 'She's got her year nine tests in the new year and she's been struggling with maths. I don't want her to get too far behind before she gets into her GCSEs. I was wondering if you might, um…'

He glances away once more and tails off. People genuinely do find it hard to ask for help.

I let it hang for a moment and he fills the gap.

'Maybe an hour or two a week…?'

'I usually do more work with GCSE, AS- and A-level students,' I say, 'but I've got the Key Stage materials for younger pupils. I'll have a look through them tomorrow. Perhaps if you send over Leah after school, then we can have a chat and I'll be able to get an idea of where she's up to?'

Gary nods along, though I'm not sure he was fully listening. He seems unfocused. 'I'll do that,' he replies. 'How much do you charge?'

'I'll have a talk with Leah first and see where everything stands. I can get back to you afterwards.'

'Have you got my number?'

'Somewhere…'

He reaches into his back pocket and passes me a card. It lists his name and police rank, plus there's a logo of the local force.

'My mobile's on there,' he says. 'Use that.'

I tell him I will and then ask him to wait a moment as I head inside to my work cupboard in the living room. I slip an interview sheet from the top and then take it to Gary at the door.

'Can you ask Leah to fill that in?' I say. 'It's best if she does it herself. There's normal stuff, like name and age – but then a few questions about favourite subjects, what she likes doing in her free time, and so on. It's more so I can get a grasp on what she might need.'

Gary scans the page and then folds it in two. He thanks me and then, as he starts to turn to head back across the road, I can't help myself.

'I saw on Facebook that something happened over on Green Road…?'

Gary stops and twists back to face me. 'Everything gets around so quickly nowadays…'

'It always has in a place like this.'

'True.'

It feels like he might turn and walk away – it's none of my business – but I think the fact that he's come to ask me to help his daughter works in my favour.

'I can't say much,' he says. 'I don't know everything anyway. I'm off duty tonight.'

'What happened?'

Gary takes a step back towards me and leans in so there's no danger of anyone overhearing. 'Hit-and-run,' he says.

'People were saying it looks bad…?'

'Who was saying that?'

'People on Facebook.'

He sighs and I don't blame him. If police officers are left having to confirm or deny every mad theory spouted by a Facebook nutjob, then they'd never have the time to do anything else.

'I wouldn't want to speculate,' he says.

'But whoever was hit is going to be okay, aren't they…?'

There's something about the way his eye twitches that sends a tingle along my spine.

'What?' I say.

'It's an ongoing investigation.' I think he's going to leave it at that but there's more. He speaks so softly that I almost miss it. 'It's not just one person,' he adds.

I stare at him and am so close to blubbing that it was me who was driving that I have to bite my lip to stop the words coming out.

'What do you mean?' I manage.

'More than one person was hit.'

It feels as if the sky is rushing towards me. The world is collapsing into a little box that's barely big enough for me. I angle sideways and lean on the door frame. It's the only thing holding me up.

'More than one…?'

I'm sure there's a croak to my voice but, if there is, then Gary says nothing about it.

'There was a child…'

'How young?'

He gulps. '*Very* young…'

I nearly say Frank's name.

'Don't worry,' he adds quickly, 'we'll find whoever it was.'

He turns to leave – and I know he means it to sound reassuring. The problem is that this is the thing of which I'm most afraid.

SIX

I can't get my head around how I managed to not see a pushchair. I suppose there could be many reasons: the dark, the rain, the fact I wasn't really looking. The decision, afterwards, to leave and not look back.

There can't be any doubt that if a child had been crying then I would have heard it. The road was still and silent – and if there was no kid sobbing, then there must be a reason why he was hushed…

Another shiver.

I watch as Gary crosses the road and lets himself into his house. There are lights on downstairs and up. He said he was off duty, so he'll probably be at home all evening. I could cross the road and explain to him that it was an accident. I don't need to mention my phone; it was dark and wet. There were no street lights and no reasonable person could have expected a woman to be *in* the road while pushing a buggy. It could have happened to anyone driving on that road. There should be street lights, or a pavement, or both.

It wasn't my fault.

But despite telling myself this, I close the front door and drift away, only now remembering the message on my phone.

The words haven't changed – *I know what you did* – but there has been no response to what I sent back. I pace along the hall, into the kitchen and back again. It feels like I need to do something, but… what? Visit the scene? What would that achieve? The road is apparently closed – plus it's dark anyway.

I don't know what to do with myself, though I know I can't sit around all evening refreshing Facebook. I'm left doing as I always do when I need to be distracted – and resolve to immerse myself in work. I find myself hunting through the built-in cupboard at the back of the living room. Neither Bryan nor myself noticed it when we viewed the place before buying. It was only after moving in that we realised there was a hidden storage area. It didn't take long for me to fill it with teaching resources. There are guidebooks going back years, plus pamphlets and booklets for the various examination boards. Everything's organised via age group, then year. I soon find the information needed to work with Leah on her maths. The problem is that when I try to scan the book, the words, symbols and equations all blend into one big monochromatic splodge. I read entire pages, though none of it goes in and I always end up back on the first line.

There's no chance of me being able to focus on anything other than the five-word text message, plus the local radio news which doesn't seem to update. Green Road is apparently still closed, although that's all they ever say. I want to see if there's anything more on Facebook but am one of that tiny minority who use a phone as a phone. The combination of the font being too small and my thumbs seemingly being too big means trying to do much more than the basics of texting and calling simply isn't worth it. I could go and ask Katie for the iPad but if she's genuinely using it for work, then it hardly reeks of good parenting to take it from her.

The evening drifts. It somehow seems to pass in both a blink and an age. I only realise it's after ten o'clock when there is a creak from the hallway. Richard is at the bottom of the stairs, rezipping his jacket. As usual, he doesn't meet my eye, though he mumbles something that could be 'goodnight' before he lets himself out.

I head upstairs and am about to tap on Katie's bedroom door when I spot the iPad abandoned on the dresser that's next to the bathroom door. When we first moved in, I was in full domestic goddess mode and would keep it full of freshly cleaned towels. Now, partly because many of those towels end up unretrieved on Katie's floor, and partly through my own laziness, it's touch-and-go as to whether there's anything in there.

I pick up the device and then knock on Katie's door. There's the all-too-familiar scuttling and shuffling that comes from announcing a presence to a teenager, and then a muffled 'come in'.

Katie is laid on top of her bed, still wearing the tracksuit/pyjama combination. The light is dimmed and her face is illuminated by the white from her phone.

'How was the coursework?'

'Huh?'

I hold up the iPad.

'Oh, right… yeah,' she replies. 'Good.'

She could have at least made it sound authentic.

'What about Richard's job-hunting?'

'That was good, too.'

'Did he find anything?'

'Maybe.'

Katie bats away a yawn, though I'm not convinced it's genuine. My daughter is too much a part of me sometimes.

'See you in the morning,' I say, taking the hint.

'Night.'

I close Katie's door and head through to my own room. Since Bryan left, I keep telling myself I should get myself some new bedding. Something fresh that's only mine. I haven't, of course. I've told myself a lot of things over these months, very little of which I've acted upon. There was even a three-day span in which I convinced myself I was going to run every day and get fit. I'd join a running club and meet some new people! I'd run the London Marathon!

Needless to say, that phase passed.

I sit on top of the bed and find Polly's Facebook thread again. There are many more comments, some confirming that Green

Road is still closed but most speculating on whether there was a hit-and-run and, if so, who was hit. Sharon is mentioned over and over. Things like Facebook have shrunk the world – and, in a community that was already small, that means rumours, both true and false, are out and around long before anything is known officially.

There is still no reply to my 'who are you?' text. If 'I know what you did' is some sort of joke, or misplaced message, then the timing is uncanny. If it's genuinely for me, then why would whoever sent it leave me hanging for more than two hours? Unless that's the point. Someone wants me to fret. Perhaps 'who are you?' is the wrong question anyway.

I type out 'What do you want?' and send that as a reply. I've barely glanced back to the iPad when my phone beeps with a reply.

Anon: *You'll find out*

SEVEN

Katie shuffles around until around half past two. She goes to the toilet once and there's the general muffled sound of something she's watching on her phone. I'll never be able to get my head around how young people can watch entire movies or TV shows on such a small device. I'm old enough to remember black-and-white televisions and VHS tapes; now people have access to more or less everything ever filmed on something that fits in a hand. When she finally settles, I tell myself it's time for me to do the same – although it's not as easy as that.

If I sleep, then it's only in five- and ten-minute bursts. Whenever I lie back and close my eyes, I'm barely a minute or two away from feeding the urge to check Facebook, or any number of news websites. As best I can tell, there are no updates from Green Road. Whoever messaged me clearly isn't ready for me to 'find out' what they want anytime soon. I type out numerous replies but send none of them. That is what whomever is trying to torment me would want.

It's a little before five when I stop kidding myself that I'm going to be able to sleep for any significant time. I head down to the kitchen, where the heating hasn't yet kicked in. There's a draught billowing around my bare feet and the windows are dusted with frost. It's going to be another cold, dark day.

I set the coffee machine bubbling, then head to the living room and grab a blanket from the back of the sofa, which I wrap around myself like a giant cloak.

The iPad battery is nearly dead and I spend fifteen minutes trying to find the charging cable. I eventually spot it coiled on the stairs, with no idea what it's doing there. Back in the living room and there are no sockets anywhere near the sofa. That's one of the things Bryan and I discovered after moving in all the furniture. I could move everything around – but it's only another thing for the list that I'll never do.

After plugging in the iPad, I end up hunched on the floor, desperately refreshing Facebook and the multitude of news tabs I have open. Between all of those and the radio news, there are no updates. No news is supposed to be good news – but that's always sounded like optimistic nonsense to me. I expect only bad news to come. It's when, not if. It feels like being on a slide. Once the decision has been made to jump, the only way is down.

Katie comes downstairs a little after half past seven. She ambles into the living room and finds me crouched on the floor, next to the reclining armchair. She's in jeans and a tight, warm-looking sweater; ready for the day, which is more than can be said for me.

She looks down curiously towards me: 'Everything all right?'

'Fine,' I reply, standing. It's definitely not an accurate appraisal of how I am.

'Is there any coffee left?'

Katie's nose twitches at the smell of the second pot that's emanating from the kitchen. I've never quite approved of her drinking coffee, though it's hard to say why, other than that she still feels like my little girl. It doesn't help that I'm a hypocrite and get through a pot every morning. I'm one of those people who laugh about *needing* a coffee to start the day. If someone says they need a morning puff on a crack pipe to get going, it would be frowned upon. Replace the name of the drug and everyone thinks it's normal.

Either way, Katie doesn't wait for a reply as she heads into the kitchen. She returns a few moments later, phone in one hand, coffee mug in the other. She puts both down on the arm of the sofa and then heads to the window, where she crouches to switch on the Christmas tree lights at the mains. Twinkling globes of pink, green and blue instantly fill the darkened room and Katie takes a step back to admire the view. Christmas has always been her thing, in the same way it was for me when I was a girl. Everything used to be built around an internal calendar of how long it was until 25 December. The worst day of the year was Boxing Day. I can't remember when I went from that to not caring.

This year, I had committed to not bothering with a tree, decorations and the like. We'd not spoken about it but, at the start of the month, Katie got this tree down from the attic while I was out one evening. She decorated it herself and I came home to find her hanging plastic baubles from the curtain rail. She was so proud of it that I didn't have the heart to say that I wasn't going to bother.

Katie moves away from the tree and slouches into the corner of the sofa, while I take the recliner. Bryan's old seat. She eyes the tree for a moment more and then focuses on her phone.

'Did you hear?' she asks, without looking up.

'About what?'

'Some hit-and-run out on Green Road last night.'

Katie looks up from her phone to take me in, which is a shock in itself. In the past few years, I've seen more of the top of her head than I've ever seen her face.

'Terrible, isn't it?' she adds. 'A baby was hit. I reckon that's why we saw that ambulance.'

I can't stop the shudder from creeping through me.

'Where'd you hear that?' I ask.

'Everyone's saying it.'

'What else did you hear?'

'Nothing… just that someone drove into a woman and her baby out there. The woman was found in the ditch and the baby ended up on the other side of the hedge.'

That's more than I'd heard from Gary but it sounds like something that's too specific to have been made up. Part of the reason things go around this town so quickly is that people working in the emergency services are all from the area. Someone attending the scene would have told a family member or friend, who'd have told someone else. Now it's morning, there's little surprise that this is common knowledge in all circles other than the traditional ones, like the radio news.

I can't reply. There's a lump in my throat and that awful tingling behind the eyes that happens a little before they're filled with tears. I fake a yawn and cover my face, willing it all away.

The poor little boy.

I hit his pushchair hard enough to send him either through or over a hedge. If I'd known that before, I'm sure I'd have called the ambulance myself. I would have done, wouldn't I? I tell myself yes.

Katie doesn't seem to notice anything is wrong with me. 'Makes you think, doesn't it?' she continues. 'If we'd gone home that way, we could've been on that road. We might have seen something.'

'Right…'

I force another yawn, though it quickly turns into a series of real ones. The tears of regret and – perhaps – self-sorrow are now ones of tiredness.

Katie has her legs curled underneath herself and is tapping away on her phone.

'What are you up to after lunch today?' I ask, wondering if we might be able to meet up for a sandwich somewhere; hoping we can do something normal that isn't talk about what happened. We've done it a handful of times since she started college but not in a few months. It feels like I need something that isn't sitting around the house.

'It's Wednesday,' Katie replies, matter-of-factly. 'I've got college all day.'

'Right… sorry. I thought it was Tuesday for some reason and you had your half-day.'

'That was yesterday.' She uncurls her feet and then stretches herself up until she's standing. 'I've got to go.'

'It's not eight o'clock yet.'

Katie glances at her phone screen as if to confirm that and then moves towards the door. 'I'm meeting Richard before I go into class. He's got a day working with his uncle and I won't see him until this evening.'

I can sense the relish with which she says this. Her boyfriend's not some work-shy layabout, despite what her mother might think.

'Has he given any more thought about retaking his A-levels?'

Katie pauses in the doorway to the hall.

'I can help him,' I add quickly, not wanting an argument.

She shakes her head but I don't catch the reply properly. That might be deliberate because the 'I've got to go' that follows is perfectly clear.

'You should eat breakfast first,' I add.

Katie picks up a bag from the floor and hoists it onto her back. 'I'll have a protein bar.' She gives me no chance to respond this time, quickly shifting out of sight. A moment later, the front door sounds and she's gone.

Now I've started yawning, it's hard to stop. One follows the other until there are tears pouring down my face. I consider going back to bed – but the chance of sleeping is slim. Even without Leah coming over later, I have work to prep anyway. That doesn't mean any of that will happen. I already know I'm going to spend the day desperately trying to hunt down any morsels of information about last night. I've been trying to think whether there's any way

I can be connected to it. The timing is a problem because Katie will know what time I picked her up – and her teammates and coach will know I was late. There is more than one route from here to the college, however, so it's not necessarily clear that I'd have been on that area of Green Road.

There might be a skid mark on the road because I did slam on my brakes after the collision. I don't know if a wet surface could have made that better or worse.

From checking over the car, it doesn't look as if there's any obvious damage, so that's one thing.

The corner shop has a CCTV camera outside that might have recorded me driving past – but that would give no indication of the route I took to collect Katie. As best I know, there are no other cameras between there and the college.

What does that leave?

I realise I'm thinking like a criminal.

It becomes almost immediately apparent that I'm not only *thinking* like a criminal, I *am* one.

Besides, it's all irrelevant if the person texting me truly does know what I did. Sometimes, when there are horrific things on television, I wonder how people can do these things and not care. When there's an assault and somebody is badly beaten, I can't help but think about the attacker and how they live with themselves. Is there an on-off switch that can make the guilt go away?

If so, I badly want it now.

As I'm thinking about that, my phone sounds again. Each notification takes me back to the road and the moment I glanced away to look down at the screen. I'm going to have to change the tone because I can't go on like this. I'll crack. I'm already fighting the urge to say something.

The text isn't from whoever's been messaging me. It's from my friend Nadia.

Nadia: Running 5–10 mins late. Soz. X

It's only when I scroll back to the earlier messages that I remember what she's on about. We'd arranged to meet for breakfast at eight thirty, which means I have barely half an hour to get dressed, presentable, and out.

I type out a reply to tell her that I'm not feeling well and can no longer make it – but then delete it before sending. If I'm going to get away with this, then I need to act as normally as possible.

Get away with this.

Already thinking like a criminal. Already *am* a criminal.

Me: Let's make it 9. I'm running late myself. LOL.

I send the message and then head for the stairs and the shower beyond. I'm not even at the top when the reply comes.

Nadia: 9 is good for me. X PS: Did you hear about Sharon? :(

The informality is one thing. Neither of us are friends with Sharon and yet we're now on first-name terms. There's an assumption that I know who she's talking about, even though I do.

Before I can respond, another text comes through from her:

Nadia: And that poor baby. Who'd do that and drive off?

Me, I think. *I'd* do that.

EIGHT

I am already at the end of the road on my way to the café when I realise I would have usually driven. The idea of getting behind the wheel again actually makes me feel sick.

The rain stopped overnight and frost now clings to the verges. The temperature is either below zero or close to it and the cold bites through my hat, gloves and scarf, leaving me shivering. I'm woefully underprepared for walking around in these conditions. I'm the type who buys winter clothes for look rather than practicality. Because they were recommended by some idiot in a Sunday Magazine photo-feature. My winter wear is suitable only for a short walk from car to shop or house. This is what I get for driving everywhere, even when it's less than a mile to the centre of town.

Because of that, I shiver my way through the twenty minutes or so that it takes me to walk into Prowley itself.

Bread And Butter is one of those cafés that only seems to exist in small English towns. It might as well be called Pretentious And Overpriced because that's certainly what it is. When it first opened the summer before last, I went around telling everyone I knew how brilliant it was. I'd bang on about how the avocado sourdough was unmissable and that the hummus lunchtime pita was to die for. I feel like a prized prat now. I'm not really a silver-lining person but if last night has done anything for me, then it's to ram a sense of perspective right down my stupid throat.

That's not the only reason I now despise the place.

For now, meeting here is keeping up with appearances. One thing that's certainly true of Bread And Butter is that it's a hub for the town's chattering middle classes. Like it or not – and there was a lengthy enough time in which I did – I'm one of those.

I'm almost at the door when Richard trails a burly bloke out of the café. We blink at each other; me because I wouldn't have thought this was his scene – and him at me because that's what he does. The man in front of him is carrying a pair of paper bags and heads towards a builder's van that's parked on the other side of the road. I presume this is the uncle with whom my daughter's boyfriend is working.

Richard pauses on the edge of the kerb but only for a second. He's seen me and we nod at each other in the way we do now. *Yes, I see you. No, I don't want to talk.* He looks out of place in a checked shirt and a pair of stonewashed jeans that are a good three sizes too big for him. His usual all-black emo gear suits his look. Day work on a building site doesn't feel like his thing. With his skinny frame and twig-like arms, I can't imagine him lugging around heavy things all day.

Perhaps for the first time, I find myself wondering whether I've been too harsh on him. At least he's doing something. He's clearly not the waster I feared he was turning into. I should probably apologise, if not to him, then Katie.

I probably won't.

I do feel sorry for him, though. A year ago and he was planning for university and a move to London. Twelve months on and he's doing a building job just as winter starts to bite. It's not how he would have thought his life was going to turn out.

Richard follows his uncle into the grubby white van where the entire bottom half is dotted with grey and brown muck. The engine roars, a cloud of something black sputters from the exhaust, and then they're off and away.

I head into the café to be met by the usual inoffensive, melodic guff of Coldplay, Ed Sheeran, or something like that. It never used to bother me but then everything happened with Bryan and here we are. All sorts of things annoy me now. At least it's not Slade or the usual drivel that's on a loop at this time of year.

It's almost ten past nine and Nadia is already here. She's sitting at one of the high tables close to the misted window at the back. It's prime real estate for watching whoever comes through the door and textbook seat selection. She grins when she sees me and it's impossible to miss the designer scarf that's draped over the third chair that's dotted around the table. It is comfortably in view for anyone who might sneak a glance in her direction. More textbook stuff.

I slip onto the stool that doesn't have her scarf across the back and we do the two-cheek kiss thing. I can't remember when it started – I definitely didn't kiss with two cheeks when I was Katie's age – but I'm not going to be the first who stops.

'I *love* the scarf,' Nadia says as I unwrap mine.

I have to ask now. It's as inevitable as day following night. 'I was just eyeing yours,' I reply. 'I don't think I've seen it before.'

'Tony bought it for me. Look at the initials.'

I run my fingers across the corner of the scarf and the material is undeniably soft. A small 'NB' has been stitched into the corner, although it's hard to be impressed by something so basic.

'Nadia Bayliss,' I say.

'It's great, isn't it? Early Christmas present.'

She wants me to push for details as to why and what for but I'm not in the mood today.

'What are you drinking?' I ask, nodding at her mug that has a crust of milky foam around the rim.

'Skinny soy latte. The usual.'

I nod at the counter. 'Anything else?'

'Don't think so.'

I weave between the tightly packed tables and slot in next to the till. There's no queue but there *is* a Dawn O'Neill, which is unquestionably worse.

She's the biggest reason I now despise the place, even though I keep coming back.

Dawn is pretending not to notice me. She is wiping down the pipes of the espresso machine, though is side-on enough that I know she can see me.

'Hi,' I say.

Dawn does a somewhat theatrical flinch. She's not ready for the West End yet.

'Jen,' she says. 'I didn't see you there.'

'Jennifer.'

A smile. 'How can I help?'

I glance up to the menu on the board behind her, even though it never changes and I already know it. I'd usually end up having some sort of cappuccino, or syrup-laced milk thing. But now it doesn't feel as if I can accept anything that might be a treat. Not after what I did. I'm only here to keep up something close to my regular routine.

'Drip coffee,' I reply.

Dawn twists and pumps down on the top of a giant kettle behind her. Thick black liquid pours into a pristine white mug and then she passes it across the counter. 'Do you want cream, or are you sweet enough?'

The cow gives a big sickly smile.

I ignore the question and dump three pound coins on the counter. I make a point to tell her to keep the change but don't add a suggestion as to where she can shove the extra 20p. Nadia recently called Dawn my nemesis, which was pretty much spot on.

Back at the table and Nadia takes in my black coffee. She eyes me over glasses she isn't wearing. 'Aren't you having the avocado sourdough?'

'Not today.'

She moves on instantly, keen to get down to business. 'Did you hear?'

'About what?'

'Sharon Tanner and her son, Frank, are both critical in hospital. Hit-and-run on Green Road last night. Everyone's talking about it.'

She nods past me towards the rest of the nearly full café. I follow her gaze to where tables of people actually are talking to one another.

'People are saying they won't pull through…'

There's a sparkle in Nadia's eye. It's not relish at what's happened, more the excitement that something noteworthy has happened in this godforsaken place. When people spend all their time gossiping about whose front garden is looking a bit overgrown, something like a hit-and-run is gold.

I don't know what to say. I think of something like 'gosh' or 'that's terrible', but it's just words. 'Critical' is better than 'dead'. That's what I tell myself anyway.

'Do the police have any leads?' I manage.

'Don't know,' Nadia replies, in her element. 'There can't have been too many people driving around those roads at that time of night. It's not like it's a main road.' Her gaze darts from side to side and then she leans in conspiratorially. 'It could be anyone around here.'

I half turn and do another sweep of the room, largely because I sense it's the thing to do. It feels like everyone's doing the same. We're all looking to one another, wondering who was driving. Nadia's right. *Annoyingly* right. It isn't as if there's a large pool of potential drivers who might have been on Green Road at night. It links a couple of housing estates on one side of town to the other. There's no A-road or motorway in that direction; no out-of-town retail park, or out-of-place McDonald's to where people might have been heading. I'd not thought of that until now.

'It could've been someone passing through,' I say.

Nadia grimaces slightly, not wanting to lose the idea that the hit-and-runner is currently in our midst. 'Doubt it,' she says. 'I bet it's a man, though. They always joke about women drivers – but it's the blokes who race around those back lanes. Don't see many women wrapping their cars around lamp posts, do you?'

It's another statement to which I'm not sure how to respond.

'There's another thing,' Nadia adds.

I peer up from my untouched coffee and realise she's staring straight at me.

She knows.

There's a moment of panic; that itching, gnawing knowledge that I'm going to prison. Except…

She *doesn't* know. She can't. I've got to get a grip on the voice that keeps whispering in my ear.

'What?' I say.

'Didn't you argue with Sharon the other day?'

'How do you know that?'

Nadia focuses on me for a moment more and then glances away towards the rest of the café. 'I can't remember. Someone must have told me.'

I wait, though she doesn't elaborate. She clearly *does* know who told her, although I suppose it doesn't matter who said what. News of my argument with Sharon in the car park was always going to go around the usual circles sooner or later. If Nadia knows, then other people will.

I'm ready to give Nadia the gossipy nugget she wants when the door goes again. It feels like everyone's watching as a pair of uniformed police officers walk in and head to the counter.

Gary spots me and offers a short nod. I recognise his colleague but don't know the guy's name.

This is nothing unusual: two workers popping into a café to get a coffee but, on this morning of all, there's a sizzle in the room. It's unfulfilled because the only thing that happens is that Gary's companion orders two coffees and then the officers hang around the counter until they're ready. After that, they turn and head back outside.

When they're gone, it's like everyone breathes out as one.

Nadia has her hands wrapped around her mug when I turn back to her.

'What do you reckon that was about?' she asks.

'Probably starting their shift and wanted a coffee to get going.'

Nadia nods shortly, though I suspect there's a little disappointment there. Imagine the scene if the officers had stormed in and cuffed someone, before dragging that person out to a police car. It would have been the greatest piece of *you-had-to-be-there* gossip this town has ever seen.

I almost have to remind myself that *I* am the driver.

Nadia hasn't forgotten what we were talking about. 'So… what happened with you and Sharon?' she asks.

'It wasn't really an argument,' I reply. 'I saw her eldest, that Josh lad, picking on a smaller kid in the car park. I told him to knock it off and then Sharon got involved.'

'Josh…' Nadia repeats the name and, though it's only a single word, there's enough context. Everyone is aware of Josh around here. If the café's customers, me included, are the chattering middle classes, then Sharon, Josh and Frank are part of the counterpoint working classes. She's got two sons from different fathers; neither of whom are in the picture. I barely know her – but even *I'm* aware of that. Not that it should matter – but for some people in gossiping Prowley, it does.

My stomach growls angrily: a reminder that I've not eaten anything today. Perhaps she hears it but it could be because I've not touched my coffee. Either way, Nadia has spotted that something is not right.

'What's wrong?' she asks.

'Tired,' I reply.

Nadia flicks a glance towards Dawn and I don't correct her. Dawn might be at the root of some problems in my life – but definitely not this current one.

She leans in and whispers quietly enough that only I can hear: 'I got these sleeping pills off the internet about six months ago. You can have a few if you want…?'

Nadia reaches towards her bag but I stop her. 'Maybe another day. I'm sure it's just a one-time thing.'

She isn't convinced and, though I am lying, it's not about the thing she thinks.

'How's Craig?' I ask, changing the subject with the deftness of a jackhammer.

'Craig…' Nadia blinks her way through her son's name as if she's never heard it before. 'He's looking forward to Christmas.'

'All kids do.'

'True. I just wish the school holidays weren't so long. Teachers don't know they're born. If it's not holidays, then they're on strike. They're off work more than they're on it. They—' She cuts herself off abruptly. I'm not a teacher in the sense of working in a school, but I am a private tutor and there is some degree of crossover. 'I didn't mean it like that,' she adds. 'You work in the holidays, don't you?'

'Teachers have marking to do and lessons to plan as well.'

Nadia bites her lip and shrinks slightly away. I don't really mind. She's always had something of a habit of plonking her foot in situations and it's usually hilarious. We were once at a charity event where she had a tipsy rant about how lazy builders were and how they all avoided taxes. The organiser's husband was, obviously, a self-employed builder, so it went down about as well as a guy with BO in a lift.

After the faux pas, she takes this moment to excuse herself, and then heads off to the toilet. By the time she re-emerges, this will be forgotten and we'll never talk of it again. That's what we do. It's what we've always done.

I take out my phone to pass the time and it's only a couple of seconds later that a new message comes through. There's no worry about who it's from this time as Bryan's name and number is still stored in my phone, despite the number of times I've thought about deleting it.

Bryan: *We need to talk*

It's almost instinctive but I glance across towards the counter, where Dawn is staring directly at me. She turns as soon as I spot her but there's no question she was watching.

Me: *What about? I'm with Nadia at B&B*

Bryan: *Not on text. It's important. Will pop round later if it's ok*

I start a reply to tell him that it's definitely *not* okay. There can't be anything we have left to say to one another that has to be done in person. I'm about to press send when another of those creeping, flickering thoughts sneaks through me.

Bryan now lives on Green Road.

When I thought I'd hit a bin, one of my first thoughts was that he lived nearby. It washed past me once I realised what I'd done.

Me: *When?*

Bryan: *5pm*

Me: *Fine*

NINE

The conversation with Nadia never gets back on track after she emerges from the bathroom. I sip at my coffee but can only taste the bitterness and end up leaving half of it. We make small talk about things like the town's Christmas tree and decorations but neither of our hearts are in it.

I feel stuck. There's a part of me that's all about the self-preservation. Someone's texting me claiming they know what I did, although there's no proof they do and I don't know what they want. Bryan wants to talk about something – although there are no clues as to what – and then there's the police. It feels as if any or all of those things could come crashing into me at any point.

I shouldn't admit this but the sense of survival is easily eclipsing what I feel for Sharon and Frank. I never thought I'd be this type of person but it's easy to judge from afar. It's not as if I'm glorifying in what I did. I'm not glad it happened and I'd do an awful lot to go back and change things.

None of that means I value strangers above myself and my own family.

It sounds terrible – but how many can truly say they'd be different? It feels like a big a step to admit that.

Trust me, nobody knows until it's them.

Nadia and I leave the café together. She asks where I'm parked and I make vague motions around the corner, without explicitly lying about how I got here. We do the double kiss thing, make even vaguer promises about catching up soon, and then she disappears off to the small car park at the back of the café.

I dig out gloves from my jacket pocket and am putting them on when I realise I'm being watched.

Sharon's son Josh is standing close to a low wall across the road from the café. He has a phone in his hands but he's not looking at that: his gaze is fixed on me. He's in a pair of scruffy jeans, with a grey hoody, which I think are the clothes he was wearing when I saw him bullying the other boy. I can't remember for sure.

He slips the phone into a back pocket and then puts his hands into the pockets of his top. With all that, his stare never leaves me.

I turn and start walking, taking the turn where I indicated to Nadia that I was parked. As soon as I'm around the bend, I quicken my pace until I'm going more or less as fast as I can without running. It's only a few seconds until I hear the steps behind me. I risk a glance backwards and Josh is there, hands still in pockets as he hurries along the pavement behind me. I've got a head start but his legs are so much longer than mine that there's no question he'll catch up.

Stopping and talking to him doesn't seem too appealing, so I take the next turn and, as soon as I'm past the corner of the wall, I run.

I was never good at PE when we were at school. Part of it was simply that I didn't care. I didn't *want* to be good at hockey, or athletics, or whatever was on that week. Being picked close to last was a badge of honour that meant I could get away with hanging around in the corner of a field and trying not to get anywhere close to a ball. The downside of that is that, aside from my incredibly brief dalliance with getting fit after Bryan left, I've done no exercise in around twenty years.

I've barely jogged the length of two houses when something in my stomach starts to twinge. I'm forced to slow back to a walk and, when I turn, Josh is at the corner. He hasn't upped his pace but it will make little difference if he continues to stride at the same rate.

His house and the hospital are in the opposite direction to where I'm going, so he has to be following me. When I check my shoulder again, there's a determined relish in his face. It's the same sort of intimidation I saw when he was standing over the smaller boy.

I take the next turn, so that I'm heading back towards the High Street. I run for as long as I can but, by the time I've slowed back to a walk and re-check over my shoulder, it doesn't feel as if Josh has lagged any further behind.

My heart is bounding – and it's not entirely from the running.

The car park for Bread And Butter is a little ahead of me and, beyond that, the High Street. I slip around the gate at the back of the car park and then slide through the narrow gap in between a 4x4 and a smaller car before making a dash towards the far side of the tarmac. When I turn this time, Josh is at the gate looking for a way across that doesn't involve jamming himself into the smaller space between the cars. It's gained me a few seconds but not much more.

Prowley is hardly a vibrant shopping hub but the one thing now in my favour is that there are people on the High Street. If Josh wants to confront me, then he's at least going to have to do it when there are others around.

Instead of heading towards Bread And Butter, I go the other way. There is no traffic, so I dart across to the far side and then pause in the doorway to the M&S Simply Food. Surely, the worst thing that's ever happened in a place like this is that someone's dropped a jar of organic marmalade.

I'm panting like a thirsty dog. Sweating like a priest in a sauna. I'm sticky and need a shower. When I look across the road this time, there's no sign of Josh.

I continue to wait. Probably a minute passes until I push my way into the shop. Even if he's not following me any longer, I figure it's best to hide in plain sight for a while.

That's when the text arrives from the unknown number.

Anon: *How was the coffee?*

TEN

The walk home that should take twenty minutes actually takes me closer to forty. I stop frequently to check behind, even though there's never anyone there. Whenever a car passes, I press to the innermost part of the pavement, while keeping a close eye for whoever might be driving. Not only is there Josh to worry about, there's also the mystery texter.

I make a mental list of everyone who saw me drinking coffee. There are the obvious people like Dawn, Nadia and Gary but, other than that, there were a lot of locals in the café too. I doubt I could name them all but enough people would know me. It's not quite true that it could be anyone – but it could be anyone from a long list.

I haven't replied to the latest message. There was no demand and no particular reason to say anything back. Whoever it is wants to intimidate me and, though they're doing a cracking job, I don't have to make it obvious that I'm affected.

When I get home, I already have the key in the lock of the front door when I change my mind. Now it's daylight, I *need* to see where the crash happened. I know that old trope of criminals returning to a scene, and if it's true, I now know why. It's a need, not a want. The people who don't do it are surely the odd ones? I want to know if there's a skid mark on the road, whether there's any sign of where a pushchair could have gone, if there are tyre marks on the verge – plus how close Bryan's house is to the scene.

Instead of going through the door, I head into the garage. My car is as it was left but, as soon as I spot it, I know I still won't be able to drive. I'm not one to suffer from anxiety or panic attacks, not even after Bryan left. I've always been one of those Keep Calm And Carry On types from the poster. I've taught students who've struggled with extreme nerves before exams. Smart children who go to pieces at the very idea of having to sit with a test in front of them.

I feel it now.

The shorter, desperate breaths; the way my mouth is so dry that I can barely swallow; the fuzziness that seems just out of reach. I'm falling and the floor is coming at me faster and faster. I tense and brace for the collision but—

My eyes are closed and I'm focusing on taking a long, slow, gentle breath. I count to ten without exhaling and then let out a long, slow gasp. Then I do it again.

When I open my eyes, the fuzz has gone. My heart is beating so loudly that it's like I can hear it, rather than feel it.

I need to visit the scene but there's no way I can drive. I move around the side of the car, into the back corner next to the tool rack. There's a rake, a spade and hoe – none of which I've ever used – and adjacent to those is a bike. It was bought in a fit of temporary madness when Bryan got himself into cycling.

Of all the things I thought would come from his earlier-than-average midlife crisis, fitness was not one of them. He couldn't just grow old, get fat and buy a convertible car or ridiculous motorbike like everyone else. He couldn't even pick up a golf obsession like all the other Pringle- and chino-wearing tosspots around here. Instead, he had to get fit and disappear off with another woman.

At the time, I bought a bike like his, thinking we'd have cosy afternoon pootles around the country lanes. I forgot that it's usually raining – not to mention that he wasn't interested in pootling. I should've had him committed the moment he started talking about cycling up things. No hill round here was big enough, so he'd go on day-long rides out to find bigger climbs.

In the time since I bought the bike, I think I've used it twice. The biggest reason is that I hate cycling; the second is that drivers around here are psychopathic.

The thought has already been and gone before I realise that I've done worse than all of them.

I wheel the bike out from its alcove and spin the wheels. It turns, which is some sort of indication that it goes. I have no idea what I'm doing. The tyres are squishy but there's an old pump of Bryan's propped against the wall and I manage to figure out how to pump them up. With that done, I spin the pedals and it *feels* like everything is in order. I guess there's only one way to find out…

I have no idea how people do things like ride a bike to work. It's not that far from where I live to the site where Sharon was hit but, in that time, I skid on a patch of mud, almost wobble into the gutter twice – and then a van overtakes me so closely that I feel the whoosh of the wing mirror passing a couple of centimetres from my head. It was already past before I really noticed, else the terror would have surely sent me spiralling.

It wasn't that long ago I was determined to try to keep doing things normally enough so that I wouldn't stand out. I'm already on Green Road by the time I realise I'm doing the precise opposite of that.

When I get to the site, it is unmissable. One side of the road is now open but there is police tape across half of the carriageway, as well as a white tent covering part of the verge. There is a second, smaller tent concealing a spot that is a couple of metres from that. Two tents. Two victims. I suppose it is true.

I can't understand how I failed to see anyone other than Sharon last night. The rumour that a buggy could have reached the other side of the hedge seems impossible. The greenery at the side of the road is dense, overgrown and far taller than me. I doubt I could push through it, while the chance of something going over has to be slim to non-existent. A pole-vaulter would struggle to get across. If there were two victims – as the tents suggest – they were both in front of me.

I had a mental list of things to look for but it all falls out of my mind as I take in the scene. A sombre rainbow of flowers has been left on the verge, a little along the lane from the tents. It's not only that: in the daylight, the road doesn't feel anywhere near as imposing as it did in the dark. It's wider and the blue sky, plus the crisp frost in the shadows, gives the sense of a burgeoning winter day.

I can see Bryan's house from here. It's further along the lane, up on the bank, on the opposite side of the road from the tents. There's a short driveway, the view of which is swallowed by hedges, although the stone property itself is easy enough to see from the road. It's one of those remote places that has its own septic tank, because it's too far from the regular sewer system. I've never been inside but I've imagined a roaring fire on Christmas morning, with smoke spiralling from the chimney. There'd be a frost on the ground outside, with a cosy Aga seeping warmth into the kitchen as dinner slowly roasts. There would be a bright, blinking Christmas tree both indoors and out.

Not that I've thought about it too much…

I can't see a house from which Sharon might have emerged, though there is a wooden pair of gateposts a little past the tents. I'd assume there's a property beyond, but it's impossible to see because of the overgrown hedges.

'I didn't know you cycle…'

I'm standing with my feet on the ground and the bike between my legs – but I almost topple sideways at the unexpected interruption. I don't know how I missed him but Gary has appeared at my side, as if he's apparated there. He's in his police uniform with a thick, long jacket over the top.

'I don't,' I reply, trying to maintain some degree of composure – which isn't easy when straddling something. 'I'm trying to get back into it.'

'Is December the best time?'

Gary is smiling and doesn't seem suspicious, even though he's right. Anyone who's taken even a passing interest in my actions this morning will know that something's up.

I pat my stomach: 'Trying to get a head start before Christmas.'

He laughs a little and pinches his own belly. 'I should probably do the same. I used to be into running but it's too hard on the knees.'

I lay my bike down on the verge and we stand together for a moment. There are two police vans parked on the other side of the scene, plus a smaller, unmarked, white car. A single officer is leaning on the back of the car, talking into his phone. Everything feels so still, so sombre. Even the birds are quiet – although the time of year might have something to do with that.

'I feel like I should've brought flowers,' I say, angling towards the bouquets that have already been left. I can't see any skid marks on the road – but it doesn't mean they aren't there.

Gary doesn't reply and, from nowhere, it feels like he knows.

I've taken a quarter-step away from him before I realise I've done it. The terror feels momentarily crippling. Is this how everything is to be from now on?

'Are you out here for any reason?' he asks, eventually.

'Exercise,' I say. 'There are no hills out this way. I like the flats.'

He doesn't reply to that either.

'Have they named who was hit?' I ask.

'I'm not sure. It isn't my call.'

'But you said there was more than one person involved. There was a child…'

He doesn't react, managing to maintain a stoic stare without so much as flinching.

'I'm sure it'll all come out in due course,' he says flatly.

I have to stop myself from rifling off a list questions that I know I shouldn't. I want to ask about any leads they might have or whether there are witnesses. About why Sharon might have been on the road in the first place and whether the gateposts are the entrance to where she lives. I wonder if he knows how she's doing at hospital; or, perhaps, whether she's at hospital at all. So much of what I've heard has been conjecture.

'Leah's looking forward to seeing you later,' Gary says.

It takes me a second to remember he means that his daughter is coming over to talk about her problems at school. Things seem to flit in and out of my mind with such ease at the moment.

'I'm looking forward to seeing her.'

It's the right thing to say, even though I doubt many teenagers are champing at the bit in order to visit a private tutor. All those hours at school are bad enough, let alone extra on top. I know where I stand.

Gary's radio hisses angrily and he reaches down to the device, which is attached to his lapel. He says 'One minute' and then takes a step away.

'I've got to get back,' he says. 'Might be best avoiding this road for a few days if you're out on your bike.'

'Okay.'

I watch as he walks off towards the tents. From the angle of his neck, it looks as if he's talking into his radio as he goes, although there's no chance of me overhearing. I retrieve the bike from the roadside and then wobble my way back in the direction I came. It's hard to take satisfaction from anything at the moment but I do relish the fact that I ride all the way home without stopping. It's only a few miles – but still more of an achievement than I'd have thought myself capable.

With the bike re-abandoned in the garage, I realise how sweaty I am. My clothes cling to me uncomfortably and I'm somehow hot and cold at the same time. When I get into the main house, the traitorous mirror in the hall shows me as red-faced and blotchy. I'm about to head upstairs to the shower when I realise I've missed a text.

Anon: *Nice bike*

ELEVEN

I can't stop myself from replying this time.

Me: *Are you following me?*

The response comes almost instantly.

Anon: *Don't have to. Do you really think visiting the scene was a good idea?!*

I don't answer this time. I shouldn't have done before – but there are a lot of things I shouldn't have done that I've found myself doing. If a test of a person is how they react while facing adversity, then it doesn't say much for me.

Who knows about the bike?

Gary is the obvious person but if he is aware of what I did, then why would he bother with texts? He's a police officer and could arrest me.

I didn't specifically notice anyone else while on the bike, though I was passed by cars. Neighbours could have seen me, too. It only takes one person who knows me to have been driving past. It's December and I didn't see another cyclist on the road – so it isn't as if I blended in.

It's not even clear why I went. I thought I'd feel some sense of closure or acceptance after seeing the scene but, if anything, I'm more confused.

I call Katie's name in case she's decided to nip home. She is supposed to be at college all day but has occasionally come home for various teenagery reasons. Sometimes I ask, sometimes it's best to leave her to it. She isn't one of those kids who's going to drop out or throw a strop because she thinks the world's against her. If she wants to skive an afternoon off here and there, I tend to let it go.

After showering, I head back to the living room where the Christmas tree lights are still on. I consider turning them off, especially as it's daylight outside, but think better of it. Although I didn't want it at first, having the tree there now makes me think of Katie. There's comfort in that she put it up.

I turn on the television and watch through the weather report until the local news comes on. It's probably the first bulletin I've watched in a good three or four years – and even back then it wouldn't have been something for which I'd gone out of my way. The idea of local television news seems so archaically quaint now, which is scary considering how it was the soundtrack of the house when I was growing up. When he was home from work, Dad would watch every bulletin throughout the day and evening.

It's probably not a surprise but the hit-and-run is the top story. A serious-sounding presenter doesn't mess around, going straight in with: 'A woman and her two-year-old son are in critical condition this lunchtime after what police are calling a hit-and-run. The incident occurred on Green Road, Prowley, at some point yesterday evening…'

Critical.

The word jumps out, confirming what Nadia said this morning. *Both* victims are critical. In terms of how police or paramedics might describe something, I'm not sure what it means. Is critical worse than serious? Does it mean life-threatening? Is it bad but stable?

She continues and then the screen cuts across to a man in a suit and tie, who is standing in roughly the same spot on Green Road as I was an hour ago. The white tents are clear in the background and the number of uniformed officers has jumped from the two I saw to five or six. A pair of police vans are also there for good measure. The word 'live' is in red letters in the top corner.

It must be drone footage that comes next, because there's an aerial shot from over the scene. As it arcs above the white tents, I can see the house over the top of the hedges where Sharon likely lives. It's such a short distance from where I hit her that she couldn't have been far outside her gates when I heard the bang. It's hard to get past how different it all looks compared to when it was dark and wet.

The camera switches back to the suited man, and then pans sideways to someone in a uniform, who is introduced as an inspector.

'This is a serious incident with what could turn out to be tragic consequences,' the inspector says. 'Sharon Tanner was walking on this unlit road with her two-year-old son.'

I already know who I hit – but to hear it officially for the first time still feels shocking. There's no dream and no mistake.

The suited man is busy playing the gormless role: 'I gather conditions were unfavourable last night…?'

'They were. The weather was wet, windy and cold – and certainly not ideal for driving.'

'Does that mean the driver might have been unaware of the collision?'

I hold my breath, waiting for the response. I'd not considered the possibility before but this could be my out. Knowingly hitting a mother and baby and then driving off is heinous – but what if that person didn't know they had done it…

My respite lasts barely a second.

'We believe that to be highly unlikely given the force with which the victim was hit.'

'Are there any leads as to the identity of the driver?'

The staged nature of the conversation is so obvious that they might as well be reading scripts. It's so bad that the inspector answers almost before the question is out.

'We are currently following a number of leads that we hope will lead to us identifying the driver.'

It sounds ominous: for me, if no one else. I wonder what leads he's talking about. Perhaps there are tyre marks that are being traced? Maybe there's a hidden CCTV camera? They could easily find out there was a football practice happening nearby – and then they'd figure out the time. From there, they could find out who was there and who was picked up. It wouldn't be a long list – and I'd stand out because I was late.

There's also nothing I can do about it.

By the time I zone back into the news, the man in the suit is talking again.

'Were the victims walking in the road?' he asks.

'We're not sure,' the inspector replies. 'There is no pavement on this stretch of the road. The verge would have been boggy last night and, because the victim was pushing a buggy with her child inside, there's every chance she was on the road surface.'

Sharon was in the road. She had to be. I wasn't aware of her but I know I didn't swerve into the verge. It could have been anyone who was driving. Anybody could be in the same position as me.

'Was there any indication that speed could have played a factor?'

The inspector shakes a head. 'We can't say at this time. What I would like to emphasise is that we know the driver is out there somewhere. That person might even be watching this. If you are, then I would appeal for you to come forward.'

I turn off the television before any more can be said. I've seen appeals like this before on the news – but never with someone talking directly to me. It's no wonder they do them. It's given me chills.

My phone is no distraction. There are no more text messages from any number, let alone the mystery texter. I'm in limbo, waiting for something to happen, rather than being in any control of what happens next. It's an unsettling feeling when a person's own destiny is in someone else's hands. Perhaps I'll get through the day and nothing more will happen – but I will still wake up tomorrow with the anxiety of being found out. Then the next day and the next. There's a little part of me that wants the police to come knocking because, if they don't, there might never be a time when I can wake up without this guilt tapping away.

For now, I go to the cupboard and pull out the guide sheets I'll likely need for when Leah comes over later. There's an assumption with teachers and tutors that we're big fans of things like textbooks and worksheets. The truth is that we often find them as incomprehensibly dull as students do. One of my old colleagues said that the biggest skill to teaching was the ability to take an idea and make it understandable to anyone. If that's true, then the people who create these workbooks are the opposite of teachers.

Just as they did last night, the words swim on the page. They blend into one another once more until it's all one big ink stain. It could be my vision. An eye test is probably overdue, although that's the last thing I want to be admitting after hitting someone with a car.

I leave the papers on the living room table and head into the kitchen. There's still coffee in the pot, so I pour it into a mug and microwave it. After a few mouthfuls, I try reading again, though it makes little difference.

I find myself back on the sofa with the iPad, reading through the local news stories about the hit-and-run. These words are unmoving on the page, so there's something deeper going on than simply poor eyesight. None of the reports seem to name Frank, although Sharon's identity is now common knowledge. The word 'critical' is repeated over and over.

Somehow, more than two hours pass. It's when the lights on the tree start appearing to glow brighter that I notice it's a little after four o'clock. It's more or less dark outside and I've wasted the entire day. When I push myself up, my head spins and my temples throb. The lights on the tree make it worse, whirring kaleidoscopically in a circle. I have to hold onto the armrest to keep myself steady.

Whenever I had headaches or dizzy spells as a child, my mum would say 'how much water have you had today?'. In her mind, water was the cure-all for everything. She'd be in her element with this.

I get myself into the kitchen and open the cupboard next to the fridge. Ever since we moved in, the bottom half has been the space crammed with various medicines and pills. There are cough mixtures in here that likely date back to when Katie was at primary school. Neither Bryan nor myself have ever been great at throwing things out when we're done with them.

Well, that's not entirely true. He threw out *one thing* when he was done with it…

I shunt the various boxes and bottles around until I find the blue box with 'paracetamol' on the side. That gets me nowhere because, when I lever apart the ends, all I discover is a pop-packet where all the pills have been pushed out.

Katie.

I have sometimes worried about the painkillers she takes at the merest mention of any ache. It's hard to be too critical, though. Children ape the behaviour of their parents and I've never been the type to grit my teeth through something like a headache. At the gentlest hint of pain, I'm busy reaching for the painkillers in the way a junkie's grabbing for a needle.

I grab my coat from the hook in the hall and re-layer myself with scarf, hat and gloves before heading back out. The temperature has crashed to something close to zero. The biting breeze gnaws at my face as I head towards the shop at the end of the road. It's not a long walk – and I take particular notice of the pair of CCTV cameras at the front. One is pointing down towards the entrance, while the other is angled towards the road. I would have definitely been caught on this when driving last night – but the corner isn't a direct route to Green Road. I could have been going anywhere.

Inside, and I grab two boxes of painkillers from the rack close to the till. When I was young, I could have bought a tub of hundreds that would've lasted for years. Now it's twelve at a time. I think that says more about my age than it does anything else.

The man behind the counter barely looks up as I tap my bank card to pay.

I pop a pair of tablets before I get outside, swallowing them without water in the way only an experienced low-level addict can.

I'm halfway out the door when I almost walk into someone who is on his way in. He's shorter than me, in a puffy dark coat, and takes a step backwards to let me past. It's only as I slip around him that I realise it's the boy who I saw being slapped by Josh two days ago. After everything from last night, it feels like such a distant memory, though I suppose it was what started this. If it wasn't for the argument I'd had with Sharon, perhaps I would have stopped after hitting her.

I can tell from his widening eyes that he recognises me. He was about to head into the shop but stops as the door swings closed.

'Hi,' I say.

He takes a step backwards towards the corner.

'What's your name?' I ask.

One thing I've learned as a tutor is that using a firm voice to ask a straightforward question can get surprising results. There's no reason for him to answer – but he does.

'Thomas.'

It's like a reflex, as if he couldn't refuse. His mouth hangs open as if he can't explain why he replied.

'What was going on in the car park the other day?'

'Nothing.'

'It didn't look like nothing.'

Thomas takes another step back. The large coat makes him look bigger than I remember him being. His hood's down and he has a shaven head. No hat, gloves, or scarf. He turns to leave but I reach forward and grip his shoulder gently. He shrugs me off, although doesn't leave.

'It *looked* serious,' I say.

'It wasn't.'

Thomas starts to walk away from the shop, changing his mind about going in, and I skip a few steps to slot in alongside him.

'Whaddya want?' he asks.

'Why did Josh hit you?'

'No reason.'

'There must be a reason.'

'Cos that's what he does!'

Thomas ups his pace and I have to reach something close to a jog to keep up. 'That's what he does to who?'

'To everyone.'

Thomas stops – but I'm moving so quickly that I'm already a couple of steps past him when I realise. It's like Wile E. Coyote carrying on over a cliff after Road Runner has skidded to a halt.

'What do you want?' he asks. He's angry now, fists balled, eyes scrunched.

'I'm sorry,' I reply.

We stand at an impasse for a moment – then he spins and races back the way we've just come. This time I don't follow.

TWELVE

As I get back to the house, there's a girl standing at the front door, checking her phone. She turns to leave as I slot in behind her and ends up yelping with alarm as she jumps backwards.

'It's me, Leah,' I tell her. 'Sorry for scaring you. I had to pop out.'

She tugs her hair straighter and moves away so I can get to the door. Her father is very much a typical police officer with the way he stands tall and authoritative, though Leah has inherited none of that. She's skinny with youth and slouches as she stands. Her arms are folded across her front.

'Cold, isn't it?' I say.

'I guess.'

I unlock the door and we head inside. I point Leah through to the living room and tell her I'll be in shortly. After that, I get rid of all my outer layers and then edge upstairs and knock on Katie's door. I call her name but if she's home, then she's not answering.

Back downstairs, Leah has curled herself into a corner of the sofa. She's all elbows and knees in the angular way that only skinny teenagers can manage.

This is work, some degree of normality. Something different to think about.

'Do you want anything to drink?' I ask.

A shake of the head. 'I've got tea at home after this.'

'What's for tea?'

She's been trying to keep a stoic face, not wanting to give anything away – but this causes a crack as the corner of her lips curl into a smile. 'Beans on Marmite on toast.'

'Is that your favourite?'

'Isn't it everyone's?'

She laughs and, despite everything that's happened in the last twenty-four hours, it's hard not to smile. There's something endlessly joyous about a youngster who makes their own jokes.

'What year are you in at school?'

'Nine. Hang on.'

She scrambles into the bag she's brought and brings out the interview page I'd given her dad. It very much looks as if it's been crumpled at the bottom of a bag and then jumped on a couple of times.

I take the page and flatten it, though don't unfold it yet.

'I gather you have some tests coming up…?'

'Yes.'

'What are they?'

'I dunno…'

She shrinks into herself, arms folded, and stares towards the floor. I already know the answers but these sorts of questions are a reasonable guide into a student's mindset.

The old compulsory SAT exams that students used to take at the end of year nine, when they are thirteen or fourteen, were abolished – but many schools still run their own end-of-year tests. It will be these with which Leah is struggling.

'What do you enjoy at school?'

Her gaze flickers up. 'What do you mean?'

'What's your favourite subject?'

She shrugs but it's the in I was after as she starts to tell me how she likes music and art. We spend a good five minutes talking about this and it quickly becomes clear that she's a creative young woman. After talking about everything she *does* like, I steer things round to what she doesn't – which is when we get onto her struggles in maths and, to a lesser degree, science. She's uncrossed her arms by now.

'Dad keeps talking about getting it right,' Leah says. 'He says that if I don't, I'll already be behind when it gets to my GCSEs.'

'Those are still two and a half years away. Lots can change between now and then…'

'He says it's the rest of my life.'

This kind of talk always leaves me in an awkward position. These sorts of tests are simultaneously important and not. It has almost no impact on a person's life as part of a bigger picture – but there are other indicators at play. The discipline of trying hard at things we might not enjoy is valuable to take forward in life. League table rankings mean schools are also beholden to results, so they have to tell their students that exams are the be-all and end-all. Parents often say they hate them, while also using the ratings to hunt down the apparent best school in the area.

Kids are pawns but it's hard to explain to anyone, let alone a young person who is going through enormous changes.

'Something like maths can be important forever,' I say, 'even if it's just to help you with things like making a budget when you're older. If you want to know how much you can spend on things you like, you'll need to have an idea of what you earn against what you have to buy, like food.'

Leah nods slowly, though I wouldn't say she was convinced.

'How would you feel about coming here once a week to work on your maths?'

A shrug.

'You don't have to.'

'Dad wants me to.'

'But what do *you* want to?'

Leah screws up her lips. 'I don't know…'

'I don't want to force you to spend time here if that isn't what you want.'

Before Leah can answer, there's a bump from the front door and then the sound of voices. Katie's head pokes around the corner of the entrance to the living room and she spots Leah before looking to me.

'I didn't know you were working,' she says.

'How was college?'

'Fine.'

She turns back to the hallway, where Richard has shuffled in behind her. He's back in his all-black get-up. Katie is used to me being here with students and knows the drill. The living room has never been her domain anyway. Without another word, she heads for the stairs and then, with Richard a couple of steps behind, she disappears up.

'That's my daughter, Katie,' I say.

'I know,' Leah replies. She pauses and then adds: 'When do you want me back?'

'Are you certain you want to do this?'

There's a small nod and then a mumbled: 'I think so.'

It's as much enthusiasm as I could expect – but at least I've got her to say it. The best way to make anybody do something is have them think it's their idea. That is especially true with learning.

'How about four o'clock on Friday?' I say, before holding up the sheet of paper she gave me. 'I'll look at this in the meantime.'

'Okay.'

'We'll start with an hour and see how it goes.'

'Okay.'

I stand and she mirrors, ready to go. I consider asking about her dad and whether he's said anything about what happened at Green Road. He might not have told Leah something specifically but she could have overheard him talking. The only thing kids like more than having secrets is telling them.

I know I shouldn't but, when we get onto the front step outside, I'm almost there. I start with 'Your dad…' unsure where the rest of the sentence is going, when a familiar car pulls up outside.

Leah looks at me expectantly and I almost talk over myself, adding: 'I'll talk to your dad.'

She nods and then I trail her to the end of the path, watching as she heads along the pavement and then starts to cross the road. The orange of the street lights is sending a mucky gloom onto the street below. While that's happening, the car doors open. Bryan clambers out from the driver's side… and Dawn O'Neill emerges from the other.

They stand in unison at that awkward distance where, to an unknowing eye, it's not entirely obvious they're with one another.

'I thought it was just you,' I say to Bryan.

'I think we all need to talk.'

It's strange to see him as he is now. He lost so much weight that even his face is different. I got used to the second chin and pudgy cheeks; now, it's all chiselled and accentuated. He looks as young as the day we married. *Younger.*

I do my best to ignore Dawn, even though I can feel her watching me.

Bryan rubs his hands together. 'Shall we go inside? It's a bit nippy out here.'

I turn and head for the house, holding the door open as Bryan and Dawn move inside. As far as I know, she's never been inside before – but it doesn't seem worth arguing over it.

As I'm about to close the door, I notice Gary in his window over the road. It's hard to tell from the distance but I think he might nod at me. I return it with a small wave, which is unreturned because he closes the curtains. I wonder if he saw me at all.

In the living room and Bryan looks out of place on the sofa. He always had the reclining armchair when we lived here together – but now he's in one corner, with Dawn sitting in the other.

I hate being the bigger person – pettiness is so much more satisfying – but I go through the motions anyway.

'Do you want something to drink?' I ask.

Bryan looks to Dawn, whose face is stony. 'I think we should probably get on with this,' she says, apparently talking for the both of them.

She continues looking to Bryan, as do I after I slink into the armchair. *Bryan's* armchair. He doesn't take the hint at first but then jolts as he realises Dawn isn't going to do the talking.

'We're getting married,' he says.

Dawn uses the moment to reach and take his hand. She turns to look at me, though I can't bring myself to return the stare. I don't trust what might come out.

'Oh…' I say.

Nobody speaks. Bryan is looking to the floor, not wanting to catch my eye, while Dawn's doing the opposite.

The Christmas lights on the tree continue to twinkle. I thought I'd turned them off but I guess not. The mood isn't captured by the joy that might usually be associated with blinking fairy lights.

'It's a bit sudden,' I add, stumbling over the words.

It's Dawn who answers. 'It's not *that* sudden.'

I don't respond to that. The timeline of when she and Bryan got together has always been a little hazy. If it was after our divorce, then it's definitely quick to be going from that to marriage. I've long had suspicions that it might have been going on for a bit longer than that.

'We thought you should be the first to know,' Bryan says.

'How very kind of you…'

The silence hangs like a fart in a lift. I want to be away from it all. Dawn breaks a second or two before I do.

'You know, you don't have to be such a *bitch* about it.'

Her voice is almost a shout. She points a finger towards me but I don't give her the satisfaction of looking at her.

'We used to be friends,' I reply. 'But you ended up being a massive *bitch* about that.'

She pushes herself up, though Bryan holds onto her hand, tugging her towards him.

'I'm going to wait in the car,' she says.

Bryan releases her and she stomps past me and slams the front door on the way out. The boom echoes through the house and I sit, staring at Bryan, who is still watching the ground.

'Did that go how you wanted it to?' I ask.

'Not really.'

'Her idea?'

'Would you rather you found out off someone else?'

I don't reply straight away. I hate it when he's right. I hate it even more when *she* is. It's bad enough I spend money in her damn café.

We sit for a while, neither speaking.

'You're free to do what you want,' I say eventually. 'We both signed the papers.'

'We were thinking about doing it in Vegas over Easter next year.'

The response comes instantly, as if it has long been the plan.

'That feels apt,' I reply.

He doesn't respond and, as we sit resenting one another, there's a vague bump upstairs, with Katie or Richard moving around.

Bryan glances up and that's all it takes. We might have been apart for a while but I know him too well.

'You tell her yourself,' I say.

'I was thinking that perhaps—'

'She's your daughter, too. You can do your own dirty work.'

'It's not dirty work.'

'So you do it then.'

He rocks back into the corner of the sofa and scratches his head. He knows what Katie's reaction will be in the same way I do.

'I just thought—'

'I don't need the details, Bryan. You told me it was important to meet but all you wanted was for me to do you a favour.'

'It's not—'

'It is. You're worried what Katie's reaction will be, so you want to run away and have someone else tell her instead.'

'I don't.'

I stand and nod towards the hallway. 'She's upstairs. I'll call her down, shall I? You can tell her now.'

Bryan stands and squirms like a child desperate for the toilet. I assume it's because he's been called out but it isn't that at all. Or, it's not *entirely* that.

'The marriage wasn't the important bit,' he says. 'That's not why I wanted to talk to you in person.'

'So what is?'

He glances towards the front of the house and takes a breath. Then, for the first time since he got here, he looks me in the eyes. 'You better sit down.'

THIRTEEN

I do as I'm told. It's that magic thing where a stern-enough voice can make someone do something they don't really think about. Bryan lowers himself onto the sofa too.

'It's about the house,' he says.

'What about it?'

'I want to sell my half.'

It feels as if the air has been sucked from the room. I stare at him, wondering if there might be some sort of punchline but there isn't. Of course there isn't.

He's not done: 'We said we'd keep everything as it was until Katie's done her A-levels. That's, what, five months away? Six? I want to start planning ahead. I was thinking you could buy me out. You can carry on living here.'

It takes me a little while to reply. It shouldn't be a shock but it is. 'How can I afford that?'

'You could get another mortgage.'

'There's no way they'll approve me. I'll be a single person on a self-employed salary.'

Bryan's jacket is on the sofa, at his side. I'd not noticed him taking it off but he's wearing a tight-fitting T-shirt underneath. Everything he wears now is either something that's designer, or sportswear. Three or four years ago, he'd have split the seams trying to fit into it – but not any longer. He's moved on. He stares off towards the front of the house, with Dawn and the new car beyond.

'Are you really going to make me move?' I ask. When he doesn't answer, I continue. '*We* picked this area together. *We* picked this house.'

He smiles thinly but what is there to say?

'Dawn owns her house outright,' I add. 'She owns a café as well. Why do you need the money now?'

It's a general question, more spewing thoughts than anything else. It's half his house and, deep down, I know he's owed this financially. There's something about the way he starts scratching his arm that feels out of place.

'No reason,' he says. He fidgets and draws in his cheek, then crosses his arms. The awkwardness is like flashing back an hour to when Leah was here.

'There has to be a reason,' I say.

He shakes his head. 'We talked about it and—'

'So it's Dawn who wants this?'

'We're getting married, Jen. What's mine is hers and vice versa. With you and me, everything was split. It's only the house that's left – and that's because we didn't want to disrupt Katie.'

'You don't think selling a house from under her while she's doing her A-levels is disruptive…?'

'Nothing needs to happen until the summer. I just want us to be planning ahead now. After her exams, Katie will be off to uni and—'

'You don't know that.'

When he next looks to me, there's something much worse than anger or annoyance on his face. It's pity.

'She's leaving, Jen.'

I know this. Of course I do. Katie is a smart girl and she won't follow her boyfriend by failing to get the grades and then dropping out. She will be off to university in about nine months. I want her to go and I want her to excel.

Except…

What then? I'll be one of those singleton spinsters living in a house – or a tiny flat, at this rate – by myself. One of those weirdo cat ladies.

I have to gulp away the lump in my throat and, from nowhere, there are tears ticking the corners of my eyes. I turn to face the tree, unable to look at my former husband any longer. I disguise a sob as a cough but am likely not fooling anyone.

Bryan sits patiently as it takes me an age to get out a single sentence: 'Could you, um… wait a bit…?'

He shakes his head. 'We've already delayed. We said after Katie's exams. If we put it back another year, then it'll end up being another six months after that. Then another six months.'

I continue to stare at the tree, thinking of Katie and the way she dragged it down from the attic herself. She's grown up here. What sort of home will I have for her to visit in the holidays?

'The housing market's in good shape at the moment,' he adds. 'It's a good time to sell if you're going to do that.'

'You're going to kick me out of my house.'

Bryan bites his lip and waits for me to look towards him. 'I'm going to *sell* half of what I own. You can keep your half and do whatever you want with it.'

He speaks kindly and I know he's being reasonable. This day was always going to come and I should have been more ready.

I stand, wanting him to leave. The house might be half his – but I'm living here.

Bryan takes the hint and stands as well. 'I'm just going to nip to the loo,' he says.

He doesn't wait for permission – although I suppose he doesn't need it. He heads past me and then disappears up the stairs. I consider calling down Katie and telling her about her father's impending marriage. She's not quite forgiven him for walking out, let alone shacking up with Dawn. She will be far from happy and, though there's a part of me that would love to see her tear a strip off her father, it wouldn't be fair.

I take in the living room and know I'm mythologising. I wasn't going to bother with a tree but now, because Katie did, I'm thinking about how this could be my last Christmas in the house. How nothing will ever be the same again.

I'm distracted by the beep from my phone. It's on the armrest of the chair and I pick it up to find a message from the unknown number.

Anon: *I want you to do something for me*

I am so angry that I first type out a list of expletives before deleting them. I think about ignoring it and I know I probably should. Instead, I send back a single word.

Me: *No.*

The response is instant.

Anon: *You're going to do something for me*

It's impossible to miss the change in tone. No longer a request; a demand. Perhaps it's curiosity, or maybe it's stupidity. Either way, I tap out a reply.

Me: *What do you want?*

The reply pings back straight away.

Anon: *Not yet.*

I wait for a few seconds, wondering if this is the first of many replies. When nothing else comes through, I try calling the number. There's a lengthy pause, then a plip and then a woman telling me that the number is not in service. I try calling a second time, only to get the same outcome. I check the list of calls and then the text, wondering if I've somehow made a mistake. I haven't. Can someone have a number that's only for messaging?

Me: *I'm not doing anything for you.*

The reply comes as the toilet upstairs starts to flush.

Anon: *I'll go to the police. Try me.*

I don't know what to type back. It feels as if it's already gone too far. I don't understand how this person can know that I hit Sharon.

Me: *What do you know?*

There's the sound of taps running upstairs and then another text arrives… this time with a photo.

FOURTEEN

Bryan is still wringing his hands when he gets back into the living room. He plucks his jacket from the sofa and slips his arms inside before turning back to me.

'Are you okay?' he asks. 'You're white.'

I put my phone back onto the armrest, trying to ignore the picture that arrived.

'I'm fine. Are you going?'

He eyes me for a moment longer, not convinced, and then says: 'Yes.'

Bryan moves past me into the hall and then I trail him to the front door. I'm hoping he's going to keep walking but he stops on the doorstep and turns to take me in. There's a second in which it feels as if I've fallen through time. We'd just exchanged contracts and had picked up the keys to the house. We stood on the doorstep and kissed, before Bryan put the key into the lock for the first time. It usually feels like an age ago – and I suppose it was – but, in this moment, it's like it's just happened. It's so close that I can smell the freshly cut summer grass.

'I'm not trying to hurt you,' he says softly.

'Just go.'

I say that because two short words is about all I can manage. Any more and I'd be a wreck.

He nods and then heads along the path to the car. Seconds later and he's gone.

I wait until the car is out of sight, then hurry to the corner of the house and pluck the garden gnome from the ground. Bryan and I bought it on a daytrip to the seaside. It was one of those impromptu days of magic that happens when people are in love. We'd got up late on a Sunday, still full of laughter from the tipsy night out the evening before. Bryan cooked us sausages and eggs for breakfast and then he shrugged and said 'Come on, let's go somewhere'. I'd never do anything like that now. I'd want to plan a route, or check weather forecasts. Back then, we simply went. We listened to the radio and sang the songs, regardless of whether we knew the words. The sun shined and, after an hour or so, we were pulling in by the beach. We played minigolf, we ate ice cream, we threw a ball for someone else's dog. We ate chips and had a sneaky lunchtime drink. We did nothing and everything. The best of days.

And we bought this gnome. It's called 'Gnomey' – original, I know – and he carries a trowel while sporting a long white beard. Underneath it is supposed to be the spare key for the house. There was a time when I locked myself out twice in a week, so we hid a key under Gnomey.

It's gone.

The soil underneath is hard through weeks of freezing and thawing. There's no way the key could have somehow sunk. I check around the nearby drain but there's no sign of it.

I hurry back into the house and grab my phone. The photo from the mystery number is of Gnomey sitting in his usual spot at the corner of the house.

Me: *Where's my key?*

It's an instant reply again.

Anon: *Wrong question.*

I stare at the two words, wondering what someone might have done with the key. Letting themselves into the house is the obvious answer, although I didn't notice anything missing.

Me: *What did you do?*

It's another quick reply.

Anon: *The scuff on the front of your car is interesting*

There *is* a scrape on the front of my car – though I'm almost certain it was already there before what happened with Sharon. Either way, my car hasn't left the garage since I got home on Tuesday night. Unless this person was paying particular attention to my vehicle before Tuesday, the only way someone could know what's there is if they'd been inside to look at it.

After me, there are only three people who know about the key – Katie, Nadia and Bryan. I don't believe any of them could be the person who's messaging me.

I head through to the garage and the car. Perhaps it's the white strip light above but the scratch on the front wing does look deeper and darker than I remember. The original scratch was from a pillar in a car park. I misjudged the angle while reversing out of a space and there was that ear-crunching grind of plasticky metal against unflinching concrete.

I still blame the pillar.

The scratch was almost the same colour as the bumper and barely visible unless someone looked closely. It's on the same side that I hit Sharon and I wonder if it is now larger because of that. I've seen enough police shows on television to know they could do all sorts of tests on this part of the car to find out for sure. There is no way I would fancy the gamble of the police examining it too closely.

I read the message back once more, staring at the photo, trying to think whether anyone else knows about the key. It's then I realise that prior knowledge is irrelevant. Lots of people leave keys underneath welcome mats, flower pots, and the like. A stranger could have found the spare key within two minutes of barely trying. Gnomey is more or less the only decoration in the garden. The only thing it shows is that whoever it is that's texting me knows where I live.

Me: *That scuff has been there for months*

I'm going to have to get the locks changed. The sooner the better. I have so many questions, wondering when this person let themselves in. Was it while I was out on the bike earlier? Did they wait until I leave and then hunt around for a way in?

Anon: *What time did you pick up your daughter on Tuesday?*

This message feels more intimate, more shocking, than the ones before. Even the knowledge that somebody has been into the house doesn't feel as brutally personal as this. It's the implication that whoever sent this knows I was late. If I was on time, then I would have been at the college when Sharon was hit, not on Green Road.

The only person I know who was definitely aware of me being late to collect Katie is Katie herself. She would likely have told her teammates that she was waiting to be picked up – and possibly another parent or two – but those people are still relative strangers.

I find myself turning towards the street. It feels like it has to be someone close. A neighbour. A friend.

Bryan…?

Another message comes quickly:

Anon: *I know*

It's more or less a repeat of the first message I ever received. If I was sceptical then, I'm not now. Whoever this is *knows* that I hit Sharon and Frank. I'm not sure what to do. Perhaps among my questions, the bigger one is a simple 'why?'. What do they want to achieve? It's not as if I have a heap of money squirreled away – but the person didn't ask for that anyway. They want me to do 'something' for them – whatever that might be.

It's as I'm thinking about that I realise it means nothing. Whoever this is *can't* have any proof. Mentioning the car wing proves nothing. Knowing something and *proving* it aren't the same thing. It's the boldness of that which has me typing out a reply.

Me: *Prove it.*

There's no instant reply this time, which gives me the first glimmer of satisfaction I've felt in a while.

I go into the kitchen and grab the bucket from under the sink, then fill it with warm water. I drop in a cupful of baking soda along with a squirt of washing-up liquid, then carry the bubbling bucket of foamy water back to the garage.

At the back of the garage is a built-in workbench that was one of the key features in Bryan wanting to buy the place. He talked about using it for various DIY projects that never happened – and were quickly forgotten by both of us. I hunt through the drawers and, among piles of items I'm certain I'll never use, I find a slip of fine sandpaper and a small tub of unused car wax. With the sandpaper in hand, I gently scritch the scuff on the wing of the car. I only press hard enough to even out a few of the rougher edges, before using a cloth to dampen the grooves with the foam. When that's done, I leave it for a moment before wiping it down with a soft brush.

After tipping the water into the drain in the corner, I then use a different cloth to rub a smear of wax into the damaged area.

By the time I'm done, it's almost impossible to see there's any damage – even when crouched next to the bumper. I doubt it would stand up to forensic examination but the patch-up job is as good as I can do on my own.

When I get back into the main house, there's another message waiting for me.

Anon: *I have more. Don't try me*

It's attached to a photo of the scuff that has now largely gone from the car. It's been taken from inside the garage, which means it must have happened today.

A second photo arrives almost instantly afterwards – this time of the calendar that's on the wall next to the fridge. The picture is focused on a single day – Tuesday. There's only one thing written in the square: 'Katie 7 p.m.' in red felt-tip.

A chill whispers through me.

I hurry upstairs, into my bedroom, and then check the drawers next to my side of the bed. Funny how I still think of it as *my* side and *Bryan's* side – even though he hasn't slept here in a long time. I pull out my underwear and drop the pile onto the bed, reaching to the back of the drawer, where…

Everything's still there.

There's almost £400 cash, plus my passport and the marriage certificate I keep telling myself to get rid of. I flip through the pages of the passport, as if to check it is what it should be – and then return everything to the drawer. After that, I take in the rest of the room before heading downstairs. Everything that's even remotely valuable is still in the house.

Whoever took the key didn't break in to steal something; they broke in specifically to look for evidence against me.

They really do know.

I try to think what that evidence might be – but the texter is ahead of me. This person *could* have more. Perhaps a house along Green Road with a CCTV camera facing the road? Perhaps one of the parents of another girl from Katie's football practice, who has put two and two together and is trying it on? I failed to spot Frank on the verge, so perhaps I failed to spot a third person on that stretch of road? The boldness I felt from before has ebbed away. Perhaps cleaning the car has made me look more guilty if the police were to check the vehicle? Especially if they were to compare it to the photo of the wing looking more scuffed than it now is.

How far do I want to push?

Perhaps it's better to turn myself in… but then there's that word which hangs over me.

Life.

Life in prison. That's a sentence for both me and Katie.

Me: *What do you want me to do?*

There's a shuffling from upstairs which makes me jump. I'd forgotten Richard was up there with Katie. I'm surprised she's not come down to poke around the kitchen and ask whether I'm making something for tea.

Anon: *Drive to the McDonald's at Bullington*

I almost wonder if this message was meant for someone else. As with the rest of the communication, it feels so formal. It could be that the person doing this is older – my sort of age – and that this level of correctness comes naturally. The other argument is that things like abbreviations and emojis could give away an age much more easily.

Me: You want me to drive to a McDonald's? Why?

Anon: Willingness. If you won't do this, you won't do anything

Me: What do I do when I get there?

Anon: Send me a pic of the M

It simultaneously feels ridiculous and worrying. This is the start. I could do a task small and irrelevant now but there will be something else around the corner. It's a line in the sand, either do what I'm told – or let whoever this is go to the police with what they know.

There is one other thing. If I'm to find out who it is that's messaging me – and what they know – the only way to do that is play along, at least for now. This person isn't asking for money, or anything more serious.

Me: When?

Anon: Now

I don't want to drive. I have avoided it all day but can hardly get away with that for long. Katie needs to go places; *I* need to go places. It will look suspicious if I stop driving completely the day after Sharon was hit.

After popping a paracetamol from the packet I bought earlier, I grab the car keys from the hook by the fridge – and then shout upstairs to tell Katie I need to go out.

FIFTEEN

The car constantly bumps into one of the potholes that riddle the roads surrounding Prowley. Every time it jolts down and up, it feels like my heart jars along with it. I can hear the sound it made when Sharon, Frank or both bounced off the front of the car. I can *feel* the vibrations.

I'm driving a good ten miles an hour under the limit, while gripping the steering wheel with such ferocity that my knuckles are white.

If I wasn't before, then I'm unquestionably in too deep now. Even if, by some miracle, people believed me that it was an accident – and not something to do with the argument the day before – I would still be done for. Who comes back from being the driver that ploughed into a baby and then drove off? I'd be in prison and then, even if I got through that, my life here would be finished. Katie would disown me – and so would my friends. I'd have nothing.

Not that running errands for some mystery person seems particularly appealing.

The quickest way to the Bullington McDonald's would be along Green Road – but there's no way I can face any stretch of that road.

Because of that, I find myself weaving through country lanes that can barely fit the width of one vehicle, let alone two. It's dark, with no street lights, and I have to use the full beams to be able to see anything. Hedges and trees block the sky and if it wasn't for the lights of my car, there would be nothing here except bleak darkness.

By the time I see the lights of a farm in the distance, it feels as if I haven't breathed since leaving the house. That farm backs onto a second, then there's a housing estate.

I've never been happier to see civilisation.

The rows of houses soon blend into another and then there's Bullington industrial estate, full of sprawling factories and red-brick office buildings. I remain below the speed limit and then continue on towards the retail park.

It's a complete contrast from the deserted back lanes to this. With nothing better to do, it seems like anyone who lives in the general vicinity has come to the cinema. There is a long row of traffic queueing to get into the park, with another line of cars snaking around the area in an attempt to get out. I follow everyone else, though struggle to stop myself from twitching as various pedestrians weave in and out of parked cars in an attempt to cross the car park. I slam on my brakes three separate times, even though the person walking in front of my car wasn't particularly close.

It takes an age to pass the cinema, though I don't mind the slow speeds. At least nobody's in danger.

I should have been thinking that the other night.

A gentle mist has fallen across the park, leaving the bright lights of the cinema and shops peeping through the gloom. There is a row of oversized outlet stores and then, around the corner, the giant yellow M burns through the fog.

I pull up towards the back of the car park and turn off the engine. Searing cold immediately replaces the heat from the vents and, in a blink, the windows start to mist. There is a separate line of cars curled around the entrance to the drive-through, while heads bob from the restaurant itself. It's one of those with a play area off to the side and I can see a couple of children hurling themselves against one of the soft walls.

This is ridiculous.

I get out of the car and struggle to unlock my phone with my already-shivering fingers. Forty-five minutes have passed since I left the house.

My first attempted picture of the M is a throwback to the days of films being developed unseen. It's a blurry mess of partially obscured red and yellow, that could be anything. The second isn't much better – but the third does at least manage to convey something yellow against the murky background. I send it to the mystery number and then get back into the car and turn on the engine again.

I wait for the warm air to return, wondering if there will be a second follow-up request. Wondering if I'll say no this time or go along again, but already knowing the answer.

A car pulls up a few rows away from me and the doors open simultaneously. A succession of children pile out, like clowns in a comedy sketch. I count six before the mother wearily hauls herself out of the driver's seat. By the time she's locked the vehicle, the kids are already bounding off towards the play area.

Five minutes pass. Ten.

There's no response to my photo.

I feel so stupid, like a teenager pressured into doing dares at a party.

I wait five more minutes and then drive back the way I came. There is almost no traffic outside the cinema now, so I assume the big release of the week has started. Not that I know what it is. When Katie was young, I'd know all the things she was into. I'd know about current music and new movies. I'd watch the cartoons and children's shows with her.

It feels like another life.

I'm passing the second farm when my phone dings. I almost reach for it. My hand is off the steering wheel before I realise what I'm doing. I don't touch the phone but I clearly have a problem. It's not a healthy reflex.

Mirror-signal-manoeuvre and I pull into a lay-by at the side of the road. It's dark and desolate, the middle of nowhere, and there's a text waiting for me.

Anon: *Good girl*

SIXTEEN

THURSDAY

Katie goes into the bathroom at least twice in the night. I would usually sleep through anything like this – but not tonight. I wonder if it's a regular occurrence, or if there's something particularly wrong with her now that I've managed to miss.

I doze in fits and starts, feeling progressively more tired after each short spurt of rest. I brought the iPad to bed and by half past four in the morning, I know I'm not going to sleep properly. I log onto Facebook, where various local news links have been shared about the hit-and-run. I know I shouldn't but I can't stop myself from reading the comments underneath.

They should bring back hanging – 24 likes

Scum – 8 likes

How can the driver live with himself? – 17 likes

Don't bother with a trial. Just give me 5 mins in a room with him – 10 likes

I have to close the app. It's another assumption that a hit-and-run is something a man would be more likely to do. Is that true?

The news story itself contains only the most basic of details about what happened. There are no updates about Sharon or Frank's condition, nor about any developments from the investigation into the driver.

Katie's door sounds again and she stumbles her way along the hall into the bathroom. I don't go out of my way to listen but it's hard to ignore the retching that starts moments later. I spool myself out of bed and cross the room, then open the door into the hall. It's like a flashback to when I was a teenager. I'd go out with my friends and roll in at a ridiculous hour – then try to stifle the sound of vomiting into the toilet. On the first couple of occasions, Mum would come to me. She would tell me I only had myself to blame and that I shouldn't be drinking at my age. That boys would think less of me and that 'anything that happens' is down to you. I didn't even realise how sinister that sounded at the time. Either way, I would go out and do it all again the next week.

Except Katie hasn't been out – and she's never spent evenings in her room drinking with Richard, so I don't know why she would start now.

I creep along to the bathroom door and press an ear to it. I've never done this sort of thing as a parent, figuring Katie deserves her privacy. My specific grumbles over her choice of boyfriend have largely been kept to myself, although 'largely' does a lot of lifting in that. At least I've never actually thrown down any ultimatums.

There's another sound of liquid splashing liquid, which is followed by a groan. When I tap on the door, there's instant silence.

'Are you okay?' I ask.

There's no answer, not at first, but then a grunted 'I'm fine' muffles through the door.

I wait, listening as the toilet flushes and then the taps are turned on.

When Katie emerges, she blinks sleepily towards me as I lean on the banister at the top of the stairs.

'What time is it?' she asks.

'Around five.'

'Ugh.'

A spot has started to form around her temple. She scratches at it and then motions to head back to her room but I reach out a hand and rest it on her shoulder. She doesn't shrug me away.

'What was happening in there?'

'What did it sound like?' She turns and rubs at her eyes, then lets herself yawn.

'Do you want some water?' I ask.

'I just had some.' She yawns a second time and then adds: 'Last night's noodles. I told Rich they were underdone but he didn't listen.'

'I've told you about eating more than noodles for tea.'

'I wasn't hungry, Mum.'

Katie stifles a third yawn and then presses back against the wall. Her skin is a reddish pink and clammy with sweat. I reach to press a hand to her forehead but she flicks me away with her hand.

'Are you sure you haven't got a fever?' I ask.

'It's just the noodles.'

'Undercooked noodles aren't going to make you throw up.'

Katie rolls her eyes, reading my true thoughts. 'I'm not pregnant, Mum. I'm not *that* stupid.'

It's impossible to hide the relief. All those dreams of Katie heading off to university were disappearing into a world of nappies and soft toys.

'Oh, I—'

'You don't have to seem *too* happy about it. It's my body.'

'I know.'

'I don't want to mess up my life.'

She sounds so angry that I don't know what to say to her. I don't know if it's fury at me for intervening in whatever was happening, or if there's something else.

Then there's the fact that I was only a few years older than Katie when I fell pregnant with her. I never felt as if I was messing up my life. She was never a mistake. It feels like the sort of thing my mother said to me when I told her I was pregnant. She was of the generation when it was expected that women would marry and settle down – but she wanted more for me, in the same way that I want more for Katie.

'I can take you to the doctor in the morning,' I say.

'It's just noodles, Mum. Go back to bed.'

She moves towards her door again.

'Did Richard stay over?' I ask.

Katie stops and rests her forehead against the frame.

'No.'

'Did your dad talk to you at all?'

'Should he have?'

Once I told Bryan I wouldn't do his dirty work, I wondered if he might tell Katie about his upcoming wedding through a text, or an email. I can't see him doing it in person. Now isn't the time for me to do it for him, either.

'I guess not.'

Katie doesn't react to this, though she does peel herself away from the door. 'Go back to bed, Mum.'

She opens her door and heads back into the bedroom, leaving me in the hall. I could go back to bed – but know I won't sleep.

I'm on my way downstairs when I remember what Sharon told me in the car park. I can hardly ask her what she meant now; not after what I did – but it didn't feel like something she'd made up on the spot.

'It's not like Katie's perfect…'

SEVENTEEN

The front door is double-bolted when I get downstairs. I wouldn't do that usually. There have been times when I've come downstairs and forgotten to lock it at all. If someone outside had pulled down the handle and pushed from outside, they'd have been in. At least whoever stole my key had no way in overnight.

I've always been a bit lazy about things like security, especially living in a place like Prowley. This is a town where youths walking across the green in a group of more than four is about as serious as it gets. I've never heard of a burglary around here, let alone anything worse than that. It's probably why I was happy to leave a spare key in what I know now was such an irresponsible place. It's also why this hit-and-run isn't going to go away anytime soon.

The hallway mirror is harsh and unforgiving. I step closer until I'm almost nose to nose with my reflection. My usually blue eyes are a pallid grey, while my dry, pale skin makes me look so much like my mother in her final days that I can barely take it. It's been a day and a half since I hit Sharon and I'm falling apart. This is why people confess to things. No matter how determined a person might be to say nothing, the guilt almost becomes a manifestation in itself.

But there's something worse than guilt.

Fear.

Fear of prison, of a stolen future. Of *my* stolen future. Of course it's selfish – but who isn't when it really matters?

I drift into the kitchen and set the coffee machine running. As it bubbles away to itself, I check my phone. I've received nothing since the head-patting 'good girl' response. That sends me back on to the iPad, on to Facebook, reading the comments about myself.

Someone should hit the driver with a car and see how he likes it! – 8 likes

More assumptions of 'he'. I scan through the responses and there isn't a single person who says 'she', or even tries to correct anyone else by pointing out that the hit-and-run driver might not be a man. I can only hope the police make the same sort of assumptions, though I doubt it.

I'm about to turn it off when I spot the most recent comment on the news thread about the crash.

Vicky: *Off to work in half hour so can't say much – but I'm the one who called the police. Was driving past and my headlights caught something. Pulled in and there she was. Can't sleep. Can't believe someone would hit her and drive off.*

There are no replies yet, likely because everyone else is in bed. I click onto Vicky's profile and, though much is hidden, I recognise her face. She has blonde hair – but it's that yellow colour from when someone's dyed it themselves. I've seen her around town but many people around this area feel familiar, whether or not I actually know them.

I scroll through the scant pictures of her that aren't hidden behind privacy settings, which is when I notice that her job is listed. She's a barmaid at the Hair Of The Dog pub, which explains why I know her. I'm not a regular pub-goer but Bryan and I used to go for a couple of drinks and a date night now and then. Vicky must have been working at that pub for at least five years – and probably more like seven or eight.

It's pure impulse that has me hurrying back upstairs to get dressed. Within minutes, I'm semi-presentable and in the car, reversing out of the garage onto the street.

A frost has formed overnight, leaving a glistening, silvery crust across the centre of the road. It's not even six o'clock yet and one of those mornings that's so cold, I can see my own breath within the car.

It's a short drive into the centre of Prowley and the streets are deserted. It's December and nobody is out at this time of the morning. Nobody *sensible* in any case.

I park opposite the Hair Of The Dog at a few minutes to six. With the engine off, the cold begins to bite immediately, so I unclip my seat belt and pull my jacket tighter around my shoulders. There are no lights on inside the pub and the only sign of life on the entirety of the street is a solitary cat that's skulking underneath a street lamp.

The clock ticks across to six o'clock, then one minute past. Condensation is starting to mist across the windows.

I'm about to start the car again when headlights flare in front of me. A small red car emerges from the mist and blurs into view, before swerving across to the wrong side of the road and stopping in a space at the front of the pub. The car's interior light goes on, leaving me squinting across the road to see if the person inside might be Vicky. It's hard to see much through the smeared condensation but, as the other car's door opens, there's a flicker of yellow – and then a woman heaves herself out of the car.

There's little time to dally. I ditch the jacket and am out of my own car and halfway across the road by the time Vicky has grabbed a bag from the back seat and locked the car. She's at the front door of the pub, key in hand, when I catch up to her.

'Are you Vicky?' I ask.

She spins and jumps a little, pressing back against the door as she takes me in.

'Um…'

'I'm Jennifer,' I say. 'Sorry, I didn't mean to make you jump.'

'Yes…'

She squints and clearly has no idea who I am.

'I think our daughters went to the same school. We've run into each other a few times at various events.'

Vicky tries to move backwards but there's nowhere to go. I know I'm sounding like a mad woman.

'I didn't expect to see you – but I read your Facebook post just before I left for a run,' I say.

Vicky eyes me up and down and, without the jacket, my leggings and long-sleeved top are just about passable as exercise gear. They're definitely *not* passable as warm winter layers.

'Oh…' Vicky untenses her shoulders, no longer as defensive.

'Everyone's been talking about the hit-and-run. I can't believe you found the body. It must have been horrible for you.'

Vicky's breath spirals out into the gap between us. She pulls her jacket tighter and glances towards the door.

'You're out for a run…?'

'I've not properly started yet. It's colder than I thought it would be. Then I saw you and thought I'd say something. I can't imagine what you're going through…'

Vicky dips her head slightly, though doesn't acknowledge the second part of the sentence. 'You must be mad…' She eyes the frosty ground and then turns back to the pub. 'Do you fancy a brew first…?'

I hadn't expected the offer – but I'm not going to turn it down.

'I'd love one.'

Vicky fumbles the key into the lock and then pushes into the pub. She holds the door and I follow her in as she scrambles on the wall to turn on the lights. As the bulbs glow and I take in Vicky properly, I realise how tired she looks. Her skin is pale and there are darkened rings around her eyes, where reddy veins puncture the white. As she turns back to me, I wonder if she sees the same in me as I see in her. I can barely sleep because of what I did – and I suspect she's in the same position.

She groans as she takes in the pub and, as I follow her gaze, I realise why. It's like walking into a landfill. The pub's tables are cluttered with half-filled and empty glasses – but that's only the start. Someone has spilled a packet of crisps across the floor in one corner of the room and there is a pool of something sticky that's formed on the bar itself. Vicky stands with her hands on her hips and takes in the room, before turning back to me.

'Staff shortage,' she says. 'I knew they wouldn't clean up properly last night.'

'Does it always look like this?'

A nod: 'I don't know how people make so much mess.' She picks up a couple of glasses and carries them to the bar, then turns back to me: 'How do you take your tea?'

'Milk no sugar.'

Vicky nods towards a booth close to the bar, which is largely free from clutter. She says she'll be right back – and then she disappears through a door behind the bar.

I sit and wait, considering the deception it took to get here. Of all the things I thought I would turn out to be, I didn't think it would be a killer and a liar. It's the ease with which it's happened that's astonishing. Have I always been capable of this?

Vicky soon returns with a pair of mugs. She places them on the table and then slots into the booth at my side before launching into a huge yawn. That sets me off and before we know it, we're each yawning at one another.

'Not just me,' Vicky says with watering eyes.

'I guess not.'

'I wasn't going to put anything on Facebook but I've been wanting to tell someone since it happened.'

'Did you really find Sharon's body…?'

Vicky loops her fingers through the handles of the mug and holds it under her bottom lip. She breathes it in as she stares aimlessly into the distance.

'The police have spoken to me twice,' she says. 'I was off work last night but my husband was more interested in the football.'

'You can talk to me.'

I hate myself for saying it but, as with so many things from the past couple of days, I'm in too deep.

Vicky nods along. 'I was on my way home. I was supposed to have finished here at six but Mike asked if I could hang around for another hour. When I got out, it had started to rain and it was *so* dark.' She pauses for a sip of the tea and then continues. 'My headlights caught something on the side of the road. I thought someone had been fly-tipping again. I stopped to look at what it was but then…'

She tails off and closes her eyes – and I'm probably the only person who could tell her I know how she feels. I *do* know because I saw it, too.

'I didn't know it was Sharon at first,' she adds. 'We're not friends – but she's in here sometimes and I know her name. I know her lad, too. That big kid. You'd swear he was old enough to drink in here but the landlord knows he's still at school.'

'Josh,' I say.

'Josh…' She repeats his name knowingly and then blinks past it. 'I'd stopped to see what was in the verge when I realised it was a person. I saw the hair at first. It was spread across her face. Then I saw that her knee was bent the wrong way. She was wearing this pink-and-green tracksuit. I went down the bank but she wasn't moving. I touched her hand, her face. I was going to take a pulse but didn't know what I was doing. I thought she was dead. That's when I called 999.'

Vicky stops for a breath. She sips her tea again and then presses back into the seat.

'I heard there was a baby as well…?'

There's a nod and then Vicky puts down the mug. 'I didn't see him. Not at first. I was on the phone with 999 when they asked something about whether there was anybody else involved. I can't remember exactly. I looked up and there was this shape in the hedge. I think I saw the wheel first.'

'What wheel?'

Vicky scratches the bridge of her nose and then rubs her eyes. She looked exhausted before but it's as if she's aged in front of me. Her hair looks more wiry than before. Her skin is greyer.

'A buggy. I had to wade through some stinging nettles to get there but, when I did, there was this little boy still strapped into the pram. I almost missed him. He was wide awake but so quiet. He—'

'He was awake?'

She nods. 'He was staring at me. I had to unclip him but, when I got back up the bank, his eyes were closed. I was trying to get him to open them again but he wasn't responding. I took him over to his mum and was trying to say it would all be fine. I didn't know if she was alive or dead – and then I realised he wasn't breathing.'

'Oh…'

I didn't know Vicky properly before any of this – but I can see she's a shell of the person she was two days ago. There's something glassy in her stare, a lack of confidence when she speaks. The sights she saw at the side of the road will never leave her. I almost tell her it was me. My mouth is open and I manage a grumbled 'I—' before I stop myself. It feels like the rest of the sentence is right there.

'I heard they're both critical,' Vicky says.

'Both alive,' I whisper.

'Yes.'

I sink lower into the seat, crippled by the knowledge of the lives I've either wrecked or am in the process of doing so. There's Sharon to start; but there's also Frank, who has barely started his life. Josh has to deal with a mother and brother in hospital. Vicky might never be the same again. Katie could lose a parent. There will be more, too. Paramedics and police officers. Second- and third-degree harm. That one second of glancing towards my phone will cause endless ripples.

Vicky's watching me, waiting for me to notice. When I look to her, she starts to speak softly. 'Do you think...?'

'What?'

'Do you think it will ever go away? That I'll be able to start sleeping again?'

I can't match the stare and turn away towards one of the muckier tables. 'I wish I knew.'

I'm speaking as much for Vicky as I am for myself.

She sips her tea again, before there's a sound from upstairs. Vicky glances up and then pushes herself out of the booth. 'I'm supposed to be working,' she says. 'You should be running. Sorry to have bothered you.'

I take the hint and clamber out of the booth myself.

'It was no bother...'

She touches my arm, which sends shame singeing through me. 'Thank you for listening. I think I needed it.'

I try to repeat 'no bother' but the words are stuck.

At the sound of another bump from upstairs, Vicky grabs a handful of glasses from the closest table and carries them to the bar.

'See ya around,' she says.

'Right.'

I head to the door and let myself out, wincing as I'm assaulted by the arctic air. My car is over the road but there's a wind blowing now and I have to duck my head to push against it. It's the sort of morning where it feels as if it might never be warm again.

As soon as I get into my car, I turn on the engine and set the heaters to their hottest and loudest. It's then that I realise I've missed a text message from the mystery number.

Anon: *I need something else*

I knew this would come but didn't expect it so soon.

Me: *What?*

The answer arrives before I can clip in my seat belt.

Anon: *Money*

EIGHTEEN

I suppose I always thought it would come down to a demand for money. It's what everything's about in the end. That, or sex.

Me: *I don't have money*

Anon: *I bet you have some hidden away. I'm not asking for millions*

I should leave this now – although it's not the first time I've thought that.

Me: *How much?*

There is no quick reply this time. I wait for a minute or so and then put the car in gear before setting off. I could wait for hours otherwise.

It's a little after seven and there is more sign of life than there was when I first drove through the centre. Someone is opening the shutters on the Tesco Express, while at least half the houses past the High Street now have lights on inside. A bin lorry is busy trundling along on the other side of the road, while a small group of men in bulky coats bustle up and down to wheel people's bins on and off the kerb. I'm already past when I remember that I once thought I'd hit a bin instead of a person. If only.

I'm on the corner of my road when my phone beeps. I don't ignore it entirely, though I do keep my eyes on the road. I check my mirror, then indicate and pull in.

Anon: £500 in an envelope at the phone box library. Put it inside the bible

My first instinct is to fire back with a determined refusal – but I know what will happen. There will be more threats of what this person knows and how they will take it to the police. I could say yes, but if I end up agreeing, then there might be another request for more money along the line.

The more I think about it, the more I see that £500 is probably the perfect amount. Most people could scrabble together that amount from savings, friends, family or the like. More than that might be pushing it; less could be too easy and a waste of an ask.

The phone box library is at the edge of the green on the end of the High Street, close to the post office that has been in the process of closing for years. At one time, it was a traditional red phone box. The phone was removed around a decade ago – maybe more – and at some point, someone put in shelves. After that, people started dropping off books and it turned into a mini library where the idea is to leave a book, then take a book. I've looked inside a few times, but it's usually fully of biographies for Z-listers I've never heard of, or crime series that have been dragging on for way too long.

Me: I don't have that sort of money lying around. I'm not rich. If you knew me, you'd know that.

I almost send the reply without the second part of the message but tag it on just before pressing the button. I'm hoping the response might give some sort of clue as to who's messaging me – but it's far simpler than that.

Anon: *Is prison worth more than £500?*

There is only one answer to that. Almost anyone would cobble together the amount to avoid going to jail. I know it's not that straightforward a choice of one thing or the other. Even if this person was to pass on whatever they know to the police, there would still be an investigation. There might be a trial if it got that far.

It's not only that.

To even be associated with this would be the end of my career as a tutor – certainly in this area. Who would pack their child off to spend an hour with a person suspected or charged with such a thing?

The truth is that I could come up with £500. There's £400 in the drawer next to my bed and a little over £1,000 in a savings account. It's supposed to be there for emergencies and, if Bryan does push through in selling the house, there's a good chance I'll need it. That's all stuff for the future, though. This is now.

Me: *I can only do this once. I don't have lots of money. If I get you £500, this must be the end.*

Anon: *This will be the last thing*

Me: *How do I know that?*

Anon: *You don't. Leave it there for 1pm*

In all this, it feels as if I'm constantly a step behind. This doesn't seem to be a plot that's been cobbled together overnight. Whoever this is seems to have a clear plan for what they want.

Me: *There's a £300 limit at the cashpoint. It can't be all today*

I'm pushing it, desperate for some control, which I'm not granted.

Anon: *I'm not stupid. Go into the bank with ID. Just for that, let's say £600 in the bible for 1pm. Don't be late*

I don't reply. There's calculated anger in the response, which seems to have cost me £100. I have the obvious thoughts about what might happen if I don't play along, even though I know I've already made that choice. I couldn't have made a bigger mess.

Lights are on in the houses all along the street now and there's a glimmer from the horizon as the black starts to turn purple. People are up and getting ready for work, college or school. If it wasn't for this, I'd have no idea what time it was. It feels late and early all at the same time. My eyes throb with tiredness and my thoughts are muddy with distraction.

It's a short drive home and I pull into the garage before heading into the main house. Perhaps surprisingly, Katie is already up and sitting in the living room with her phone. She looks up as I get in and frowns.

'Where were you?' she asks.

'We were out of teabags,' I reply.

I instantly regret it, seeing as I've come in straight from the garage and clearly don't have teabags with me. I wait for Katie to point that out, though she looks back to her phone. I'm about to head into the kitchen to warm up some coffee when she speaks again.

'Why did you ask if Dad had talked to me?'

I wait in the doorway, wondering if there's an easy way out. I should have left it to Bryan and not said anything.

'I'm not sure if it's my thing to tell you.'

Katie sighs and mutters something under her breath. 'Do we have to do this again? It was bad enough with the two of you the first time. I don't—'

'He's getting remarried.'

'You—oh…' Katie stops herself mid-sentence, not expecting the interruption.

I suppose it was always going to be me who told her. Bryan knew it and so did I. It's why he asked.

'*Married*…'

'That's what he and Dawn came round to say last night.'

Katie puts down her phone and looks around the room. It feels like *her* room with the Christmas tree lights twinkling. She must have turned them on when she came down.

'I didn't realise he and Dawn were so…'

She tails off again but the point is made. I also didn't think they were that much into one another. It's not as if I thought he'd come back, nor that I wanted that… not really, even if my dreams sent me drifting to those places. I thought Bryan and Dawn would be some sort of quick fling that would soon be over when either or both of them moved onto other things.

'When?' Katie asks.

'He said Easter, then mentioned something about Vegas.'

A slim hint of a smile creeps onto Katie's face. 'That does seem like them.'

There's a wicked glimmer in her eye and, in that second, it feels as if I've never loved her more than now. The sparkly, neon fakeness of a place like Las Vegas really *does* seem like them.

Katie catches my eye and I allow myself a snigger to match hers. I've tried to rise above the me versus him that comes with a divorce – but I do allow myself this moment. It feels so satisfying… at least until I remember the other reason for Bryan's visit.

Katie must have seen something in me that I didn't know I'd let on. 'What?' she says.

'I might have to sell the house.'

Katie has always been a person who wears her emotions openly for anyone to see. Like me, I suppose. Her mouth hangs open as her eyes widen. It isn't only her acting out of character. I'd never usually have blurted out something like this without carefully thinking through what to say. I'm losing who I am.

'Why?'

'Your father and I own it jointly. We agreed that, after your exams, he'd get his share of what it's worth. I can either buy him out, or we'll have to sell. I'm not sure whether I'll be able to get a mortgage to cover buying him out. If not, it will have to go on the market.'

'So you'll be homeless?'

'If we sell the house, I'll have half of whatever it goes for. I'll be able to get somewhere with that.'

'But you'll still have to move? You'll be somewhere smaller?'

'Maybe…'

Katie is so outraged that she pushes herself up until she's standing: 'But that's not fair. *He's* the one that left.'

'I know but it's still our house. He owns half of it.'

'He left that half!'

'That's not how it works.'

She paces across the room and wraps her arms around my back. I allow myself to fold into her and it's not clear who's comforting whom, nor why. It's not only the house that makes me want to keep holding on to her.

By the time Katie pulls away, the lump in my throat is back. 'Nothing will happen before you've gone to university,' I say.

'*If* I get the grades.'

'You will.'

'That's what Richard thought – and look what happened to him. He's stuck clearing houses with his uncle.'

It feels odd to hear Katie talking so clinically about her boyfriend. She's always been his defender. I suppose, in the end, the truth is the truth.

'He should have applied to more than one place,' I say. 'He'd have got in.'

Katie shakes her head. She sounds tired – but perhaps it's because she's exhausted of this topic. 'You don't know him, Mum. It wasn't about going to university. He wanted to move to London. It was that or nothing. Nobody wants to waste their lives here. It's—' She stops, although it's not a surprise that this is how she feels. She takes a breath. 'Sorry… I didn't mean it like that.'

'You did – and it's fine.'

Katie presses her lips together. There was a time roughly a year ago when I knew Richard had applied to City University and I assumed he'd get the grades needed to go. With Katie being a year younger than him, I thought she might move with him. She would drop out of college here and pick it up there. I never told her how much of a relief it was that it didn't happen – though I suspect she knows. That's what happens when mother and daughter wear their emotions on their faces.

'He's got an interview later today,' Katie says, unprompted. 'He won't tell me where in case it jinxes it.'

'Things aren't working out with his uncle?'

'I don't think building and house clearing is his thing.'

'No… I can see that.'

She puts her hands on her hips. 'He's not a waster, Mum.'

We stand facing each other and it's hard not to wonder how much I've underestimated my daughter. I know she's smart enough to get the grades she needs to go to whatever university she chooses – and yet I've struggled to let myself believe she can pick a boyfriend for herself.

'Mothers aren't supposed to like their daughter's boyfriends…'

I mean it as a way of saying sorry, even though it isn't. We've never had full-on shouting matches over Richard but I've rarely failed to let my disapproval show.

Katie waits, perhaps wondering if a real apology might be on its way.

It isn't.

'I've got to get ready to go out,' she says as she takes a step towards the door. 'You look like you need some sleep.'

She has a point and there's little to say as she moves past me and heads for the stairs.

I fight away a yawn and drift into the kitchen, switching on the radio absent-mindedly. I'm immediately brought back to reality by the newsreader's voice.

'…and her two-year-old son are still in critical condition after a hit-and-run outside Prowley on Monday night. Police have this morning released a description of a car they believe might have been in the area at around the time of the collision. They are looking for the owner of a silver, grey or white hatchback that was spotted close to the scene. A spokesman said…'

The words are almost past me before I realise what's been said. The police are looking for a silver hatchback… like the one currently sitting in my garage.

NINETEEN

I check my phone, wondering if there might be something from the person who's been texting me, only to see there has been nothing since that demand for £600. Vicky didn't mention seeing a car, only that she found Sharon and Frank. She doesn't seem to know it was me – but somebody must have seen a car like mine in the area. I wonder if it's the person who has been texting me.

The radio news rolls onto the weather and traffic and then returns to the presenter, who is waffling on about whether people prefer toast to be blackened. I browse around the news websites, though there seems to be no mention of the silver hatchback. Incredibly, there is a full twenty-five minutes of toast talk on the radio – including listeners mad enough to phone in and give their opinion. They eventually get back to the news bulletin and I listen properly second time around, although there is no more information than there was the first time.

I switch off the radio and move into the living room. The Christmas tree lights are still twinkling and I leave them be as I find myself drawn to the window. The bleakness of earlier morning has passed as the sun rises higher. The frost looks crisper in daylight, a crinkled white blanket across the street.

As I take that in, I realise that Jonathan across the road has a silver VW parked on his drive. I knew that before but it's one of those things I wouldn't have thought too much about.

I head outside without my jacket and the cold immediately slices through me. The sky is blue and it feels like it's going to be another of those days that's glorious as long as nobody has to venture outside.

When I reach the end of the path, I look along the street towards Polly's white Audi. Then there's Gary the police officer's silvery-grey Vauxhall. Of all the cars on the street, somewhere around half would fit the vague description of the vehicle from the radio. When I bought my car, it wasn't because I was set on having something silver, it was because most vehicles on the lot were that colour.

It's a small relief – but I'll take that for now. If this is all the police have, then they won't be banging down my door any time soon.

I'm about to go inside when a battered blue van pulls in outside the house. A man gets out of the driver's seat and checks something on his phone before taking me in.

'Are you Jennifer?' he asks.

'Yes.'

He offers his hand. 'Lee's Locksmith,' he says. 'I'm a bit late but there's a load of ice on my road. Nightmare to get out.'

His hands are rough on mine. When he was alive, Dad would have said this was the sign of a person who'd 'done a day's work'. I'd forgotten that I'd arranged a locksmith for this early – but so many things are going on that my thoughts have muddied into one another.

'How long do you think it will take?' I ask.

'Just the front door?'

'Yes.'

'Not long. I'd love a brew though.'

He finishes with a grin that could've come from a cheeky fifteen-year-old and, as he goes to the back of his van to fetch his tools, I head into the kitchen and turn the kettle on. Katie is already in there, taking a banana from the fridge to go into her bag.

'What's going on?' she asks.

'I'm having the locks changed. The key that was under Gnomey is missing and I don't want to take any risks.'

Katie seems unbothered by this and says she'll see me later, before heading to the door. I don't catch what she says to Lee but there is a brief sound of their voices before the whirr of an electric screwdriver eclipses everything.

By the time I take Lee his cup of tea, the old lock is already out of the door and on the floor. He thanks me, has a sip and then gets back to work. I leave him to it – but it's not long before there's the drone of a mini-vacuum. A few minutes later and he's in the kitchen with an invoice and three new keys.

'Told you I wouldn't take long,' he says.

When we go back through to the hall, the only sign that any work has been done is the old lock mechanism on the floor. I half wonder if he has a side business in cleaning – because he's done a better job with this house than I do. He shows me that all three keys turn in the lock and then hands across a business card, asking me to pass his name on to any friends I know who might need work. It seems like something of a long shot, especially in a place like Prowley – it's not as if there are houses full of students always losing their keys, or new places always being built – and I wonder how someone in a specialist job such as his manages to keep going.

Lee is pulling away when I spot Gary over the road. He waves across, beckoning me to wait as he trots across the road. For a police officer, he has one hell of a dad-jog about him. It's all raised knees and exaggerated elbow movement, like he's mashing potatoes while having a fit.

'Cold, isn't it?' he says, as he reaches the front of the house.

'Very,' I reply.

'I know it's early but can I have a word?'

'Sure… is it just a word for out here, or…?' I half turn towards the house, hoping he'll decline – but he's already at my side.

'This might take a little while,' he says.

It should be innocuous but there's something about the way he deliberately avoids looking at me that sets my mind racing.

Perhaps the 'silver hatchback' line from the radio was only the start and the police already know which car they're looking for…?

When he gets inside, Gary takes the time to wipe his feet on the mat in exaggerated fashion.

'Shall I take these off?' he asks as he lifts his feet, although it's impossible to miss the tonal implication that he'd rather not.

'It's fine.'

He hovers in the hall as I shut the door behind us and then lead the way into the living room.

'Do you want anything?' I ask. 'Tea? Coffee?'

'I think I should probably get on with it…'

It sounds ominous and I slink onto the sofa, grabbing a cushion and using it as a shield while he takes the armchair. He says nothing at first, simply watching me across the room, before he clears his throat.

'Can you tell me about your relationship with Sharon Tanner?'

It's so direct, so unexpected, that I find myself cough-laughing for no reason.

Gary doesn't react. He's not dressed as an officer; instead he's in jeans and a red, knitted dad jumper, as if he's popped to the shop for some milk. No big deal.

'Sharon…?' I say.

'Do you know the name?'

'I guess… I heard about what happened with the crash.'

'But did you know her before…?'

'I, um…'

I have to fake a cough to gain a few seconds in which to compose myself. In all this, Gary is unmoving. I want to ask if this is some sort of official interview, but fear that will make me seem guilty.

'We went to school together,' I say, 'but that was thirty years ago. Our kids were at the same school, so we would've seen each other here and there. You know what it's like around here. Everybody kind of knows everybody else.' I try to smile it away, as if this is obvious to everyone. Me, her, Gary himself: we're all in one big club.

He nods but I don't think he's broken the stare since walking into the room. I wilt under it and find myself gazing away towards the pair of Christmas cards that are in the windowsill. In years gone by, there would have already been dozens of the things dotted around the living room. They seem to be going out of fashion. One of the two is from the local hairdressers, while the other is from Mrs Dawson at the end of the road, who gives one to every person on the street.

'Fair enough,' he says. 'Can you tell me about your relationship with Ms Tanner?'

It's a repeat of what he opened with, except for the formality of the 'Ms'.

'We didn't really have a relationship,' I say.

'You're saying you don't know her?'

'Not really.'

He presses back into the chair and then crosses his knees, as if sitting for story time. There's a stoniness about his movements. It all feels very wrong.

'Is that why you're here?' I ask.

'I understand you and Ms Tanner had words on Monday…?'

I suppose I knew it would come to this sooner or later. I'm still telling myself that if it was anybody else in the gutter, then I'd have called the police. Maybe it's true. I'm not sure how much is me lying to myself any longer.

'Do I need a lawyer, or something like that?'

I want for something friendly. A chummy 'of course not'.

'That's up to you,' Gary says. 'You've not been cautioned, or charged. This isn't an official interview and I'm not taking notes. This is very much informal. That said, we can make it formal if you prefer. I can fetch my notebook, or we could go to the station. Whatever you feel most comfortable with.'

I wonder if this might be a trap. I *have* seen plenty of police shows on television but that doesn't mean I know what's realistic and what isn't. Is this a friendly, neighbourhood chat – or is something else going on?

'Sharon's son Josh was bullying another kid in the car park,' I say. 'I saw him slap the other boy.'

Gary waits. It's not the answer to his question.

'I noticed Sharon loading her car with shopping, so I went to tell her what I'd seen Josh doing.'

'What happened then?'

'I don't know, really…'

I wait for him to say something but he continues to sit impassively, giving no sign that this is either new to him or something he already knows. I can't stop myself from breaking the silence, trying to keep to what happened. The more truth I tell, the less there is to worry about.

'We had a conversation,' I say.

Gary gives the smallest of nods, but it feels like it's more to say he's heard than that he accepts the explanation. 'Just a conversation?'

'Yes.'

'Were your voices raised?'

'We were outside in a car park, so probably.'

'Was it an argument?'

'I wouldn't say that. She was angrier than me. I was only telling her what I'd seen with Josh.'

He nods again, barely a dip of his chin, though it feels somehow dismissive.

'It wasn't an argument,' I repeat. 'You should talk to Josh, though.'

'We have.'

'Oh.' I'm not sure why I should be surprised by that but it stops my flow of thinking. 'What did he say?'

'I'm sure you understand that I can't talk about that.'

For the first time since he sat, there's a glimmer of movement in the way Gary's eyes twitch from side to side. That's all it takes.

'Josh told you about me…?'

He pauses for a second, which is the real answer. 'I'm sure you—'

'You should ask him about the boy he was bullying!'

Gary is wearing that slim sort of smile that adults use when humouring children. *Yes, you can stay up late if you eat all your peas.* He holds the stare for a second too long and then he slaps his knees and stands.

'I think that's everything,' he says. 'Sorry for all this. I'm sure you understand that I had to ask.'

I find myself standing too, guiding him back towards the front door until we're standing at the precipice. I was somehow expecting more.

'How was Leah yesterday?' he asks.

The abrupt shift in topic has me gasping. In the moment, I had forgotten about his daughter.

'Fine,' I say. 'She's back tomorrow and we have some things to be working on. She's a smart girl. I think it will work out.'

Police officer Gary is replaced by father Gary as a smile spreads across his face. 'That's fantastic. How do we do payment? Do you invoice, or—'

'I'll send Leah home tomorrow with an invoice containing my bank details. Everything should be on there.'

'Sounds good.'

Gary opens the door and the blast of cold immediately surges inside. I wrap my arms across my front instinctively, ready to close the door, but he isn't done yet. He turns back to me and I already know what's coming.

'Sorry about this,' he says. 'I'm sure you understand but I have to ask where you were at seven o'clock on Tuesday.'

There's a knot in my stomach that squeezes and won't let go. I wonder if this was purposeful, even down to opening the door and letting in the cold.

'I was picking up Katie from football practice. She failed her driving test and still needs ferrying around.'

Gary gives the same, non-committal nod that he's been offering for the past fifteen minutes. He's quite the expert at it.

'Where was her practice?'

'Saint Catherine's. They have all-weather pitches out there.'

'Which route did you take?'

I almost blurt out 'Green Road', simply because it's in my mind and it's the truth.

'Through the industrial estate,' I say. 'Past the tip. I think it's the quickest way.'

One more little nod. 'It probably is at that time of night.' He half turns, then offers a small wave and a 'thank you' before ambling off along the path with his hands in his pockets.

I've lied to a police officer and, even though – as he said – there was no caution or arrest, I don't know if I could now be in trouble for that alone. There are probably CCTV cameras on the industrial estate that would be facing the road. If the police were to check, they could easily find out that I definitely wasn't in that area on Tuesday night. Would they bother?

As Gary crosses the road, he takes his phone from his pocket and starts tapping something into the screen. I have no idea what's just happened – but can't shake the feeling that it's not only me who knows far more than I'm letting on.

TWENTY

There's always one, isn't there?

No matter what I queue for, there's always someone at the front who shouldn't be allowed out in public. If it's not a woman in the supermarket who's forgotten her PIN, it's a dullard at the petrol station who's dumped a load of unleaded into their diesel tank.

This particular time involves a woman berating a teller at the bank for having the temerity of stopping a payment when she was already £250 overdrawn. I know all this because everybody within a few hundred metres has overheard the one-way slanging match.

It doesn't help that the bank only has one person at the counter to serve the ever-growing line of people. This is despite the fact that there are tens of staff milling around, wondering what all the shouting is about.

By the time I get to the front, I've been in the bank for almost twenty-five minutes. I'd rather not dip into the cash I have at home, so ask the cashier for £600 from my savings account. I pass across my driving licence, unused chequebook, two utility bills, passport and part of my dignity. For this one thing at least, I came prepared. There's no way I'm going home, only to come back and line up again.

The clerk holds my passport up, comparing the photo to my actual face.

'No one takes a good passport photo, do they?' I say, to zero reaction. Tough crowd – but if I keep making jokes then I can't be the sort of person who'd hit and run.

The clerk passes across a slip of paper and asks me to sign and, with that done, she counts out the money in the rushed, manic way only someone who works in a bank can manage. She moves so quickly that there could be anything from £60 to £6,000 in the pile she pushes underneath the window. As it is, when I check it, there is the correct amount.

'Could you tell me how much is left in the account?' I ask.

She taps something on her keyboard and then looks up. 'Ninety-four pounds and fifteen pence.'

I'd been moving over small amounts each month but this is definitely less than I thought. It's not a lot to show for someone who's in her forties. I have half a mortgaged house but almost no savings. It's hard to know where the money has gone. There are the basics, like car payments, the mortgage and food. But what about everything that's been wasted? The DVDs never watched? The unlistened to CDs? Those magazines I never read? The food from M&S because I didn't want to be seen going into Lidl? The thrice-weekly coffees and lunches with Nadia just because?

I stuff the cash into one of the bank-branded envelopes and bury it in my bag before heading back onto the High Street. The message said to leave the money in the phone box library by one o'clock, which gives me a little under an hour to make the five-minute walk to the green.

There's a big part of me that can't believe I'm going to do it. It's blackmail and I know that there might never be an end point to what the texter is asking for. I suppose that's the beauty of the crime. What other choice is there? I could go to the police and show them the messages – but what's the penalty for blackmail compared to the one for what I did? If not that, I could ignore the messages and hope for the best – but there seems like a very real chance that I still end up in the deepest trouble imaginable, while the blackmailer faces no punishment. It's like being asked if I'd prefer to be punched or kicked in the face. There is no good option.

I could leave the money and go home but I don't want to do that. I also don't want to spend the best part of an hour hanging around in this Siberian corner of the country. I find myself back in the car, driving out of Prowley with no particular plan. Or, perhaps *that* is the plan.

Before I know what I'm doing, I'm on Green Road once more. It's the first time I've been back here in a car since what happened. I expect waves of déjà vu but, in the daylight, without the sideways rain lashing the windows, it feels like a different place. Even the road doesn't feel as narrow and dangerous as it did at night.

The properties are intermittent, with hundreds of metres between each driveway. There are no other cars on the road, which gives me a chance to slow as I pass each house to look for signs of a camera that could be pointing towards the road. If there are any, then I don't spot them.

As I near the site of the collision, I slow to a stop on the other side of the road, which gives me a full view of the scene. The white tents from yesterday morning have gone, as has the police tape. It's as if nothing ever happened here.

I know there's a big part of me that wants this all to go away, that wants to absolve myself of all responsibility – but, now I'm back here, I cannot fathom how it could have happened. There is the hedge that acts as a border between the field beyond and the verge. The verge itself dips down sharply but then rises up to be level with the road. There's a patch that's perhaps a metre wide that is relatively flat, on which people could walk if they wanted. After that, there's the road itself. If Sharon had been walking on the verge, there's no way I could have hit her. There are no tyre marks of where I would have swerved off the main carriageway. That means she must have been on the road, in the dark, in the rain. If that's the case, then can this really all be on me? Is that fair?

There is still one thing about this area of which I'm unsure. I edge the car along for a couple of hundred metres until I am level with a pair of gateposts on the other side of the road.

Sharon's house.

There is no actual gate to block the bumpy, dirt drive, which leads down to a ramshackle house. It's the sort of property that would have been glorious when it was built in decades gone by.

It's not now.

The once-grey stonework is overrun with greeny-brown moss and dirt, while I can count at least half a dozen slates missing from the roof. There is a car on the drive – but it's caked with rust and propped up on breeze blocks, with no wheels.

Bryan and Dawn's house is about a half mile along the road. The two places are closer than I thought.

The good news is that there is no sign of a CCTV camera anywhere near either the house or the gateposts. If there was, any footage would likely be damning.

I'm about to pull away and head back to the green and the phone box library when the front door opens. It's too late to pull away because I've already been spotted.

Josh stands tall in the door, his head almost reaching the top of the frame as he folds his arms and stares. He doesn't need to say anything because his body language is saying everything needed.

What are you doing here?

TWENTY-ONE

I'm still edgy as I pull into a space on the edge of Prowley Green. There was something about the way Josh's gaze bored through me that is impossible to forget. Part of it is undoubtedly his sheer size. It's hard not to be intimidated by someone who is so much taller and stronger than me. The other thing is harder to define. It's the sense that he knows what I did. Not only was he following me yesterday but it sounds as if he's already put Gary on to me. If there was all that pressure for something I hadn't done, I might feel a sense of aggrievance. The problem is that I really *did* put his mum and brother in hospital. How am I supposed to defend myself against that? If Josh put the police on to me, then he had every right.

I reverse into one of the hour-long bays that is on the edge the green. It's opposite the hat shop, which probably says a lot more about Prowley than I ever could. There can't be many towns in which a shop selling only hats has enough business to prosper.

Before I get out of the car, I check my phone. It is five minutes to one and there have been no more texts from anyone since this morning, let alone my mystery texter.

I get out of the car and step onto the path that rings the green. It is a busyish place at lunchtime, even in the winter. I suppose it's people who want to get out of their offices for lunch, no matter how cold it might be. In the summer, there are cricket matches played here at the weekends, with impromptu picnics taking place throughout the week. People come out to lie on a blanket and read their books, or perhaps have a kickaround in the corner by the trees. At the moment, the grass is coated with a thin layer of frost that has melted into dew. There is a woman with a dog on the far side but, other than that, everyone is sticking to either the path or the benches.

The green is surrounded on all four sides by various buildings. There are shops on three of the four edges, with houses on the other. A war memorial sits in the corner, with a withering poppy wreath left on the steps from Remembrance Sunday. Next to that is a large Christmas tree that's as tall as the memorial cross. The lights are off but there are more zigzagging around the lamp posts that surround the area.

There are probably thirty people dotted around at various intervals and, as I take them in from a distance, it's hard not to wonder whether one of them is my blackmailer. The best place to hide is surely in plain sight. There are men and women, older and younger. Some in suits, others in jeans. A mix of everything. It's always felt like the person trying to blackmail me was a man, though I have no particular reason to believe that. It's no different to the Facebook posters who believe the hit-and-run driver has to be a bloke.

My stomach gurgles as I start to walk around the green. It doesn't matter too much whether it's hunger, nerves or both.

The phone box is on the corner directly opposite the Christmas tree. Although it's no longer in service, someone takes the time once or twice a year to clean and paint it, meaning it's the same classic red as it's always been. There can't be many more things that are as distinctly British.

It's 12:59 when I open the phone box door. The shelf of books occupies the back wall; where the phone itself used to be stretches from head height down to my knees. There are rows of books with battered, split spines – the philistines. As well as the biographies and crime books, there is a mix of popular titles and junk that people would've otherwise thrown out. Tucked into the corner on the lowest rung is a hardback Gideons Bible with a brown cover. I run a finger along the rest of the rows, making sure there are no others, though this appears to be the only one.

When I take the Bible from the shelf, the back cover falls away and I have to pick it up from the floor. Aside from that, the pages look in decent enough nick, as if the book has never been read. I suspect that sums up the vast majority of holy books left hopefully in public places.

I check behind and, when I'm sure there's nobody watching, I slide the envelope of money in between the pages, before returning the Bible to the rack. With the addition of the cash, the cover bulges wide, splaying into the adjacent title. I squash everything together as best I can and then turn and leave, hurrying away with my hands in my coat pockets.

With my head down, I'm almost at the car when a tap on the shoulder makes me yelp and almost tumble into the road. I stumble into the people carrier that's parked too close to the kerb and bounce off, gasping into Gary's arms.

'Sorry,' he says as I step away. 'I didn't mean to startle you.'

He's in the same outfit as earlier with a jacket over the top. I assume it must be his day off. Either that, or the police have started making everyone dress as if they're off for an afternoon of discussing geography trends over warm beer.

'No bike today?' he adds.

'It's a bit colder than it was.'

He moves on without question: 'Sorry about earlier. I realise it was all a bit sudden with the questions and everything.'

I say it's fine, even though I'd rather tell him to do one. It feels like he's waiting for me to ask him something but I don't, which leaves us standing awkwardly on the edge of the green.

It's Gary who breaks the impasse. 'Anyway… I should be getting off.'

He does precisely that, edging between a pair of parked cars and then crossing the road. He stops and looks over his shoulder straight towards me and then, when he realises I'm still watching, he ducks into the barber shop.

The past two days has seen us exchange more words than in all the years we've lived on the same street. Perhaps it's just his way – but it isn't the first interaction with Gary today in which it's felt afterwards as if I've missed something that was right in front of me.

When he doesn't re-emerge from the barber, I head back into my car and lock the door. I slide down into the driver's seat, giving me a clear view of the phone box, while making it unlikely anyone could see me unless they were close.

Although there are still people dotted around the green, the corner on which the phone box sits is clear of anyone. The closest people to it are the boys playing football – although they have no interest in anything other than their game.

There are two women chatting by the war memorial, both in long, thick jackets. The type of thing bought in by the town's boutiques one at a time. I vaguely recognise one of them as being married to the bloke who does pottery out of a studio on the same row of shops as Bread And Butter. He was featured in a ninety-second light-hearted news report a couple of years ago and everybody's been treating him like a celebrity ever since.

I have no idea what she does.

The more I think about this stuff, the more I wonder how anyone can afford to live here. Almost nobody has a real job – and I don't necessarily exclude myself from that. I suppose much of it is old money. These houses have been inherited from parents and, in turn, will be shuffled on down to children.

That's definitely not going to happen with mine.

The two women hug in the way people do when they would rather have no physical contact. It's all arse-out, shoulders in, until they separate and head in opposite directions. The one who's married to the pottery guy slips on a pair of gloves from her pockets, looks both ways, and then strides along the length of the green towards the phone box. I don't think we've ever met and I definitely don't know her name but, as she gets closer to the corner, I find myself holding my breath, wondering if she's about to grab the money.

My mind is already racing ahead to confrontation and conflict – except that she continues walking past the phone box without breaking stride. Seconds later and she's across the road and out of sight.

It's almost ten past one now – and she's the only person who has gone anywhere near the box.

I continue watching as the clock on the dashboard reaches quarter past. It's not as cold as first thing this morning but my breath still twists and disappears. My knuckles are beginning to tighten from the cold, or what is probably the onset of arthritis. I haven't been to the doctor because I'm not ready to hear what he has to say. *Old* people get arthritis.

Twenty past one. People have been steadily drifting away from the green, back to work or wherever else it is they go. The phone box is still unopened. This is hardly an MI5 operation and I'm wondering whether I should leave when the text arrives.

Anon: *You seem to think I'm messing around. Go home*

I shuffle up a little in the seat, which sends sparks along my spine. Even the football-playing boys have gone now and I can't see a single person on or around the green.

There aren't a lot of choices. I could message back, but what would that show? Whoever this is knows I'm here. The chances of someone else going to the phone box and flicking through the

Bible seems minimal and there's no reason to think someone's going to collect the money right away.

I switch on the engine and pull away from the space. There is no traffic, so I don't hurry. I squint towards the surrounding buildings, wondering if there's anyone I've missed who might be watching me. The glare makes that largely impossible and by the time I get to the corner, I remind myself that I should probably be watching the road anyway. That's how I got into all this in the first place.

It's a short, uneventful drive home. For the first time since I was a learner driver, I feel as if I'm actually paying attention to all the things I should.

Which is why I'm half a street away from my house when I spot the familiar figure waiting on the wall outside.

TWENTY-TWO

I ignore him for now, pulling onto the drive and then getting out to open the garage. By the time I've driven in, Josh is standing on the path to the house, watching. Fear ripples through that he might burst into the garage and then… I don't know. Something bad.

When he doesn't shift, I consider closing the garage door behind me, leaving him outside and then heading into the house to make sure everything is double-locked. It's probably what I should do. He's on the path and I suppose that means he's trespassing. I certainly don't want him here. The problem is that he's seemingly already told the police about the argument I had with his mother. He has to be suspicious…

Instead of going inside, I head out of the garage onto the path to where he's standing with his arms folded. At least we're in public. I could really do with some nosey neighbours.

'Why were you at the house earlier?' he asks.

His voice isn't as deep as I thought and his tone is calmer than his body language belies.

'I was driving past. I saw the flowers and slowed to look.'

He doesn't react, not at first, and seems anything but convinced.

'I know what you did.'

It's word for word what the anonymous messenger sent me – except that Josh's delivery is so unflinchingly confident that I've taken half a step back before I know I've done it. He's pushed me without ever touching me.

'What do you mean?' My reply is so lacking in conviction that I can't even convince myself.

'I know.'

In an instant, he strides past me, dismissing my 'hey' and heading into the garage. He stops at the front of the car and crouches by the wing, where he runs his hand across the area near the headlight where I sandpapered away the scuff.

I follow him in, though he ignores my 'What are you doing?'. I almost tell him the scuff came from a pillar in a car park – but there's no need to say anything. The mark can hardly be seen now.

Josh stands and steps away from the car. 'I'm on to you.'

'On to me for what? I haven't done anything.'

He stands defiantly and I wonder what comes next. He's trespassing in my garage and I suppose this is the test of how far he's going to take this.

It happens so quickly that it's almost over before I knew it was going on. He feigns a lunge towards me and, as I reel away, he stretches forward and touches his index finger to my forehead. No punch, no slap; barely even a pat.

'You don't fool me.'

With that, he walks around me and paces out of the garage back to the street, heading in the direction of the town centre without looking back.

I watch him go and then have to press onto the car to steady myself. It's hard to describe but there was something almost more intimidating by that gentlest of touches compared to if he had been violent. It might have been the calmness of his tone, or the precision of the way he tapped my forehead while barely applying any pressure, but it's left me trembling.

I wonder if he *really* knows, or if he's guessing. Pulling up outside his house earlier won't have helped.

Whoever's texting me seemingly knew I was at the green, watching to see who picked up the cash from the phone box. There's no way Josh could have got from there to my house on foot in the time it took me to drive, so does that rule him out from being the blackmailer? If it was him, surely he wouldn't be talking to the police? He didn't seem to hesitate when it came to checking the front wing of my car – and whoever's been messaging has a picture of what it looked like before. I don't know how long he'd been waiting outside the house – but, with me not here, he could have guessed I was waiting at the green.

I check my phone again to re-read the message.

Anon: *You seem to think I'm messing around. Go home*

It doesn't *specifically* say the person knew I was at the green. It could have been sent by someone who knew I wasn't home.

While everything was happening here with Josh, I have also missed a call from Nadia. There is a follow-up text.

Nadia: *Can we talk? Sort of important. Call me.*

My first thought is that Bryan claimed it was 'important' that we talked. It's a little different with Nadia, though. If she was after a natter and a coffee, she'd have said so.

I call and she answers after barely a ring.

'Hey. I missed you,' she says. 'Are you home?'

I look around the garage and then focus on the door to the rest of the house. I'm not sure it feels like home any longer. It's partly because someone used the spare key – but also because of everything with Bryan. A home should be a sanctuary and I'm not sure this is. At least the locks were changed.

'I can come to you,' I reply. 'Is everything all right?'

'Yes,' she says, not sounding as if she means it. 'It is important, though.'

'Shall I come now?'

'Yes.'

Considering my vow to not drive is barely twenty-four hours old, I've done an awful lot of driving since.

Nadia lives at the other side of Prowley, on the edge of the final housing estate before the town becomes the hedge-lined banks of Green Road. It is probably one of the newest houses in the town. After it was built, the council later went all NIMBY about anything or anyone new invading our little corner of the country. Don't want to let the riff-raff in and all that.

I'm not even thinking as I park on her drive and let myself into her house through the front door. Nadia once told me it was too much trouble to have to get up whenever someone wanted to come in – so she has always left her front door unlocked. It's easy enough to get away with here – but I do wonder how long either of us would survive in a big city.

I find Nadia in the conservatory at the back of the house. She's half sitting, half lying in one of those circular half-globe chairs, where it's about seventy per cent cushion. Her attention is taken with her phone – and she's jabbing the screen while frowning at the device. There's a romance paperback on the table next to her, with a photo of a topless man on the cover. A half-empty glass of wine sits next to the book. It certainly doesn't *look* as if she needs anything urgently.

'Jen,' she says, looking up from her phone.

With anyone else, I might say it's an accident – but I know my friend too well. She waggles her right index finger for no particular reason, other than to show off the sparkly new ring that she's wearing.

Before she can say anything, there's a huge bang from behind me and then a football fizzes past my side and cannons into the frame of the conservatory.

Nadia drops her phone and angles her head so she can see around me. 'Craig! What have I told you about playing football in the house?'

Her son emerges from the living room behind me. I've known Craig his entire life to the point that I saw him the same day he was born. Aside from his parents, I was the next person to hold him. It's easy to say in retrospect but, even back then, there was something about that wriggling ball of energy that I suspected might be a handful. The following twelve years have been punctuated by Nadia insisting that he's going to grow out of this 'excitable' stage.

He's not got there yet.

Craig looks nothing like either of his parents. He has a wide, freckly face with the type of smile that those related to him describe as 'cheeky'. I lean towards the other school of thought that thinks it's more 'pain in the arsey'. He's in a full football kit, down to the socks that go over his knees.

'Sorry,' he says, as he dashes past me. It's obvious to me, if no one else, that he doesn't mean a bit of it. He shows this by racing to the ball, flicking it between his two feet and then dribbling it back into the living room and the hall beyond. There is a pair of thuds, which quickly becomes a steady, intermittent thumping of what I assume to be ball on wall.

Nadia nods me across to the second chair next to her and I slot into the seat, wriggling to get comfortable. Despite the protest moments before, she makes no attempt to stop her son playing football in the house.

'Do you want a drink?' Nadia asks. She produces a bottle of wine from behind the chair and waves it towards me.

'I've got to drive home later.'

She returns the bottle to the floor and then stretches for her glass, before gulping down a large mouthful.

Thump-thump-thump.

Nadia glances towards the hall and then back to me. 'You know what Craig's like. He gets like this when Tony's away.'

I say nothing. There is unquestionable truth in that Craig is harder to control when his father is working away – except that the greatest reason for that is because of Nadia's lack of parenting skills.

I've obviously never told her that.

There are a lot of things like that I've never told her, partly to maintain the friendship but also because I'm certain there's plenty she could tell me that I wouldn't want to hear. It's an odd thing on which to build a kinship – but we've been doing it for decades. Perhaps that's *why* we're friends? Neither of us want uncomfortable truths.

'Where is Tony?' I ask.

'South Africa. He's trying to put together some project. God knows what. He flew out there on Monday. Typical timing, really. We'd talked about trying to keep Craig off his PlayStation for so many hours – but now, instead of playing football on that, he wants to play for real.'

The drumbeat *thump-thump-thump* is quite the testament to that.

'Is that why you called me…?'

Nadia shakes her head and then has another slurp of wine. 'Sort of. Craig's still having hyperactivity problems at school and—'

She's cut off by a crash from the hallway. There's a momentary silence and then a return to the steady thumping.

'He's on a final warning,' Nadia adds. She hasn't moved, despite the clatter. 'He's still on that ADHD medication but it's not calming him down.'

'I think that's more an issue for the doctor.'

'Do you know anyone at his school that you could talk to? Perhaps put in a word and tell them he's not a bad kid? I thought with you being a teacher yourself…'

I look across to her, though Nadia is gazing aimlessly towards the back garden. I want to be angry about the fact that she doesn't seem to know what my actual job is. We could get into a whole thing about how being a teacher has little in common with being a private tutor – but if she doesn't understand my career by now, then there's little point in pushing it. We're destined to have this sort of relationship for as long as we're friends.

'I know a few people at the school,' I reply, 'but not in the sense that would help Craig. Is he still seeing the educational psychologist?'

'Yes – but she's always so far booked up. There are always long gaps between visits – and I don't think it's making much difference anyway. She keeps talking about pills and doesn't seem to understand that Craig's dad works away, so he's bound to play up a bit.'

There's no sense of self-awareness in anything Nadia has said. There's another bang from the other room and she rolls her eyes. Ignoring problems makes them go away in her world.

'Craig came home with new trainers the other day,' she adds. 'He said he'd been out knocking on doors and asking people if they wanted their cars cleaning – but I didn't know he could make that much money.'

She lets it hang.

'I'm not sure what you're asking me.'

'I don't want to say anything to him. He's got this whole budding entrepreneur thing going on that comes from his dad. If he *has* been making money from washing cars, or whatever, then great. But I think he might be up to something.'

'Like what?'

'I don't know.'

There's another hanging, extended pause.

'What are you asking?' I say.

'Can you talk to him? Seeing as you're his godmother and all…'

There it is. I suspected the request might be on the way. I *am* Craig's godmother – but that isn't supposed to replace a real mother.

'I'm not sure if I'm the best person,' I say.

'You're better at this stuff than me. You work with children all the time. You know what to talk about.'

I want to say no. I *do* work with children – but Nadia actually *has* a child. This one! I *should* say no – but, in this week of all weeks, I could do without alienating everyone in my immediate orbit.

I tell her I'll see what I can do – and then head through the living room into the hall. Craig is busy booting his ball against the front door. I stand in the doorway behind him, watching as he commentates on himself as if he's in the Premier League. The excitement in his voice is undoubtedly charming and sweet – but it would likely be sweeter and more charming if he was doing this outside.

'Hey,' I say.

Craig turns and grins, then rolls the ball in my direction. I try my best to pass it back – but only succeed in shanking the ball into the pile of nearby coats.

'You're better than me at this,' I say.

'Do you play football?'

'It's not my thing. My daughter does.'

'Girls don't play football.'

'They definitely do. Some of them are better than you.'

He shakes his head: 'Nah…'

Craig walks awkwardly along the hall. He's pigeon-toed and trips over his own feet, almost careering into the banister before he rights himself.

I crouch, so that we're at the same eye level.

'I've heard you've got quite the car-washing business on the go…'

'Who told you?'

'Lots of people with very clean cars.'

He brims at the praise, puffing out his chest.

'Do *you* need your car washed?'

I should have expected this question. I'd happily say yes and give him some money – but there's that tiny niggle of a worry that, in doing so, I'd make him an accessory to my crime if he washed away any evidence. Incriminating a child would be a great little extra to go on the charge sheet.

'I'd love that,' I say, 'but not right now. Maybe in a week or so?'

'Okay.'

'How much do you charge?'

'Dunno…'

'What are you doing with the money you make?'

The change is instant. He recoils backwards along the hall, breaking eye contact and grabbing for his ball.

'Is it for something special?' I press.

'No.'

'Those are nice trainers…'

I nod to the bright white shoes he's wearing and it's suddenly as if he wants to hide his feet. He moves to the stairs and disappears around the corner, so that only his head is poking around the side.

'Did you buy them with the money you made?'

'Yes…'

I've never heard a 'yes' sound more like a 'no'.

'Are you sure?'

'Yes.'

I suppose it does show that Nadia has a right to be worried – although I'm not sure what I can do about it. The bigger issue is that she will still be in her chair, with the wine at her side. Even if I could tell her exactly what's going on with her son, I doubt she would do anything about it. I've seen her tell him he's grounded for a week, only for her to then let him out to play again an hour later. As with most children, Craig knows where his boundaries lie – and they are miles and miles away from this house.

'I have to go home now,' I say. 'But I'll be back another day. You can wash my car then if you want. I'll bring you some money.'

'Okay.'

I push myself up and my creaking knees let me know they object. 'I'll see you soon.'

I'm about to head back to the conservatory when Craig stops me by saying my name. I turn and he's sitting on the stairs, his knees tucked to his chest.

'Do you know when Dad's coming home?' he asks.

'You'd have to ask your mum.'

'She says soon.'

'Then it will probably be soon.'

Craig nods but then dips his head. 'But she always says soon…'

He's sitting a few steps up, which means we're more or less at the same eye level, even though he's now looking at his feet. He doesn't need to say anything else because I can feel the sadness. Worse still, I know there's nothing I can do.

TWENTY-THREE

The car parking bay next to the green is still free and there's a new wave of déjà vu as I pull in and turn off the engine. It's quieter now; colder, too. The sun is almost set and the curtain of darkness is beginning to wash across the village.

I head along the path to the phone box and then reach for the Bible. I know before picking it up that the envelope of money has gone. It's substantially thinner than when I left it. I check anyway, opening the book and holding the broken back cover in place, only to see confirmation of what I already knew. Even though the cash has been taken, I have no new messages from the anonymous texter.

I'm on the way back to the car when I notice the poster that's been pinned to the nearest telegraph pole. It wasn't here earlier, so must have gone up in the last couple of hours. The words at the top read 'WITNESSES WANTED' and there's a brief description of the collision, naming Green Road and listing the time as 6.50 p.m. to 7.05 p.m. on Tuesday. There is a phone number for potential witnesses to call. Underneath is a picture of a silvery-grey car that, with mine parked on the road behind, looks similar without being exact. It *could* be my car – but it could also be one of many models and makes. There's a similar vehicle parked in one of the bays on the far side of the war memorial. There is no manufacturer listed on the poster and no mention of a registration plate. If this is all the police have, then it's nothing damning. The worry is the way the separate pieces of information link together. Gary already knows about my argument with Sharon. He'll also know I have a silver car – and that I was picking up Katie from football practice, which isn't too far from where Sharon was hit. There must be suspicions. It's not one thing, it's the totality of them all.

It takes me a few seconds to realise that all those thoughts are about myself. There's a woman and her baby in hospital – with family members and friends devastated and concerned. Is it normal to think of myself first?

As I get back into the driver's seat, my phone rings. There is no name listed – but it's a different number to the one that has been texting me. When I answer, there's a brief pause and then a man's voice asking for 'Mrs Hughes'. The 'Mrs' makes me wince. It's only after something like a divorce when a person realises how many things they are signed up to. I still get letters most days addressed to 'Mrs' – plus these marketing calls.

'That's me,' I reply. 'I'm a bit busy, though.'

'It's Luke from Prowley MOT. Do you still own the silver Ford Focus?'

There have been so many moments from the past couple of days in which it's felt as if time has momentarily stood still. I had assumed it was a marketing call. I was mentally ready to tell whoever was calling that, no, I didn't have time and that, yes, they could try another day, even though, no, I didn't know what time might be best.

The ol' polite piss off.

Instead, I'm stuck making gagging noises as nothing comes out.

'Mrs Hughes?'

'Yes… um… I do own that car.'

I'm ready for him to mention something about the collision. The police have been round the local garages, asking about silver cars – and they've passed on my details for investigation.

That's not what comes.

'We've been trying to contact you because the MOT is due. I was wondering if you might want to book it in…?'

It's at the mention of this that I remember the third text message I got on Tuesday night. There were two from Katie, wondering where I was – and another from the garage, reminding me that the car was due for its check-up.

'Um...'

'We're booked up for the next three weeks but there is a cancellation for tomorrow, so the slot is yours if you want it. We won't be able to get you in before the MOT expires otherwise.'

'Right... um... yes.'

He's caught me off-guard, partly because no sensible person walks around with details of a car's service history in their head – but also because of the timing. Do I really want someone poking around my car so soon after what I did? Perhaps I do. Maybe they'll give the whole vehicle a clean? It also gets my car out of the way for a day.

'Shall I book you in, then?' he continues. 'You'd have to drop it round by half seven in the morning.'

'I can do that.'

'Great. We'll see you then.'

I end the call and then sit for a moment, overanalysing what just happened. I remember that the car's MOT was due at this time last year, because it was a chunk of money I had to spend a little before Christmas. This is all normal and above board. Nothing with which to be concerned.

The sound of the radio punctuates my short drive home. The hit-and-run has been relegated to the second story, below something about a comment made by one of the local MPs that has upset some woman who sounds like she's professionally offended. Essentially, things are back to normal. For the first time since the accident, I'm beginning to think that things might turn out all right... for me, at least. I just need Sharon and Frank to wake up soon – I can't even consider the alternative – and then that nothing period between Christmas and new year will help the story drop out of public consciousness.

By the time I get home, it's clear Katie is already back from the college. She has an innate ability to play her music at a volume that's just loud enough to be heard at the bottom of the stairs, without being gaudy enough to be noticed anywhere else in the downstairs part of the house. It's that borderline thing teenagers pull off with such aplomb: driving a person to near insanity but not quite over the edge.

I call up to ask if she wants anything to eat. The music is momentarily dimmed for the usual exchange of 'what?', a repetition of what I asked in the first place, another 'what?', another repetition, and then a final 'no', before the music is restored. This is what we call a 'conversation' in this house.

It does give me yet more sense of normality.

I make myself a cup of tea and then head through to the living room, where I search through the cupboard for the work folders I need. The doorbell goes at a couple of minutes to four – but I'm expecting it this time. Amy has been coming over for almost three months to help with preparation ahead of her GCSE maths exam. She's close to the perfect student in that she wants to succeed and is happy to get on with the necessary tasks. She also has a self-awareness of the things she can and can't do, which is rare in anyone, let alone someone so young.

We've been working for twenty-five minutes when I realise I've not thought about the accident since Amy arrived. There's a part of me filled with relief. Perhaps I will be able to sleep? The guilt will subside over time and my life doesn't have to be defined by this.

Then I'm riddled with more shame because many other people's lives – Sharon, Frank and Josh to name a few – might well be defined by this. I *should* struggle to sleep. I don't deserve to be let off.

It's Amy who brings me back to reality. She looks up from her workbook, across to where I'm sitting with a pen poised over a piece of paper she'd handed back to me.

'Is everything all right?' she asks.

I tell her it is – but the flow has already been interrupted and, from having almost half an hour with my mind free of culpability, suddenly I can think of nothing else other than Sharon in the gutter.

I'm so lost that, when the doorbell goes again, Amy says it will be her dad to pick her up. The second half of the hour blitzed past with me barely noticing.

I take her to the door and we go through the usual ritual, with Amy cringing as her dad asks how she's getting on, while I tell him enough to make him feel this is all worthwhile but not enough to break any of the trust Amy and I have developed. I've found over time that this is one of the hardest parts of the job. Parents deal in absolutes – their children *will* pass the exams – while children deal more in progress. They did better than last week.

After Amy leaves, I head up the stairs and knock on Katie's door. The music has been turned off now and it's so quiet that I wonder whether Katie went out while I was working. It's only the delayed, muffled 'yeah' that lets me know she's in.

I nudge her door open a crack and lean against the frame. Katie is sitting in bed with the covers over her. Her fingers are poised, ready to type on her laptop, while a movie or TV show plays on her phone.

'No Richard tonight?'

She lifts her glasses onto her forehead and shakes her head wearily. I half wonder if I woke her up from a doze. Her drooping eyelids make her look as tired as I feel.

'He's been working with his uncle and said he was tired after work.'

'How did his interview go?'

'I'm not sure. He hasn't said.'

I've been around long enough to know that this isn't a good thing. Someone who has had a good interview is happy to talk about it.

'Have you eaten yet?' I ask.

'I had a protein bar.'

'You can't live off those, Katie. You need some real food. I can—'

'I'm fine, Mum. I might have something later.'

'I just—'

'I'm fine.'

She pulls the cover up higher and tucks it under her chin.

'How was college?'

'Fine.'

It's one of *those* conversations but there is one more question to ask.

'Has your dad called you yet?'

Katie glances away from her screen, taking me in. She releases the cover and it slips to her waist. She's still in the clothes she wore to college. 'I've not heard from him since last weekend.'

She sounds annoyed, something in which I do revel. I want to be the adult and not have her pick sides – but I still love it when she picks mine.

'I'm sure he'll tell you about the wedding soon enough.'

'He's not going to invite me, is he?'

'I don't know. It sounded like it was going to be just them. Did you want to go?'

'I'd take the free trip to Vegas. I'm not fussed about the wedding.'

Good girl.

'Do you want anything?' I ask.

She shakes her head. 'Just some sleep.'

It's only five o'clock but I know this feeling all too well. It doesn't help that it gets dark so early at this time of year. When I was Katie's age, I would often doze in the daytime and then stay up through the night. When it came to getting a proper job, it was quite the shock to have to be up each and every morning.

I consider saying something about how she should eat well but I was her age at one time – plus she's on my side for once and I don't want a needless fight.

With that, I leave her and head downstairs. I've barely eaten in two days, something of which my rumbling stomach is keen to remind me. When Bryan was living here and Katie was a bit younger, I would regularly cook for the three of us. It didn't always mean we would sit down as a family, like I did with my parents when I was young, but there was a satisfaction from all being together. Since he left, I've felt the urge less and less to cook anything that goes above the necessary expertise of a university student.

I'm looking in the fridge, hoping something might grab my interest, when there's a bump from the back of the room. I stop and turn towards it, but it takes a couple of seconds for me to realise the noise has come from somebody knocking on the back door. It wouldn't be so much of a shock if it wasn't for the fact that there is no way for someone to get into my back garden…

TWENTY-FOUR

I've not been into the back garden for weeks. In the summer, it's doused in sun throughout the afternoons and Katie will take herself out there to spend hours lying around while not doing very much. Because there's no gate at the back – and the fence only backs onto a patch of wasteland – there's little reason to be out there at this time of year.

It takes me a good thirty seconds to find the key. It's usually kept in the cutlery drawer, but I spend the time shunting things around while cursing Katie for moving it. That's when I find it underneath a pile of spoons.

The chilled bleakness of the night bristles through the open door, immediately sending shivers along my bare arms.

There's nobody there.

'Hello?'

My voice is swallowed by the darkness. The lawn is already covered by a slim dusting of white from the frost, although it's hard to see much more than that. The only light comes from what's seeping around me from the kitchen and the clouded moon. There are no street lights back here.

There's a rustle from the end of the garden. It could be the wind – but is then immediately followed by the sound of something slapping into wood.

I move onto the lawn. The dew soaks through the bottom of my slippers and the grass is long enough to envelop them from the top, instantly leaving my toes damp and cold.

'Hello?'

There's no reply and I figure I'm already wet, so might as well continue. Each step seems damper than the last until it's as if I'm wading into the ocean.

The second bump is louder than the first – and it's accompanied by what sounds like a grunt. It's hard to see much of anything – but, even in the dim light, I know an arse disappearing over a fence when I see one.

'Hey!'

I rush towards the fence that runs along the side of my house and then use the top to push myself up, giving me a glimpse into next door's back garden. They ripped up the lawn a couple of years back, replacing everything with a patio that meant I had to listen to the sound of a cement mixer for a couple of weeks. The area is dimly lit by light seeping from the doors at the back of the house. It's not much – though it's enough to see the shape of a very tall young man vanishing over the fence into Polly's back garden.

Josh.

The chance of me catching him is zero and even if I were to give chase, I don't know what I'd be hoping to achieve.

Aside from a bobbing head hopping over the next fence, he is quickly out of sight. One more fence and he'll be back on the street.

I drop down and return across the lawn. My feet are drenched and the slippers are going to need a wash at best, a throwing out at worst. As I move across the lawn, I try to figure out why Josh bothered to knock. The answer comes as I get to the back door.

He didn't.

What I thought was a bump on the door frame was instead a clay pot tumbling to the ground. There is soil across the decking at the back of the kitchen window and the fuchsia plant stalks are lying sideways on the ground. The plant was given to me by a parent after I'd tutored her daughter for her GCSEs a couple of years ago. Aside from pouring in a little water whenever I remember, I barely touch it. In spite of that, it bloomed a bright pinky-purple last summer.

I pick up the largest part of the broken pot – but it doesn't seem like the kind of thing that's retrievable. There are at least a dozen small splinters of clay on the ground, plus likely more that are too small to see in this light.

I prop the pot against the wall, leaving the plant the right way up. When I turn back to the garden, there's nobody there – or at least nobody on the main part of the lawn. The shadows stretch deeply along the sides and I have that sense of being watched, even though I simultaneously feel alone.

I should call the police and report Josh for trespassing, if nothing else – except there's no specific proof he was here. Even if there was, I'm not sure I want to be drawing attention to myself at the moment – especially not by linking myself to him.

When I get inside, I lock the door and then push the bin up against it. If someone's coming in from the back, they're at least going to make a noise. I throw my slippers into the washing machine and then grab a towel to dry my feet.

The house is quiet.

I've still not eaten, though my stomach has stopped trying to insist that I do. I drift into the living room and pack away the workbooks from earlier. I'm tempted to check Facebook and the local news sites for updates about Sharon but fight the urge and instead settle on the sofa underneath a blanket. I switch on the television and don't bother flicking through the channels. Anything will do for now; the more mindless the better. Luckily, there is a quiz show on. There's nothing more perfect for establishing self-esteem than watching a parade of people fail to grasp the most basic pieces of trivia.

The yawns begin almost immediately. Despite feeling on edge from seeing Josh, from remembering the way he touched my head, I've hardly slept in two days and with the heating turned up and the cosiness of the blanket, my eyelids are almost instantly droopy. There is a question about what baby swans are called and then…

It's five minutes to eleven.

There's a crick in my neck and twinges along my side. I've ended up twisted around a pillow, with my head in the crook of the sofa. The blanket has been discarded on the floor and the darkened room is lit eerily by the bluey light of television. I turn everything off and then yawn my way upstairs with the blanket under my arm, before heading for the bathroom.

When I come out, I catch the stifled sound of music or a show coming from beyond Katie's door. It's late, even for her, especially as Richard isn't staying over. I tap gently on her door and the sound mutes before there's a weary-sounding 'yes'.

I open the door a crack and it doesn't look like she's moved from earlier. She's still sitting in bed, half under the covers, with the glow of the laptop screen illuminating the lower half of her face. She yawns as she looks over the screen towards me.

'Have you been working all night?' I ask.

'Some of it.'

'You should get some sleep.'

She takes off her glasses and puts them down on the side. 'Snap.'

'Do you want anything first? Hot chocolate?'

'I've got some water.'

I eye the glass to her side and try to imagine myself at her age. Mum would ask about how much water I'd had to drink – but my friends and I would get through gallons of Diet Coke. Or, more likely, the cheap supermarket knock-off version. I'd have never thought about drinking water as a first option. But teenagers today are more into health and fitness and detoxing and everything else than we ever were.

Katie has snapped closed the lid to her laptop and I realise I'm still hovering.

'Were you after something…?'

'I was reading about the hit-and-run,' I find myself saying. 'The woman is Sharon and her little boy is Frank. Do you know the other son, Josh?'

It's a question out of nothing but Katie takes it in her stride.

'He was the year below me at school. Everyone knows him because he's so big. I think he was six foot by the time he was eleven, or something like that.'

'But you don't actually *know* him?'

Without the light of the laptop, Katie is only a shape on the bed. She shuffles but I can't read her body language. 'He's a bully, Mum. Everyone knows that.'

'Has he ever bullied you?'

'Not me.'

I almost miss the implication. The reply feels very deliberate.

'But you know someone he's bullied?'

She pauses before replying. The words feel very chosen. 'Everyone does. He didn't mind if someone was older or younger than him. Some of the teachers were scared of him.' There's a breathy pause and then: 'Why?'

I don't respond because I'm still focused on what she said before.

'Did Josh do something to Richard?' I ask eventually.

'No.'

It's too quick and I know my daughter well enough to see there's some sort of connection there.

It's one of the things parents learn. When children are younger, there's the constant coaxing to tell the truth. If a person is religious, it's right there in the ten commandments. If not, there's Santa and his naughty list. All those constructs and many more in an attempt to force children to be sincere. It's always left me wondering whether honesty is the default. If it was, would it really need to be taught so forcefully? Perhaps we're meant to lie, cheat and steal?

Things change when they become young adults. It's sometimes best not to know what's really going on. Some things need to be private – and pushing for anything else is only ever going to cause an argument. Or lots of them.

'Have you heard from Richard yet about his interview?'

Katie sighs before replying. 'You don't have to pretend you're interested. We know you don't like him.'

She sounds so aggressive that I take a small step backwards.

'That's not fair, Katie. You're my daughter and—'

'And what? He's my boyfriend, Mum. He tries his hardest.'

'When did I ever say—'

'It's not what you say. That's what you always used to tell me when I was in trouble, isn't it? "It's not what you say, it's how you say it".'

'How do I say things?'

'Not just that…'

Perhaps it's because I'm tired, or maybe it's because we're talking through the dark and I'm not taking in Katie's expression. Either way, I suddenly realise what all this is about. I don't know how I missed it all these months when it was right there.

'I tried to help him,' I say, stumbling. 'I tutored him for free. I wanted him to pass.'

'*Did* you?'

'I…'

It was ten or eleven months ago that I started to help Richard with his work ahead of his A-levels. It wasn't formal hour-long sessions with my official students, more fifteen or twenty minutes here and there. I shared some past papers with him and talked him through the sorts of things examiners look for in coursework. I thought I was helping. He'd *asked* if I could help. Or, more to the point, Katie asked if I could help him.

'What do you think?' I add. 'Do you think I deliberately undermined him?'

The silence through the darkness is Katie's answer.

'Is that what *he* thinks?' I say.

There's still no reply, only a sigh – which might be a yawn.

'I'm tired, Mum. Can you let me sleep?'

I wait for a moment but then tell her good night and then reluctantly close the door. There is truth that I was worried Richard would go to university in London – and that Katie would want to follow. None of that affected the work I did with him, though. If I had any sort of serious problem, I wouldn't have offered to help in the first place. The truth was that I never felt as if he wanted to do the work. In his mind, he'd applied to his dream university, been offered a conditional place, and was already there. Everything in between was a formality – until it wasn't.

I shuffle along the hall into my room and then allow a yawn to overtake me. It feels like I might sleep tonight.

My head is barely on the pillow when my phone lights up with a new message. I should ignore it – but curiosity gets the better of me.

Anon: *I need one more thing*

When I left the money in the phone box, I knew it was unlikely to be the end of this. What I didn't suspect is that it would take only a few hours more for the request to come.

Me: *I don't have any more money for you! You said that was the last thing.*

Anon: *I know. I did mean it. Not more money. Something else*

I wait, resisting the urge to message back with a 'what?'. It's like one of those pathetic people on Facebook posting cryptic updates and waiting for their sheep-like friends to pile in with questions about what's going on.

There's no instant reply and the tiredness I felt has now gone. I'm on alert, waiting for whatever the request might be. It's almost fifteen minutes before the message comes and, when it does, it's true that the person doesn't want money.

It's much worse than that.

TWENTY-FIVE

FRIDAY

It's not only me who sleeps in unsatisfying bursts. Even when I manage to drift off, I'm awoken by Katie clumping along the hallway into the bathroom. She possesses many talents – but the grace of a ballerina is not one of them and neither is an ability to sleep through the night. None of this is unusual.

In between her trips back and forth, I'm haunted by what comes next. If it's not the fear of the police knocking, then it's of what the anonymous texter wants. I can't think of a way out that doesn't involve me ending up in serious trouble. Is that worse than the trouble I'd be in if I went to the police now?

It's a little after five in the morning when I reply to the most recent message with a straightforward 'I'm not doing it'. It's been hours since I received the request and I don't know if I should expect a quick reply. Staring at the phone screen doesn't do much and so I drift downstairs, into the kitchen, where I turn on the coffee machine.

After switching on the radio, I sit at the table with my eyes closed, listening to the bubbling of the machine interspersed with the news. The hit-and-run is even further down the running order. The first story is the MP's offensive remark that's as tedious as it is predictable. Then there's something about a reality TV star who's staying in the area because they're in panto. I'm grateful that somebody of whom I've never heard is busy dragging the attention away from me.

The hit-and-run story is third. I've heard the same details over and over to such a degree that I almost miss the significance when the newsreader says that the two-year-old boy is out of intensive care. As best I can tell, Frank hasn't been named – but this is new information and I feel a surge of relief of which I'd forgotten I was capable.

Thank goodness he's getting better. I never wanted anyone to be hurt. Things will hopefully start to calm down. He will recover and so will Sharon. That's what I tell myself.

I feel too awake to sleep but too tired to do anything of note. I drift around the house, drinking coffee and listening to the radio. It's a few minutes before seven when I remember I have to drop off the car for its MOT. There's no sight or sound of Katie, so I start to write her a note. I'm halfway through when I realise I could simply text her and she'll see it when she gets up. I continue writing anyway, saying I hope she has a good day, and then I leave the message on the kitchen table before heading out to the car.

It's still dark when I get to the MOT garage. Hazy orange light seeps from the deck at the back and there are a pair of men in overalls who are busy lugging something heavy into a large bin.

I get out of the car and make the usual small talk with the mechanic, who turns out to be the Luke that called me yesterday. We go on about it being cold, dark and early. Yes, the shortest day is around the corner. Yes, the days do start getting longer after that. Yes, it will be summer before either of us know it.

When all of that is out of the way, I edge my car forward into their dock and then, when I get out, Luke is eyeing the car. I have to fight the worry that he automatically knows what I did. He can't. He works in a garage. Of course he's eyeing the car. He has to work on it.

'Any concerns with the vehicle?' he asks.

'It squeals every now and then when I'm turning right.'

'Only right?'

'Yes.'

He nods, as if this all makes sense. Mechanics have an incredible ability to make anybody feel stupid with a well-placed silence, while simultaneously making anything sound plausible. If he turned around and said that it sounds like a problem with the left-sided large oddie shifter, I'd nod along and ask how much one of them tends to cost.

'We'll see what we find,' Luke says. 'Anything else?'

I almost tell him about the scuff on the front, figuring I'll cut off any questions before they might come. I'll mention the pillar in the car park and give it the ol' *women drivers, hey?* smile.

Then I realise that's exactly what children do when they're trying to act as if they haven't done anything wrong. I stop myself just in time and offer a short 'no'.

Luke's barely paying me any attention anyway because he's already fiddling with something in a toolbox. 'Can you check in with Helen at reception?' he says. 'She'll make sure everything's up to date, then we'll give you a call later.'

It's only as I'm heading through the garage into the waiting area at the front that I remember the 'Helen' he's talking about is Richard's mother. We've met a couple of times before but have never had anything other than the same kind of weather-temperature conversation that I just had with Luke. Until people's children get on with marrying one another, I suspect that's the way for most parents whose kids are in relationships.

The reception is a browny-grey throwback, with curled, sun-damaged posters of cars across the walls. Helen is the only other person present and she's busy typing something into her computer when she speaks without looking up.

'Did you want the Bosch? They're out of stock.'

'Um…'

She turns and blinks at me with confusion. 'Sorry, I thought you were someone else.' Her eyes narrow and I can feel her trying to work out who I am.

I let it continue for a few seconds and then say, 'It's Jen. I'm Katie's mum.'

'Oh… yes, of course.'

She glances to her computer momentarily and then looks to me expectantly.

'I've just dropped off my car,' I say.

Helen checks the details they have for me are correct and says someone will call when the car's ready.

'I only work mornings,' she says. 'So it might not be me.' I thank her and am about to leave – but politeness gets the better of Helen and she adds quickly: 'How is Katie?'

'She's fine,' I reply. 'Working hard and looking forward to the Christmas break. How's your husband?'

'*Ian* is good.'

I almost laugh. I thought I'd covered the fact that I couldn't remember his name. 'What about Richard?' I add.

'You probably see him more than me.'

I laugh at that. 'You're probably right. How was his interview?'

The second I've said it, I know it was the wrong thing. Helen's nose twitches and then one of her eyes narrow. 'What interview? He's doing some work with his uncle.'

I shrink away and unsuccessfully try to cover myself with a cough.

'Right, um… yes. I know. I thought he had an interview yesterday. I might have got the dates wrong, or Katie was maybe talking about someone else…'

Helen's not convinced, nor should she be. We both know what's happened – Richard has told Katie and *only* Katie about an interview. He didn't think she'd tell me and he definitely didn't think I'd tell his mum.

I know this is going to end up with an argument between me and Katie. I can even hear her voice.

Why did you tell Richard's mum?
I didn't mean to. I thought she knew.
Of course she didn't know!

I suppose this will lead to another evening of us not talking to one another.

'I have to get going,' I say, 'Great to see you.'

Helen doesn't reply and I scuttle off through the door, not daring to turn back.

Being without a car for the day could be a blessing in that I won't be tempted to do anything stupid, like visit the crash site, or Josh's house. I can stay in and do some work.

That idea comes crashing down when I'm barely a minute away from the garage. I didn't expect an enthusiastic response from the person who's been texting me, especially after my 'I'm not doing it' reply.

The first text is a simple message.

Anon: *This isn't only about you*

I'm wondering what it means when the photo appears directly underneath. Since everything happened, there has been moment after moment in which it felt like a new line had been crossed.

This is something else.

It's a picture of Katie standing on the doorstep in her pyjamas. The photo has been taken from somewhere on the other side of the road opposite our house. I can't be certain but the confused look on Katie's face makes it look as if she's answered the door after someone rang the doorbell and then disappeared.

By itself, the photo is sinister enough – but with the preceding messages, it is outright chilling.

Me: *Don't touch her.*

I want an instant reply this time, though it doesn't come. I set off towards the house at as close to a run as I'm going to get. I try calling Katie while moving but stab the wrong button and instead call someone named Kevin who is directly below her in my contacts list. I can't even remember who he is – probably the parent of a former student – but I end the call before it connects.

I'm trying for Katie a second time when the text message comes through.

Anon: *Everyone is safe and will stay that way if you do as you're told. Do it today*

TWENTY-SIX

I call Katie but, after six or seven rings, it redirects me to her chirpy voicemail message.

'Hi, it's Katie. I'm doing something that's not this, so do whatever you need.'

I try again but it doesn't ring this time. My heart is thundering when the rational part of my brain kicks in to say it's probably because her line is still connected. I press to call a third time – and this time Katie answers on the second ring. She sounds confused.

'Mum…?'

'Are you all right?'

'Um… yeah. Of course I am.'

'Where are you?'

'At home. Where are you?'

'I just dropped the car off for its MOT.'

There's a gap and then: 'Why are you calling…?'

I don't have an answer. Nothing that sounds sane in any case.

'I couldn't remember whether you have college this morning…'

There's another pause and then: 'You know I do on Fridays. I'm trying to get ready. I'll be leaving soon.'

'Okay, great. Have a good day.'

I don't catch what she says after that, although I don't blame her for sounding confused. She probably thinks senility is starting to kick in. When I was a teenager, I thought anyone older than thirty was just about ready for an old people's home.

I hang up and then re-read the text. I think about calling Katie back to tell her she should stay home for today – but have no idea what reason to give. I doubt she'd listen anyway and, even if she did, what about tomorrow? Or the day after? I can't watch her forever.

I scroll back to last night's request – and it seems so childish. It's not something I can actually do… is it?

There is no trust in the person who has been messaging me, especially after the so-called 'final' request. Despite that, I also don't see how harming Katie, or anyone, could be in that person's best interest. They would surely end up in trouble with the police, too?

Is that a risk I'm willing to take?

Perhaps this person has a way of hurting Katie that would make it *seem* like an accident? Am I willing to risk her safety against keeping my secret?

No.

After everything from the past few days, I think this is the line I won't cross. It is also why I suspect the person who sent me the photo did so. I am going to be left doing whatever they want in order to keep Katie safe.

Instead of heading home, I walk towards the centre of town and the site of my third 'task'. It's hard to wonder about how many more will come.

The sun is on its way up and a spectral purple glows across the horizon. My stupid coat and scarf are offering little resistance against the wintery morning breeze and it feels as if small pinpricks of ice are jabbing into my skin.

I have just passed Bread And Butter when I spot Dawn hurrying along the street from the other direction. She has a large shopping bag over one arm and is sporting a pair of fluffy pink earmuffs that are hard to miss. She spots me a second or two after I see her and, in that instant, I think we both know what's about to happen. It's been coming ever since my former husband told me he was moving into her house. The only surprise is that amicability has lasted this long.

We stop a metre or so away from one another, staring through the gloom. It's like a stand-off in a Western – but with less sunshine and more hummus in a shopping bag.

It's Dawn who starts: 'Let's hear it then.'

'You must know what this is all going to do to me.'

'The *wedding*?'

'Of course not the wedding. I don't care about you getting married – it's the house.'

Dawn shifts her weight from one foot to the other and puts the bag down on the ground.

'You don't *have* to sell your house.'

Dawn makes it sound as if this is an option I had somehow overlooked.

'I can't afford to buy him out. There's no way I'll get a new mortgage when it's just me on one self-employed salary.'

'So get a smaller place. What's the problem?'

I don't know what I expected – but there's something about the matter-of-fact tone that has me seeing red.

'That's easy to say when you're the one inheriting houses.'

I spit the reply and know it's cruel. In this moment, I don't care.

Dawn gasps gently, steps back a fraction as if pushed. I've said the unsayable and can feel the fury bubbling from her.

'My parents died in a car crash,' she says, while barely moving her lips. 'I didn't *want* their house, *or* their savings. You don't know how hard it is to live in a place that reminds you so much of them.'

'So get a smaller place. What's the problem?'

Dawn seethes and I feel ripped down the middle.

There's such anger within me but it's more for myself than her. I'm furious at everything I've managed to do to myself and others in the past couple of days – but it's so much easier to take it out on Dawn.

There's a very specific emotion that comes from being a child and I'm not sure it exists much for adults. I once had an argument with Mum when I was about eight or nine. I can't remember any of what it was about – but it ended with me shouting that I hated her. In the second that followed, her face fell and there was such impossible sadness that it felt like I'd broken her. In that same second, I would have done anything to take back the words. It's that sense of disappointing a parent that feels like nothing else. The knowledge that time cannot be rewound and that the person who probably loves you the most has been hurt directly because of your actions.

For the first time in decades, I feel a twinge of that same emotion. I've deliberately said the thing that I know will be the most hurtful.

I can't stop, though. It might be irrational and unfair, but I hate her.

'That's low.' Dawn's voice cracks but I'm not done.

'Is it as low as sleeping with someone else's husband?'

There's a sniffle and then Dawn pushes herself up so that she's as tall as she can be.

'We didn't do *anything* while you were together. We barely knew each other then.'

'You're only kidding yourself.'

'Why would I lie? It doesn't matter to me. I don't care about you.'

It sounds brutal – but it's true. I'm her husband-to-be's ex-wife. I'm a customer. Why should she care about me?

Dawn continues, not waiting for a reply: 'We're getting married anyway, so why would you care about the where and the whens? He's not coming back to you.'

'I don't want him back.'

'So what's the point in any of this? Why are we arguing on the street?'

It's my voice that cracks now.

'Because selling the house is going to turn my life upside down.'

'It's half his. What do you expect?'

I hate that she's right – and not only in this respect. There *is* nothing wrong with a single woman living in something other than a large three-bedroom house. It's much more than I need – so why would I pile on the debt to keep it?

Except I know the answer to that, too.

It's pride.

To move out would be an admission that I've lost and that Bryan has won. That Dawn wins as well.

I take a step to the side, wanting to get off this section of pavement.

Dawn must see the weakness.

'Do you know why he left you?'

I should walk away – I *want* to walk away – but she has me now. This is her moment and, after I hurt her, it's time for the payback. There's no question that I deserve it.

There was no particular reason that Bryan told me he was leaving. The best I got was 'It's not working any more', which quickly led to 'I think we should take a break'.

It was unexpected for me. I *didn't* understand what wasn't working and *didn't* want to take a break. In the end, it wasn't up to me. After he said that, I always knew the 'break' was going to be permanent. It wasn't long before he came back and said he'd been looking into getting a divorce. I went along with it because there was little other option. It's not as if I could force him to stay with me – and who'd want that anyway?

I can't speak.

'It's because you were *boring*, Jen.' Dawn speaks with absolute assurance. 'You were *boring* him and he'd had enough.'

It's the truth that I always knew, offered with the callous delivery of a person revealing that the sky is blue and that two plus two is four. I hate her for being the one who actually says it.

It's a miracle my voice remains calm as I correct her. 'It's Jennifer.'

She's not done.

'Bryan was *bored* of you and the way you were turning him into a boring, dull version of himself. He didn't want to end up throwing himself off a bridge, knowing that he'd wasted his life, so he left you.'

I wish she sounded meaner, that there was a condescending sneer to her tone. Instead, it's an unemotional confidence that this is a fact.

'I'm not…'

I can't finish the sentence.

Dawn picks up her bag, ready to head to the café that she bought with the inheritance money left to her by her parents. That's the other thing with a place like Prowley. Bread And Butter is Dawn's redemption arc. She went through the horror and pain of losing both her parents at the same time – and then rose from the ashes to launch the most popular café in the area. Everyone knows her story. It's horrible, I know it is, but her parents dying was the best thing that ever happened to her. She has everything – and I'm months away from having nothing.

My voice is a croaky mess. 'Why do you need the money?'

Dawns rolls her eyes and doesn't answer, so I try again.

'Why does *Bryan* need the money?'

'Ask him.'

'I did.'

Dawn shrugs. 'I don't know what you want me to say, Jen.'

'It's Jennifer. I don't want to have to move.'

She turns and takes a couple of steps towards the café. 'I guess you have to figure something out then. See you around, *Jen*.'

TWENTY-SEVEN

Boring.

I'm not sure how I'm going to get past that. The worst insults are the ones with a stabbing needle of certainty to them. There are definitely times when I've thought that about myself. When we were younger, Bryan and I would have date nights at the cinema, or in town for drinks. We'd have weekends away and impromptu meets for lunch. That all ebbed away over time and I thought it was down to both of us. We got older and that's what happens when people age. Life becomes more settled, more predictable, more… boring.

Now I find out that it was only me who felt that. We weren't a couple becoming set in our ways: I was an individual who was doing that.

I don't know if I should be angry or sad. I'm boring because I have a sensible job and because I wanted to give Katie a stable upbringing.

Last night's request from the anonymous texter reads differently now. I said I wasn't going to do it – but perhaps that's what someone who is deathly dull might say.

I follow the path past the phone box library and along the edge of the green. I pass the Christmas tree and the war memorial, then continue until I'm on the riverbank. There is a rocky trail that follows the edge of the water, heading towards the woods in one direction and the industrial estate in the other. In the mornings, it's mainly used by people walking their dogs. By the evening, especially in the summer, there are clumps of teenagers with illicit bottles of cider, trying to avoid the accusing stares of people who don't remember what it was like to be young.

The bank is crusted with frost and I stick to the edge of the path that's furthest from the water as I walk towards the industrial estate. The word boring is still rattling around my head as a golden retriever bounds out of the trees and stops in front of me. I nuzzle the dog's ears as its owner appears from the bushes. We offer mutual hellos – and then they're off and away in the opposite direction. It's only when they've gone that I remember I came this way to be seen by as few people as possible.

The path soon loops up and away from the river, poking through a copse of trees and emerging onto a cul-de-sac at the back of the industrial estate.

The larger factories are further away from the centre and the line of offices here are blocky and grimy. There are seven or eight companies operating in a terrace of buildings that is so dirty, it would likely be cheaper and easier to knock the whole lot down than it would be to try to clean.

There is a pair of cars at the far end of the car park but no other sign of life. I almost start to head along the front but then spot the CCTV camera perched above the main entrance. To avoid that, I move around to the side of the building and then into the back alley. A long line of trees sweeps across the rear and there are no cameras here. There's not much of anything, other than rubble, bins and overgrown bushes. When there are TV news pieces about rats thriving, this is the type of scene on show.

There's a plaque above the back door of the first office that mentions a cleaning supply company, so I continue along the line, checking each door as I pass the offices for a lawyer, a pet food supplier and then AD Investments.

I've never heard of the company and have no idea who runs it. Whenever there is talk of stocks, shares and investments on the news, I blank out. I don't think I know anybody who cares.

I check last night's text one final time, even though I know the name of the business already.

Anon: *Smash the windows at AD Investments. It's on the edge of the trading estate*

Searching for details of the company online threw up almost no information, other than the address. I didn't know what to think when I got the message last night. It's a backwards step from asking for money. At first I thought it was childish and, to a degree, I still do. But then I realised that a company like this might have cost an individual money through bad investments, or poor advice. It might be petty revenge to break a window – but it's still revenge.

Crucially, whoever has a grudge against this company isn't acting upon it themselves. They are using a proxy – *me* – to do it for them.

It's only when I figured that out that this task made any sense. After my run-in with Dawn, it now seems logical. If I had someone at my disposal who was willing to do whatever I told them, would I use that person to carry out small acts of retribution on my behalf? I'd like to say no – but I'm not sure that's true. Perhaps I'd have someone put through the windows of Bread And Butter if it couldn't be traced back to me…

Spiky thorns criss-cross the alley, growing out from the bushes at the back. In among those are scores of crumbling half-bricks, as if whoever built these offices dumped whatever was left at the back. I nudge a few with my shoe before opting for a rock that's the size of my fist. The surface is smooth and cold as I pick it up and wonder if I'm really going to do this. I shouldn't – but there's the implicit threat to Katie and I can't ignore that. One of the reasons I told myself I left Sharon at the side of the road was to protect my daughter from having a mother in prison. Now she might be in even more danger.

I've not thrown anything since the javelin at school. I was terrible then and can still remember the wrenching pain in my shoulder as I launched it barely a few metres. It's still hard to comprehend how schoolchildren are allowed to wander around with spiked poles that are taller than they are.

There's a sound of tyre on gravel from the other side of the building. It might not be someone who works at AD Investments – but there will be someone here soon.

It's now or never.

I picture Dawn's face through the gloom of the morning.

Boring.

And then, just as requested in the message from last night, I throw the rock through the window of AD Investments.

There's a moment in which it feels as if everything has slowed to a stop. The rock goes through the pane in silenced slow motion, leaving a rounded circle in the glass. Then, in an instant, there's a crash and the piercing howl of an alarm.

I'm frozen for a second – but only that – because then I turn and run.

TWENTY-EIGHT

I don't run for long – but I don't need to. My lungs are fire as I burst back onto the towpath next to the river. I slow to a steady walk and try to catch my breath as I head back towards the centre of Prowley. I expect sirens and shouting, chaos and confusion, but there's nothing. There are no dog-walkers in sight this time; no sign of anyone. I keep walking back past the tree, around the green and then – for a reason of which I can't quite fathom – I head into Bread And Butter.

The café is quieter at this time of the morning. It will fill up as all the yummy mummies finish dropping off their kids at school, before they head here for a debrief over a skinny latte or a green tea. Aside from the couple sitting in the window with matching green juices, I am the only other customer.

I've not smoked since I was a teenager and even the thought sends me spiralling back through time to the days when I'd hide packets in my shoes overnight. At school, my friends and I would sneak into the gap at the back of the English hut, which bordered the tall hedges at the back of the field. We thought we were smart to create our own little smoking den, somehow missing the somewhat obvious outcome that smoking creates, well… smoke. And smell. Everyone knew what we were getting up to back there, though even the teachers didn't think it was worth interfering. I can see why now. Why would they want to interrupt their own break times in which they managed to find a few minutes of freedom each day? As long as we were out of trouble and only poisoning our own lungs, they didn't care.

The craving for a cigarette now is so intense that I can almost taste it. I almost ask the couple whether either of them has one I could pinch.

I just about stop myself as the voice behind the counter calls across to me:

'Can I help?'

I was expecting Dawn – but it's not her. The café is open six days a week – seven in the summer – and she doesn't work here every day.

Iris is older than Dawn; the type of woman who's a fixture in towns like Prowley. She's lived here all her life, knows everybody, and can whinge like nobody I've ever met. If there was ever a World Cup for moaning, England could recruit Iris and she'd captain the team. If she won the lottery, she'd find something to complain about.

I drift across to the counter and eye the board to waste a moment of time.

'Black coffee, please.'

I pay and then Iris huffs for no particular reason as she passes across the drink.

'Where's Dawn?' I ask.

'Haven't you heard?'

'Heard what?'

Iris glances past me for show, as if she's about to impart a national secret. 'She's giving it up.'

'Giving what up?'

She holds out her hands, indicating the café. 'This.'

I seem to spend a lot of time being dumbfounded at the moment – but this is truly a surprise.

'I only spoke to her this morning,' I say.

That gets a dismissive shrug. 'I found out last night, then she was in this morning dropping some things off. She's going to be moving down to three days a week for now – but she wants someone to buy her out.'

'Did she say why?'

'Said she's getting married in three months and wants it all sorted by then. First I'd heard of it.' She pauses and reels back a fraction as she remembers who she's talking to. 'You did know about the wedding… didn't you?'

'I'd heard.'

'Oh… good. I just thought what with you and her – and him. Y'know… all that.'

I nod, unsure what to say. *All that* is certainly one way to put it.

'I don't think I understand,' I say. 'Why does she want to be bought out?'

'Don't know. It came as a shock to me. She asked if I want to be manager for a few months.' With most people, this revelation might have brought a smile. Not Iris.

'That sounds good for you…?'

'Lotta work, isn't it?'

'I suppose. People don't usually give up their businesses because they're getting married. Did she say if there was another reason?'

'Not to me.' Iris pauses and then a slim smile creeps across her face. It's not mean as such – but there's a hint of mischief-making. 'You could ask her.'

'I don't think we have that type of relationship.'

'No… not with you and her – and him. Y'know… *all that.*'

I should be annoyed but there's something deliciously sly about the way she's repeated herself. Such wonderful spite for no reason whatsoever. I almost admire it.

I take my drink and start to move towards a table when I spot the poster that's been taped to the counter.

'Dawn dropped that off earlier,' Iris says.

A SERVICE OF PRAYER AND CHARITY
Join us in praying for the health and welfare
of Sharon and Frank Tanner
Friday – 7.30 p.m.
St Jude's
All welcome

'It's all over Facebook,' Iris adds, although I'm surprised that she knows what Facebook is. It's like when my mum once mentioned a DVD and I was surprised because she'd never got her head around VHS tapes.

'Church isn't really my thing,' I say.

'Me either. He's only a wee babby, though.'

I nod along but can't fathom going. How could I sit and listen to that sort of service while knowing what I did?

I'm saved from a longer conversation by the sound of the door and the usual gaggle of mothers blustering their way inside. I scoot across to a seat in the window, out of their way, and sip my drink while listening to the usual one-upmanship about whose child is the best. Billy got some award for his handwriting, while Charlene – who's a brat, by the way – has entered a flute competition because she's predicted to be some sort of prodigy. The mothers go around in a circle, each trying to passively aggressively outdo one another. It's exhausting to listen to. Their poor kids are going to end up on a therapist's couch in twenty years, wondering where it all went wrong.

I wonder what a therapist would make of me smashing windows and leaving someone to die in a ditch. I don't think I want to know.

It's not long before the green juice couple disappear out the door to go and do whatever it is people do after drinking something that looks like it's used to declog a drain.

I check my phone for anything from either the anonymous texter or Katie – but there's nothing. I send a quick message to Katie, asking what time she's likely to be home. It's more to check that she's safe, without having to ask something so specific. The reply pings back almost immediately:

Katie: *About 5. X*

I'm wondering whether I should respond when my phone starts to ring. The number of the garage flashes and when I answer, it's Helen's voice.

'Is that Jennifer?'

'Yes.'

'I'm calling to let you know your car's ready.'

'That's quick. I was expecting—'

'It passed its MOT but Luke has a query or two.'

The significance almost passes me by before I realise what she's said. He's noticed the scuff and put two and two together. If not that, then there was a piece of evidence I missed.

'What kind of query?' I ask.

There's the faint sound of typing and Helen sounds uninterested, like she's doing a few things at once. 'I don't know. You'll have to ask him. Are you on your way?'

TWENTY-NINE

Luke is in the well underneath a blue car when Helen waves me through to the area at the back of the garage. He heads up the steps and ducks underneath the rear of the car before going to the sink and washing his hands.

The radio at the back of the garage blurs one eighties hit into another as he turns and dries his hands on a towel.

'That was quick,' I say, forcing a smile.

'You were first up,' he replies.

Luke leads me out the back door of the garage, where my car is sitting in a bay next to the gate.

'Did Helen give you the papers?' he asks.

'Yes… but she said you had a query…?'

Luke stops at the front of the car, standing by the wing. His knee is almost touching the scuff. It feels like he's about to crouch and ask me why there's a dent, or some blood I missed…

'I couldn't see anything that might be causing the squealing sound you mentioned,' he says.

'Oh.'

'I had a good look around but there's nothing obvious it might be. If it keeps happening, maybe make a note of exactly what you're doing and then come back.'

He licks his lips. There's more to come – and then he crouches so that he's almost level with the graze. Just as I think he's about to ask what happened, he starts to tie a lace that's become undone.

'Your gearbox feels looser than it should,' he adds.

'The gear*box*?'

It comes out as if I've never heard of one before, even though it's more from surprise that he hasn't mentioned the scuff.

'The gearbox isn't checked as part of the MOT – so your car passed – but I noticed it while I was moving the car around.'

'Does it need replacing?'

Luke winces a little as he stands. 'Not at the moment. I'd keep an eye on it, though. If you're having problems with changing gear, you should come back as soon as possible.'

'Should I be worried?'

He shakes his head. 'It should be fine. If we don't see you before, then someone will call you in eleven months.'

I thank him and he waves me out of the back gate with a big whirring arm, as if I've never reversed a car before.

The drive home sees me obsess over whether the gearstick feels any different to how it did before. I conclude that it definitely doesn't and am lost in thoughts of Katie and anonymous texts and smashed windows when I notice Josh sitting on the wall outside the house. He's wearing a cap, with his head down and hands in jacket pockets – but the way his legs stretch long onto the pavement makes it unmistakeably him. I've fretted at the things of which he might be capable – but one thing he most definitely cannot do is blend in.

I park in the garage and then turn and walk back along the path to where Josh remains on the wall. He's turned to face me and the house, but is still sitting.

'Why are you here?' I sound wearier than I thought.

'Free country, innit?'

'It's my wall.'

Josh stands and takes a step back until he's on the pavement. 'Happy now?'

The fire and anger I felt around Dawn earlier have ebbed away to the point that I almost can't remember how it felt. I'm so exhausted.

'How's your mum?' I ask.

His cap is pulled down so that the peak is covering his eyes – but because I'm so much shorter I can see the way they're glaring down. 'Are you joking?'

'I heard your brother was out of intensive care.'

'You've got some nerve.'

His jaw is clamped and he speaks while barely moving his lips. His hands are still in his pockets, though I have no doubt his fists are balled.

'What do you want me to say? You're outside my house. You followed me into town the other day. You were in my back garden last night.'

He shuffles on the spot, which makes him look uncertain. He doesn't deny it. He replies with a quiet growl. 'Admit what you did.'

'I didn't *do* anything.'

Josh lifts the peak on his cap and stares past me towards the garage and the car beyond.

'I know you were driving.'

'You *can't* know that – because I wasn't.'

He rocks on his heels and I feel certain he's about to tell me he saw me stop after hitting them. If he was at home, he would have been right there. Of everyone, he is the most likely person to have seen what happened.

'How can you live with it?'

I can see his face fully now – but there's no anger. His eyes are twitching and his throat bobbing. It looks like he might cry.

At first, I wonder if this is some sort of ploy but then it clicks that he's still a teenage boy. His height has almost robbed him of that fact. He's a boy whose mum is in hospital, along with his baby brother.

He looks me in the eyes and I'm welded to the spot.

'You can keep saying you didn't do it but, deep down, when you know you did, how do you live with it?'

His voice falters and it's then that I realise he's not talking about me. Or not *only* talking about me. He twists away so that I can't see his face.

'What did you do?'

My question hangs and there's a haunting silence. Josh no longer feels like the towering young man I saw in the supermarket car park. It's like he's shrunk in front of me.

His reply is a husky whisper. 'You don't know me.'

'You can say…'

When he turns back, it's like a switch has been flicked. The vulnerability has been replaced by steel.

'You're losing it,' he says.

'Losing what?'

'You know what you did.'

A smirk flickers onto his face and the moment of vulnerability is so far lost that it's like it was never there – and then the question comes, unprompted and unthought. Stupidity personified.

'Have you been texting me?' I ask, and then a hasty 'It's you, isn't it?'

He looks at me curiously but amused. 'What's me?'

'The messages.'

He snorts and steps backwards. 'It's the guilt. That's why you're losing it.' He takes another step away and then points a finger towards me. 'You're going down for this.'

THIRTY

Josh crosses the road and strides around the corner without looking back. I can't fathom why he's so certain it was me that caused the accident. It *was* me – but how can he know? And if he somehow does, then why are we dancing around it?

When I get inside, the lights from the Christmas tree are blinking through the open living room door into the hall. I call Katie's name instinctively, even though she said she was going to college. When there's no answer, I head upstairs and knock on her door. There's still no reply, so I nudge the door and peep inside. I don't like going into her room when she's not home, largely because I remember how much I hated my mother coming into my room. She'd think she was helping by picking things up from the floor and generally tidying up – but it meant I was rarely truly comfortable in my own space.

There is no sign of Katie and I can't stop myself from sending her a text.

Me: *How's your day going?*

I don't expect a quick reply but I get one nonetheless.

Katie: *I'm in class. Are we going to church later?*

I have to double-check the message is actually from my daughter. I've never known her mention church – and it takes a few seconds until I realise she's talking about the prayer service for Sharon and Frank. She's assuming I already know about it – which I suppose is fair enough, considering that I do. I wonder how she found out about it. Is it really a hot topic at her college? Iris said it was 'all over Facebook', so Katie could have heard from that, even though I know everyone her age thinks it's really a tool for old farts.

There's no obvious reply – so I let it rest for now. It's usually Katie who leaves me hanging when it comes to messaging, so she can hardly complain.

I get out the iPad and check the local news sites. I'm hoping for better news on Sharon but the only update is the same as earlier which has upgraded Frank's condition out of 'critical'. He's still only referred to as a 'two-year-old' – even though his name is freely visible on the prayer service posters.

Another text comes through from Katie.

Katie: *I'd like to go tonight. Are you going?*

Even from just these few words, I can tell that she's frustrated I haven't responded. She's used to me replying instantly to any messages she sends. It isn't only with her – that's how I am with anyone. I think it's a generational thing. I'm not one of those who talks about how useless young people are. The *can't-even-wire-a-plug brigade*. Those complainers always seem to forget that young people don't set their own school syllabuses. If they've been failed by education, it's hardly their fault.

I still don't reply to Katie. I don't want to go but can hardly tell her that. What explanation would I give?

As I swipe away from that message, I load the one underneath. There's still no acknowledgement from the anonymous texter for what I did at AD Investments. I'm not going to initiate a conversation unless absolutely necessary and wonder whether whoever it is knows what happened. Unless they work on that estate, there's every chance they haven't heard. Putting a rock through a window is hardly likely to get much media attention, either.

I type AD Investments into Google, wondering if I'll have a clearer idea of what I've done now that it's daytime and I'm not trying to stay awake. The company's home page is the top link. It's functional but basic. There's an image of someone grinning manically at a computer screen in a way that nobody has done in the history of technology. After that there's a graph where the Y axis has no label and the X says 'profit'.

The gumpf at the bottom is like reading an economics essay by someone who didn't do the reading. It talks about 'making your money work for you' – as well as a host of other clichés. As best I can tell, there are no other links or pages to click. It's just this, with an email address and a phone number at the bottom. I know nothing about building webpages but even I can tell this has been slapped together by someone with little idea of what they're doing.

I go back and then press the next link, which is a pair of reviews for the company.

5* Amazing people. Brilliant company. Doubled my investment. Recommended.

It's from eighteen months ago and has likely been written by someone who works for the company. Either that, or a full-stop fanatic.

1* Terrible company. I lost almost £5,000 with them – and then they used their 'terms and conditions' to stop me withdrawing what was left. Have been talking to the FSA about what happened. Avoid. Avoid. Avoid.

– G Porter

It's generally the way with reviews that things are all or nothing – but the two extremes are exaggerated even by the standards of the internet. I almost click away from the page – but then I notice the name underneath the review. I'm sure I know someone called Porter.

I remember seeing the name recently… but have no idea where.

I try Facebook first, searching through my friends list, though there is no Porter there. The contacts list on my phone is little use, largely because almost everyone is stored by first name and, at best, a single initial. There are three Martins – a Martin F, and Martin T and the person who is presumably the original, because he's simply known as 'Martin'. That would be fine except I can't remember knowing a single person of the same name.

My previous caller list has no further clues, neither does the stack of miscellaneous mail that has amassed on the table next to the front door. I try googling the name – but 'G Porter' throws up the name of a singer, plus some sort of GPS device. Nothing that helps.

It's only when I open my work cupboard that the memory returns. Sitting on the interview pile is Leah's sheet from the other day – and written at the very top in neat capital letters is the name 'Leah Porter'.

Is G Porter… Gary? The police officer? My neighbour? How many G Porters can there be that would have an issue with a local investment company? They can't be many more than… one.

I move across the living room, stepping around the Christmas tree and shifting aside the net curtain at the window. There is a single light on upstairs in Gary's house but, other than that, it looks empty.

I've moved away from the window when another thought occurs. I head outside this time, phone in hand as I scroll back to the text from the anonymous messenger that had the photo of Katie.

Hours later and it's as eerie as it was. Katie is standing in the doorway, still in her slippers as she stares bemusedly to the side. I can picture her doing it: looking both ways and wondering who rang the doorbell. We have one of those wireless devices that occasionally rings either by itself, or because someone in the general vicinity has a bell that uses the same frequency. She probably put it down to that, and then went back to her room.

I cross the road and shift a few houses down until I'm outside Gary's, then I check the photo once more and compare it by looking up to my own front door.

There can be no doubt: whoever took this photo was standing on Gary's driveway.

THIRTY-ONE

I don't know Gary very well. I'm aware of him in the way that neighbours are – a nod here and a wave there. The occasional 'hi', or moan about the weather. Mum used to talk about street parties and 'community spirit', saying how sad it was that things weren't like that any longer. But then she voted for Thatcher and 'no such thing as society', so she didn't have the right to complain. She and Dad used to argue about that all the time, right up until the end. If she'd told me that his last words had been, 'I can't believe you voted for that hag', then I'd have believed it.

Using my phone, I take a photo of my own house and then return across the road and head inside. When I swipe between the two images, there's no question they have been taken from the same spot. That isn't proof that it was Gary who sent it – but there is the second link from him to AD Investments.

From the first text message, the biggest thing I struggled to figure out – except for the sender's identity – is how that person could know what I did. There were no other cars on the road. The entrance to Sharon's driveway was only a few metres from the collision, so I could perhaps understand Josh seeing something, even if his reaction to me would be a curious one.

Whoever has been messaging saw me on a bike – and Gary's the one person I know that definitely did. He also has a simple way of keeping an eye on everything I'm doing because he lives over the road. If it is Gary who's playing with me, then perhaps he has access to a traffic camera somewhere that would have recorded my number plate?

If the footage is something that can be accessed by the police, then it would be hard to understand how *only* he has access to it. I don't know enough about their processes. It's still the same question – how could he know?

Then there's what is perhaps a bigger question: *Why?*

The journey to take a photo of the McDonald's sign is explainable in the way it was outlined. It probably *was* a way of finding out if I'd do what I was told. But is £600 and the smashing of some windows worth the potential loss of a police officer's career?

I scroll through the entire text thread and then type 'anonymous text messaging' into Google. It quickly becomes apparent that I have probably misunderstood everything that's going on. I'd assumed someone was messaging me from a phone – but it's seemingly easy to create a fake number and then send messages to a real one. There are apps and websites built to do precisely that – and all of them promote 'privacy' as their biggest selling point. If it truly *is* anonymous, then even if I was to report the messages, it seems like the authorities might struggle to trace the sender. If that's the case, perhaps it *does* make sense that Gary would have me carry out a petty piece of revenge on his behalf?

When it comes to blackmail, certainly in something like a movie, there is always a request that seems impossible. The biggest one is that the blackmailer wants a huge sum of money. Whoever this is must know me well enough to realise that something like that is utterly beyond my capability – £600 is about the limit of what I could get. Everything asked of me has been broadly realistic and enough to keep me going along with it.

Not for the first time, I'm distracted by a message from Katie.

Katie: *Richard is going to church with me later. Can you drive us in? Loads of people are going.*

She still hasn't specifically mentioned the prayer service and is assuming I know what she means. When she says 'loads of people', she will be talking about college friends and people from her football team. If that's true, there will also be a large number of locals attending, too. It would look weird if I wasn't there. *Suspiciously* weird.

It's a typical Prowley occasion – a chance to be seen and perhaps get into the back of a photo for the local paper. There was a funeral last year for the bloke who was mayor for most of the eighties. I can hardly complain because I was at the church – but that was because *everyone* went. Every seat was taken and there were lines of people along both sides, plus a five-deep crowd at the back. The heart of a black hole would have had more light on display than was on show in the outfit choices that day. People I've known for years – people I'd consider friends – were bursting into tears at random intervals, even though they didn't know him personally and he had no effect on their lives.

There was an eight-page pull-out in the local paper, though – plus photos were plastered across the town's Facebook page. Grieving photos are for life, not just for a funeral.

With that in mind, I check the town's Facebook page. Sure enough, the top post is an event that's listed as: 'Prayer service and fundraiser for Baby Frank and Sharon'. The person who posted it has advised people to 'spread the word' – and the poster layout has been put up for people to print. There are already two hundred people listed as going – and many of them will have partners or children who haven't RSVPd. There will be more who've heard about the service away from Facebook and won't be listed. I have no idea how everyone is going to fit in the church.

I message Katie to tell her I'll drive her and Richard to the church later, then get an instant 'ty' as a reply.

Late morning turns into afternoon as I wile away the hours. I separate a few guidance sheets I'll likely need for Leah's tutoring session later – but it's hard to focus. The house feels emptier than usual and, as I sit in the living room with the Christmas tree lights blinking, I realise how much I'm looking forward to Katie's college going on break for the holiday. She might spend time outside with Richard, or her other friends – but she's no more a fan of winter than I am. She will be home a lot. My daily routine, if it can be called that, will be punctuated by muffled music and company. If I agree to buy her something, she might be up for a day of shopping, with a stop-off for lunch while we're out.

It's the sound of the doorbell that jumps me back to the present. I'm not sure whether I drifted off to sleep on the sofa, or if the afternoon passed me by.

Leah is at the door, with a backpack over her shoulder. She smiles nervously as I welcome her in – and it's hard to get a word out of her at first. The difference comes as soon as we start working. She's bright and emerges from her shell very quickly. In terms of pure academia, it's hard to know why she's been having problems at school. On her form, she said that maths is her least favourite subject – but she has a clear grasp on how things work, plus knowledge of as many terms as she needs to know.

In reality, ability isn't the only thing that's needed. It's easy to be distracted by other people at school – or there can be a clash with a specific teacher. When someone is young, small criticisms or offhand remarks can feel massive. A person's entire outlook on a subject can be turned by a single thing that happened years before. I've found that few of the people who 'fail' at school do so because of the actual work. When they're in a one-on-one environment such as this, they tend to realise that they're a lot better at their supposedly troublesome subject than they believe.

The time passes so quickly and pleasantly that it's five minutes to five when I first look at the clock. I check the final line of Leah's page of work – which is perfect and correct – and then say we're done for the day.

'How do you feel?' I ask.

She slips her pen into a pencil case and zips it shut, then retrieves her bag from the floor. 'Good,' she replies. 'I think I get it better now.'

'It's been a really productive hour. You're much better at this than you think.'

She shrinks a little, slightly embarrassed, although the creeping smile shows off her true feelings.

'Do we do this again next week?' she asks.

'If you're happy with that. I don't think we need to try for more than once a week.'

She nods along but there's something about the glance towards the window – and her house beyond – that doesn't feel right.

'Are you okay with that?' I ask.

'Yes.'

'I can ask your dad if you think there's a problem…?'

Her gaze flickers back from the window. 'No… um, yes. I mean… it's just that he's been at work a lot this week.'

'Is that normal?'

'It's because of the crash and the baby and everything. He's not at home at the moment but when he is…'

The sentence drifts away to nothing.

'What?' I ask.

She shakes her head. 'Nothing.'

Leah picks up her bag and motions to the door.

'If your dad's not home, you can stay here for a while, if you want? I have bread for toast and Marmite if that's what you want…? And beans.'

'There's leftovers from last night in the fridge.'

She steps towards the door, although it feels reluctant.

'Are you going to the service later?' I ask.

'Dad said we should. Everyone I know is going.'

'I think there's going to be a lot of people there.'

'That's what Dad said.'

Perhaps more than any other age group, teenagers can have an uncanny way of giving away their feelings through only body movements. I think it's because they're still growing. Sometimes their arms and legs have a life of their own. Probably without meaning to, the way Leah cringes makes it obvious she doesn't want to go.

'I'm not much of a church person either,' I say.

She shakes her head.

'Not that?' I ask.

Leah's engaged now and she bobs on the spot, caught between saying something or walking away.

'Do you know Josh…?'

She looks away, not wanting to catch my eye in case she's misjudged the mood.

'Sharon's son?' I ask.

A nod.

'I would imagine he's going to be there tonight,' I add.

'Exactly.'

I'm so slow on the uptake sometimes. 'Have you had some sort of run-in with Josh…?'

'I, um… not me…'

'Who?'

Leah hoists her bag higher and steps away. It's unnervingly close to what I heard from Katie. She's started towards the door, likely regretting saying anything.

I start to follow her: 'Does your dad know about Josh?

A shake of the head. 'Don't think so. He's busy a lot. But he did say it should all be over soon.'

I'm confused by what she means: 'What should be over?'

'I'm not supposed to say.'

'I'm not going to tell him.'

Leah reaches for the front door and pulls down on the handle. Cold air blusters inside to fight with the warmth of the house.

'I heard him on the phone. He said they have an idea of who was driving. That's when he said it should be over soon.'

It takes me a moment to take it in. As if I've heard incorrectly. 'What do you mean?'

A shrug. 'I don't know…'

With that, she darts through the door and scrambles along the path, probably wishing she'd not said anything in the first place.

THIRTY-TWO

I start to call after Leah but she's already off the end of the path and on the way home. I have the sense she'd been waiting to tell someone what she'd heard – but didn't have the confidence in her friends that they would keep it to themselves.

Can it be true?

If the police have an idea of who was driving, then why haven't they spoken to me in any official way? When Gary talked to me, it was more of a chat and certainly not recorded. I suppose they could be building the evidence before the arrest. The clock could already be ticking.

There is an alternative.

Through everything that's happened since Tuesday, I've not thought about what I might do if the wrong person was to be arrested. I've seen documentaries and news stories about people who have been released from prison after spending years – decades – behind bars, even though they turned out to be innocent. Every new case feels as shocking as the last. We all only get one go at life – and there can't be much worse than unjustly giving up a percentage of that.

I want to believe that if the police arrest the wrong person, then I'll hand myself in. If not straight away, then by the formal charging stage. I definitely wouldn't wait for anything to get to trial…

Except maybe I would.

Everything I've done since Tuesday has been to minimise what I did. Could I *really* let someone else take the blame?

I'm thinking of that when I remember that at least one person seemingly knows what I did. Could Gary really be my blackmailer? There's still no message since I put that rock through the window of the investment company.

So much of this seems surreal.

I'm back in the living room when the front door sounds. There's a breathy heave and then another gust of cold air before Katie's voice fills the hall. I go through to meet her just as she's closing it. Richard is standing off to the side, pretending I'm not there. He's back in his black gear today, though it's hard to know if it's because he's off to the church later, or if this is what he put on this morning.

'Hi, um, Mrs Hughes,' he says.

'I've said you should call me Jennifer.'

He nods, but I know he won't.

Katie takes off her jacket and turns to hang it on the peg.

'Wait here a minute,' she says, talking to Richard. She disappears along the hall and lets herself into the garage.

Richard glances up towards me but then instantly turns his gaze to the floor when he realises I'm watching him.

I remember what Katie said about the tutoring sessions we did and wonder if I should bring them up. Tell him that I genuinely wanted to help. He was always reluctant to talk and nervy during those sessions: much like now. I assumed it was because I was his girlfriend's mother – but some people are simply like that until they really get to know a person. He can't be like this when it's only him and Katie.

Then I remember that I accidentally told his mother that I knew about his interview. I wonder if I should tip him off, or whether that would create a problem between him and Katie. It seems clear she wasn't supposed to tell me.

Instead, I do neither of those things.

'How's the job with your uncle?' I ask.

'A'right.'

'It sounds like hard work.'

'Yeah…'

There's a purply-grey bruise in the crook of his neck and he's standing with a slight hunch. He definitely doesn't seem the sort who would embrace manual labour unless necessary – not that I'm any different. I did agency work for a little while when I was around his age and the production line shifts left my quads and calves burning at the end of every day because of the standing around, plus the lifting and carrying.

Bryan was never one for manual work, either.

Bloody Bryan.

He's there in my thoughts again. I suppose he's never completely gone. I'd almost forgotten about everything with Dawn this morning. It feels such a long time ago, even though it was hours.

He thought I was boring…

Katie breaks the awkward impasse between Richard and me as she returns from the garage. She closes the door behind her and then turns to me.

'What time are we leaving later? The service is at half seven.'

'Seven o'clock, then.'

'Can we go earlier? There won't be anywhere to park. They're setting up a tent outside the church because they're expecting so many people. I don't want to end up standing in that.'

Me either, I think, but don't say.

'Six thirty…?' I reply.

'Okay, good.'

She turns for the stairs but I'm not done as I motion towards the garage.

'What were you doing in there?'

'Looking for my winter boots. They're not upstairs. Have you seen them?'

I tell her I haven't, though, if I'm honest, I don't ever remember her having any boots specifically for winter.

Katie pulls a face and then nods back to the stairs. 'I need to get ready.'

She disappears upstairs with Richard trailing behind like a kicked puppy. I wait for the sound of Katie's door closing and then head into the living room. The Christmas tree lights have been on all day and are starting to grow on me. I'm already picturing where the tree can go next year when I'm reminded that I probably won't be living here in twelve months. I turn and take in the room and know that it's not only the house I'll miss. Wherever I end up will have a different layout. I wonder if the furniture will fit, or if I'll have to get rid of some things. Then there's the hassle of actually shifting everything. When we moved here, Bryan and I had very little. We were able to move everything with the help of some friends and the backs of their cars. There'd be no chance of that now.

So much hassle.

I'm sure Bryan will be at the church later – and it won't be the time then – but I wonder if I might be able to persuade him to let me put things off until the end of next year. One more Christmas.

It's then that I realise something that should have been obvious. I didn't think of it before but, now I have, it seems inconceivable that there isn't a link. Dawn is selling her café, presumably because she wants the money – and now Bryan is also keen on getting his money out from the house.

What are they planning to do?

There has to be something going on. I'm busy thinking of that as I drift across to the window. It's dark now and I start to draw the curtains, which is when I spot a car pulling onto Gary's drive. The vehicle's lights go off and then he gets out from the driver's seat and pats his pockets. He starts towards his front door but then, almost as if there are eyes in the back of his head, he stops to glance backwards towards my house. I don't know if he can see me from the distance, especially in the dark, but he pauses for a second longer – and then heads for his front door.

THIRTY-THREE

Katie was right about leaving early. The streets around the church in the centre of Prowley are like IKEA on a bank holiday. The roads around the green are already chocked with vehicles, with all the latecomers – like me – pouring into the side streets.

Katie is in the passenger seat and lunges against the belt to point towards a gap between a pair of parked cars.

'There's a space there.'

'I'm never going to get this car in there.'

'What about that one?'

She points towards a different space further down the line. We're on the streets a little away from the shops, where homeowners have an aneurysm over someone parking in front of their house. It's such an issue that there was a front-page article about the 'epidemic' in the local paper last year. In reality, it was two mardy-faced busybodies having a whinge – but someone still wrote about it.

I edge along the road towards the space Katie indicated and then pull into it front first. I'd usually at least try to parallel park – but someone's driving too close to me and I suspect they'd try to take it. Whoever it is honks their horn as they pass which, when it comes to Prowley, is the equivalent of knife crime.

After they've passed, I have to fiddle around with going back and forth to fit into the space. It's when I hit the kerb that Katie finally cracks.

'I failed my test for less than this,' Katie says.

'That's what you said the other day.'

'And yet it's still true.'

Richard is in the back seat and hasn't said a word since we left the house, though I can sense him wondering how I've made such a mess of it.

When I eventually level everything out, we all get out of the car. Katie and Richard set off towards the church side by side with me trailing a few steps behind. The pair of them are both dressed in black, while I've gone for something that's dark purple. It's not a funeral, no matter what the mood of the town.

As we get closer to Saint Jude's, I realise that almost everyone is also in black. There are a handful of people in purple, dark red or brown – but we're very much the outliers.

We have to go around the phone box library to get to the church and I find myself watching it as we pass, knowing that the person who took the money is likely going to be at the church this evening. It has to be someone who knows me, even if I don't know them particularly well. Whoever it is will no doubt be watching for me, wondering how I had the gall to turn up given what I did.

We continue on around the green, past the memorial and the tree and over the road towards the church. Saint Jude's is one of those huge, stone churches; the type of which don't seem to have been built in centuries. The steeple soars high above the town, while the stained-glass windows wrap around from the front to the sides.

Katie was right that a massive tent has gone up. The huge, white monstrosity is at the side and it looks like it's been dragged straight out of summer fete storage. I have no idea who they roped in to make all this happen so quickly.

The three of us continue along the main path to the church and I doubt I'm alone in hoping not to be shunted off towards the consolation area of the marquee. When we get to the soaring heights of the large wooden door at the front, I'm braced for the man in a suit to usher us around to the side but he instead waves us inside.

As soon as we cross the threshold, I spot Nadia off to the side. She's using her hand to try to pat down Craig's hair. Being the twelve-year-old that he is, Craig is fighting against this with every fibre of his being. It probably doesn't help that he's wearing a suit which is a good size or three too big. Nadia spots me and attempts a wave, though all she succeeds in doing is to release her wriggling son, who then darts along the aisle down towards the front of the church. Nadia attempts to follow but is hamstrung by her heels.

The inside of the church is, if anything, more impressive than the outside. Enormous gothic beams soar high before curving into giant arches. An organist is at the front, playing subtle classical music that echoes around the stone walls. There are two lines of wooden benches, with a carpeted aisle along the centre that leads to an altar and pulpit at the front. As well as the central door at the back of the church, there's another off the side. I've never seen it open – but it is now. There is a man in a suit standing in the entranceway, with the darkened shade of the marquee behind him.

I've never been religious – but there has always been something special about this place.

When I turn, I realise Katie and Richard have stopped to watch the scene unfold with Nadia and Craig.

'I'm so glad you weren't like that as a child,' I say.

Katie doesn't acknowledge the point, instead nodding past me towards the flower arrangement that's been laid across the back of the church. Bryan and Dawn are standing together, looking every inch like the type of couple who'd appear in an advert for overpriced cars. I can picture the pair of them in chunky-knit sweaters with a fluffy dog and Aryan kids, all rushing out of a house to jump into a too-clean people carrier.

Bryan gives me the silent nod of acknowledgement that we've nailed since the separation. It's impossible to ignore one another in a community like this, so whenever we spy each other across the

M&S Food Hall, or at the petrol station, we'll do this mutual nod. *Yes,* we were once married; *Yes,* we do have a daughter together; *Yes,* we did live together for a long time; *Yes,* I acknowledge your existence.

I blank him.

'I'll be back in a minute,' Katie says. She reaches for Richard's hand and then guides him around a group of people who are standing in a circle chatting, as if this is a coffee morning.

They're too far away for me to hear what's being said but there's something about the way Katie's standing rigidly away from her father that cheers me. At least he's getting a hard time about leaving it to me to pass on news of his wedding.

I'm watching them when there's a tap on my shoulder and I turn to see Gary standing tall in a suit. Leah is at his side, in a black dress that makes her look older than she is.

Gary acknowledges me in the way people do when they're at a funeral: a gentle nod combined with a closed-lip smile. There is no indication that there's anything behind it, or that he knows what I did.

'Good to see you,' he says.

'You too.'

'Leah says you had a great session today…?'

I look to Leah but she's embarrassed and eyeing the floor.

'I thought it went well.'

'That's so good to hear.' He smiles a little too much, like a used-car salesman trying to foist a chopped-together death trap on an unassuming old lady.

He looks between Leah and me as if expecting us to have some sort of in-depth chat about the work. It only takes a second or two for Gary to take the hint. He claps his hands together and then rubs the palms into one another.

'Probably not the time,' he says.

After that, he guides Leah back towards the front of the church. I continue watching as he twice breaks to look over his shoulder in my direction. It might be nothing… or it might be everything.

I lose sight of the row he enters because a man stops directly in front of me. I vaguely recognise him as being on the council, or maybe one of the school governors. That sort of thing. Someone whose name I should probably know.

'Collection for Sharon and Frank,' he says.

He's carrying a black bucket. If this was for charity, it would be rattling around like a pair of false teeth on a rollercoaster. This being Prowley, when I look down, it is full of notes. I dig through my purse and drop in three ten-pound notes, which gets a blink of surprise from the councillor/governor.

'Bless you,' he says.

If he only knew that I was the cause of this, he'd know this is the absolute least I should be doing.

There are thousands of pounds in the bucket and when I look up, I can see two more people collecting on either side of the church. I don't begrudge Sharon a single penny of the money – but it's also hard to overlook the hypocrites who have been emptying their wallets. Nobody cared when they were gossiping about the woman with two kids from two different fathers, with neither of whom now in the picture. It was all a big joke then. Sharon was a person to be ridiculed.

I know I'm not one to talk. I'm not pretending to be a good person – but the duplicitous pretence is sickening. We're all hypocrites, it's just that I'm the biggest of all.

There's no sign of Dawn and Bryan over by the flowers any longer; nor Katie and Richard. When I turn back towards the pews, I realise Katie and Richard have joined a group of people their own age. I recognise a few of her football team and there are a few boys I don't know. Either way, they've managed to grab themselves a pair of benches on the right side of the church, not too far from the entrance to the marquee. There's little surprise that Katie would want to sit with her friends and I realise this is why she wanted to come – but there's still that little stab of disappointment that I'm by myself.

I try to look for Nadia but it's already too late because anyone who was still standing is now heading for the benches. I allow myself to be swept along with the crowd and find myself about three-quarters of the way back, crammed in between a woman who used to work in the library and a man who presumably hasn't heard of deodorant. As well as the bulging rows, there is a crowd that's at least five deep standing at the back of the church – plus everyone in the marquee. Unless there's an unseen camera system, they must only be listening in there.

The service itself is awkward. The priest begins with a prayer for Sharon and Frank's well-being – and then he beckons Josh forward to do a reading.

Josh is in a suit that's too small for him, with white socks visible at the bottom of his trouser legs. He stoops awkwardly to fit underneath a low hanging beam and then takes his place in the pulpit. Even with everything, it's hard not to feel sorry for him. He stares at a sheet of paper and speaks so quickly that all the sentences run into one another. It's almost impossible to take in what he's saying – and it's not helped by the fact that he doesn't look up once.

Our row is so tightly packed that it's hard to look anywhere other than directly ahead – but I do manage to wriggle myself to the edge of the seat, where I glance across to Katie. She's whispering something to Richard, who is staring stonily towards the front of the church. When I look more closely, I realise there's an unquestionable split between the older people who are listening and the younger ones who are almost all muttering quietly among themselves.

Back at the front, Josh is still rattling through his Bible reading. He consistently trips over the words and then tries to correct himself. When he finishes he scrunches up the page and then walks back to his spot, still without looking up.

I suddenly realise that he has to be staying with someone – or someone must be at his house. He's only sixteen and, with his mother in hospital, there has to be an adult around.

When Josh is back in his seat, the priest returns and asks us all to stand. I mouth the words to 'Amazing Grace' – and then it's time to sit and listen to the sermon. It's during this that the low rustling begins. People only want to be here to show their faces among a community where *everyone* is out showing their faces. It's not as if anything close to this many people ever turn up on a Sunday – and listening to an old man read from the Bible isn't many people's ideas of how to spend a Friday night. I'm the same, drifting in and out of what's being said until it feels as if the priest is talking only to me.

'…if we confess our sins, he is faithful and just to forgive our sins – and to cleanse us from all unrighteousness…'

I missed the first part of what was being said but the second leaves me paralysed. I can feel the heat of my face as I turn red and the voice at the back of my head is saying that everybody knows. The priest said this specifically to target me.

I should confess. I knew that then and I know it now.

It's only when people start to stand that I realise the priest has stopped speaking and that it's time for another hymn. I have to force myself up as my body rebels. As I stand, I notice that Gary is sitting two rows ahead and has turned to look at me. I check behind in case there's someone there but there's no one recognisable and, when I turn back, he is again facing the front.

After the hymn, there is another reading from someone who is on the council. There is one final hymn, a prayer – and then the priest wishes us all a safe journey home.

Everyone starts the slow shuffle to get into the aisle – and then people start filing towards the back of the church. The violence of the cold air is quite a shock as I get outside. Some people are heading off to the side streets and their cars, while other groups have made a beeline towards the pub. I move towards the church sign and wait underneath that, keeping an eye for Katie and Frank.

I watch as Josh emerges from the church with a grey-haired woman clinging to his arm. She's got to be in her seventies and I assume she's his grandmother. He continues along the path, past anyone in his way, and heads for a battered Vauxhall that's parked next to the gates.

It's hard to describe the feeling of being watched, even though everybody understands it. It's almost like a buzzing that allows a person to turn towards whoever it is that's doing the spying.

In my case, it's Gary. He's standing next to a gatepost close to the graveyard entrance. There's no sign of Leah but when I spot him watching, he glances down to the phone that's illuminating his face with a blueish glow.

A moment later, I feel my bag vibrating. I reach in and grab my phone, where there's a new message waiting.

Anon: *I can't believe you came*

When I look up, Gary is no longer staring at his phone and is talking to a woman I don't recognise. Over by the gates, Josh is in the passenger seat of the car, although, because of the angle, it's impossible to see any more than that.

I put the phone back in my bag. It's the first message I've had since breaking the window – and there's no acknowledgement of that. I'm not going to respond unless I absolutely have to.

It's only another few seconds and then Katie emerges from the church alongside one of her friends that I recognise from her football team. Richard trails a little behind, as do a few of the other boys.

Katie spots me quickly enough and starts to walk across.

'We're going to stay out for a while, if that's okay,' she says.

I think of the photo I was sent of her on the doorstep in her pyjamas.

'Would it be better if you stayed in tonight?' I reply.

'Why?'

There's no answer to this. None I can give, anyway.

As well as I know her, Katie knows me well enough, too. She takes my lack of reply as consent and starts to turn away.

'We won't be too late,' she says.

She takes a step but then turns back and leans in to kiss me on the cheek. 'Thank you for driving us in,' she says.

'You're welcome. Will you make sure you're with someone all the time – and that you can get a lift home…?'

'You don't need to worry, Mum. This is Prowley. I'll see you later.'

With that, she says something to her friend that I don't catch – and then the group heads off towards the green.

THIRTY-FOUR

Gary isn't home yet.

I know this because I'm sitting in my living room with the lights off while watching the road for any sign of him and Leah. I wish I could ask him outright if what Leah said is true. Was he sitting in the service the entire time, believing he knows who hit Sharon? Believing it was me…?

I've still not replied to the last text from my anonymous messenger. It's almost as if it's my own conscience that's been getting in contact. I can't believe I went to the service either, but what other choice did I have? There is only two: own up to what I did, or continue as if life hasn't changed.

My stomach is grumbling once more and my head is thumping. I can't remember the last proper meal I had. There has been the odd sandwich here and there, some toast, some breakfast cereal… but that's about it. I go through stages of the day when the adrenaline gets me through but this is the crash. I'm so tired but I know that the moment my head hits the pillow, I will stay there, staring at the ceiling as the guilt runs amok.

This must be why people hand themselves into the police. When people say 'how can you sleep at night?', they don't realise how close to the truth they are. The simple answer is that I *don't* sleep at night. Is this what it's like for everyone who has committed a crime and possibly got away with it? There's little consolation that I seemingly have a conscience. If I didn't, then I wouldn't care.

I wait at the window for another five minutes or so, all the time wondering what I'm doing. If Gary does pull onto his drive, so what? If he glances towards my house, then so what? Even if I knew with one hundred per cent certainty that he was the person messaging me, then what could I do about it?

After drawing the curtains once more, I head through to the kitchen and open the cupboard next to the fridge. There's an array of out-of-date cough mixtures, cold packs, hot packs, and all sorts of other things. The older a person gets, the more pills they need to take in order to pretend they're a functioning human being.

I pick up the box of paracetamol but instantly have a flashback as I squish the sides and realise it's empty. There's a second box but that's empty too. It wouldn't be as annoying if I hadn't specifically bought more the other day.

I head up the stairs into the bathroom and check the cabinet. Most of the medicines are kept downstairs but the odd one is left in here when neither Katie nor myself can be bothered to go back downstairs. Not that it makes much difference because the only contents are an almost empty tube of Deep Heat and some hair-removal cream.

My bedside cabinet contains a blister packet with only a single pill – which almost certainly means that Katie has again been pilfering the painkillers. I should have said something to her long ago. This can't be healthy.

I'll mention something in the morning – perhaps even ban her from having painkillers in her room. There will be an argument but it's one of those issues that's probably worth it.

I wait at Katie's door. Those memories of my mother going through my room are so close that I can almost smell the stale dust from the vacuum bag when she used to clean up after me. It's been a long time since I've entered Katie's room without permission. I genuinely believe that young people should be allowed to have their own space that isn't invaded by adults. That is unless they abuse the privilege… Besides, I have a headache and she hoards the paracetamol.

The door scuffs on the carpet as I push it open and turn on the light. I'm not sure what happened during the process of Katie getting ready to go out this evening but, since I last saw this room, it's turned into a TK Maxx at closing time. There are clothes all across the floor, with even more on the bed. There are textbooks scattered in the corner and shoes spilling out from under the bed.

I'm not a clean freak but I've never been one to leave masses of things lying around. That's largely because, when I was young, Mum would refuse to give me pocket money for a week if I had left too much clutter around the house.

More recently, Bryan was more insistent about cleanliness than I was. He came from a home that was run by a full-on 'cleanliness is next to godliness' dictator, in the shape of his mother. There would be twice-weekly inspections of his room to make sure everything was in its place and if it wasn't, he wouldn't be allowed out until it was. He told me about how he thought everyone's house was like that, until he started going to friends' birthday parties, when he realised not everyone was into tidiness.

With the pair of us as her parents, I'm not sure from where Katie's messiness comes.

I edge into the room and spot the candles on top of her dresser. The wax has dripped over the rim of the saucers and dribbled onto the wood. I don't mind that – but Katie and I have had conversations about lit candles being left unattended to the point that I banned them from the house at one point. Banning things only makes teenagers want to do them more, so that decision was quickly reversed.

There is no obvious sign of a blister pack of painkillers on top of any of the surfaces, so I try the top drawer of Katie's dresser. I don't want to snoop too much – but there is a pile of underwear on one side and two make-up bags on the other. Behind those, pushed to the back, is a small stack of opened, colourful envelopes. I almost reach for them, wondering what the letters inside might say, but then I stop myself. It's not what I'm here for – and it's not fair to Katie.

The next drawer down has a packet of cigarettes wedged into the side, half buried underneath a pair of pyjamas. They've been opened and there are only three left inside the packet of twenty. Smoking was certainly something that almost everyone tried when I was Katie's age – but I didn't know *she* smoked. Perhaps she doesn't? They could be Richard's, or another friend's… but even as I consider this thought, I know it's the kind of lie parents tell themselves.

This is the problem with snooping: I don't actually want to know what Katie gets up to in her free time.

There is an irony in that the cigarette packet – with the photo of a diseased lung emblazoned across the front – is sitting next to Katie's blue asthma inhaler. Underneath that is a packet of unopened cigarette papers, next to a small sandwich bag that contains slim strands of green that are packed tightly into the bottom. I hold the bag up to the light, although the faint aroma tells me what the contents are.

I wish I'd never started hunting around.

If my mother had found anything like this in my drawer, then she would have likely packed me straight off to a convent. Those were 'different times', of course. In my own seventeen years of being a parent, I've constantly compared myself to how my mother did things. It's impossible not to. Is this a big deal? It could definitely be worse – but, if that's the benchmark, then nothing means anything. There's always something that's worse.

I'm about to close the drawer when I hear a rattle. I pull the drawer out further until it's almost falling from the rails. The source of the rattle is an orange tub at the back. I retrieve it and then close the drawer, before moving under the light to examine the tub properly. There are six or seven small round pills inside, each of which are a browny-orange. The label on the tub has been largely scratched off, although I can just about make out the word 'PRESCRIPTION' across the top.

This is the first I know of Katie having a prescription for anything in recent times. I'm not even sure I can remember the last time she went to the doctor. She's old enough to book her own appointments without needing me – although I thought we had a decent enough relationship that if she had a problem, she would say something.

I rotate the tub once more and look more closely at the label. It has definitely been scratched away on purpose, with that gluey white residue left clinging to the plastic. It's the sort of gummy gunk that can only be fully removed via some sort of nuclear detonation.

It's then that I realise the bottom part of the label is still almost intact – and that this prescription isn't Katie's. The 'BA' of the last name is gone – but the 'YLISS' at the end makes it clear who the pills belong to.

Bayliss.

Why does Katie have a prescription that's been issued to Nadia?

THIRTY-FIVE

I jump awake a little after six in the morning. I reach across the bed but there's nothing there except for crumpled covers. No *one* there. This is the most I've slept since the collision on Tuesday. I didn't draw the curtains last night, though it doesn't make much difference because the sky is a gloomy blend of navy blue and black. It's not the hazy orange of the nearest street light that has woken me.

After creeping into the hall, I nudge open Katie's bedroom door without knocking. I didn't hear her get in – but she's now asleep on her bed, clutching a pillow tightly to her chest. She breathes steadily in and out and I find myself watching her, remembering when I used to do this after she'd been born. She wouldn't fall asleep unless she had something to clutch onto, so Bryan and I would leave a small finger puppet in her crib. We found it in a charity shop one time when we'd been ambling around town, looking for something else. It was pink, with a pig snout on the tip and Katie would hold it all night long. In a blink, I'm back in our old one-bedroom flat, with Katie's crib in the corner of our room. Everything felt so much easier then, even though we had a lot less money and space.

I close Katie's door as quietly as I can and then head back to my room. I'm drawn to the window, where I stare out towards Gary's drive. His car is parked there now, though I have no idea what time he got in. Not that it matters.

With him on my mind, I pick up my phone from the side table where it's been charging. There's a text message waiting for me.

Anon: Better hope she can't ID the car…

I read it through three times but have no idea who the 'she' might be. It's only when I visit the town's Facebook page that I spot the top post from late last night.

Alison Smart: All our prayers tonight have been answered! Sharon has woken up – and Frank is doing well, too. The doctors are very pleased with their progress. No word on if/when they can go home – but let's keep up the prayers. The service earlier was beautiful and God must have been listening. Peace and love.

Alison was the person who first named Sharon on the Facebook page – so she must have information coming from somewhere. She ran for the district council last year and sits on the board of at least two charities. She is probably the most connected person in the village – and unquestionably the one who sticks her nose into the most people's business. I suspect every town has an Alison.

The conflicting emotions leave me weak at the knees and I have to perch on the edge of the bed to steady myself.

Thank goodness Sharon is alive.

There is deep and genuine relief that she's awoken. Josh and Frank will both get to grow up with their mother in the frame.

There's relief for myself, too, of course. Even if the worst happens, it won't be manslaughter, or death by dangerous driving. All my worst fears – not just prison but *life* in prison – now shouldn't happen.

That wave of happiness, however, is offset by the message I received overnight. What if Sharon *does* remember my car? What if she saw me in the driver's seat in the moment before I hit her?

I consider waking Katie under the guise of telling her the good news about Sharon. That wouldn't be the real reason, of course.

There's the matter of the prescription pills she's been hiding away. If it was a weekday, I might have done – but it's rare that I see my daughter before midday on a weekend. It's one of the skills of youth. When I was Katie's age, I could easily sleep for fourteen or fifteen hours a day if I needed to, then survive from three or four when I had things on. As an adult, I'm lucky if I can sleep for seven without being awoken by anything from a car passing three streets over, to the desperate call of a bladder.

Instead of waking Katie, I head downstairs and set the coffee machine running. While it's bubbling and popping, I send Nadia a message.

Me: Let me know when you're up. Can I come over?

I drink two mugs of coffee while scrolling through the comments underneath last night's Facebook post about Sharon. The top few are all similar in tone to the first – relief that she's now awake – but it isn't long before it degenerates into people calling out the police for not finding the driver yet.

After that, it's a slippery slope. Someone names their neighbour as having a silver car and adds that the driver was 'definitely out' when Sharon was hit. That brings out even more responses of people wondering why the police aren't doing anything.

I'm about to pour a third cup of coffee when Nadia's reply comes through.

Nadia: Just up! Will put the kettle on. CU soon

I send Katie a short message to say I'm going to Nadia's and then head out to the car.

The drive to Nadia's takes me past the church, where there is already a group of men helping to take down the marquee. By the time most people are up and about, it will be as if it was never there.

When I get onto Nadia's street, I hear Craig before I see him. He's on the drive at the front, ramming his football into the garage door, which creates a booming clang. Each time it rebounds, he dribbles the ball in a circle and then crashes it back into the door again.

The neighbours must be delighted.

I park in front of her house and then get out of the car. Craig is in the same full kit as when I last saw him. The ball has been abandoned in a nearby flower bed as he approaches me.

'Do you want your car washing now?' he asks.

I'd forgotten about my promise to let him do this. At the time I refused, it was because I thought having him clean it could end up making him some sort of unwitting accessory to my crime. It's been to the garage for its MOT since then, so that's already an interference.

'That would be great,' I tell him. 'How much?

'Twenty quid…?'

The sheepish grin is that of someone who knows he's trying it on.

'It's less than that if I go through the machine at Tesco.'

'Nineteen…?'

I open my purse and pull out a five-pound note. 'You can have that now and another when you're finished.' I'm still paying over the odds.

He scrunches his lips together, making it clear he's not entirely satisfied about this. He still holds out a hand for the money, though.

'Deal.'

I hand him the cash and then he leads me into the house. I follow him into the kitchen, where he grabs a bucket from under the sink and then squirts a good quarter-bottle of washing-up liquid into the bottom.

As he returns outside, I move through to the conservatory. Nadia is still in her dressing gown and slouched in her chair, with a mug and filled cafetière at her side. Steam pours from the top, filling the air with the bitter smell of caffeine.

'Was that Craig?' she asks, angling towards the kitchen.

'He's going to wash my car.'

She nods at this but I can see she's already moved on. 'Did you hear about Sharon waking up?'

'I saw it this morning.'

'Wouldn't it be exciting if she knows who hit her…?'

Nadia sounds thrilled at this prospect, though, in fairness to her, I doubt she's the only one.

I opt for a somewhat obvious change of subject.

'How's Craig been?'

She sighs and rocks back into her chair, before pouring herself a coffee. Nadia holds up the cafetière but I wave it away.

'Hyper,' she replies. 'I'm still trying to get him another appointment at the educational psychologist. He was a nightmare at the church last night. He wouldn't sit still. I'm surprised you didn't hear him. I kept having to tell him to stop talking.'

'When's his dad due back from South Africa?'

'Wednesday, I think. He didn't seem clear when I spoke to him yesterday. He said next weekend at the latest.'

'Does Craig have many friends to keep him occupied?'

This gets a partially dismissive shrug. 'He *did*… I think they fell out.'

'Why?'

'Probably because he's so…' She whirls a hand, searching for the word, before settling on: '*intense.*'

I'm not sure what to make of it. I can't imagine ever describing Katie in the same terms but then she didn't provide the same difficulties that Craig does. Whenever Nadia talks about her son, there seems to be a distance between them that Katie and I never had. He's a daddy's boy… except that his father is often away.

It feels like the conversation has run its course. Tony will be back in a week – and then Craig will settle down until he's gone again. This has been the pattern for years and I'm certain it will continue to be for years more.

I open my bag and take out the tub of pills I found in Katie's drawer, then place it on the table next to Nadia's mug.

Nadia picks it up, rolls it around in her hand and then pouts a bottom lip. 'Where'd you get this?'

I ignore the question for now. 'What are the pills?' I ask.

She flips the bottle around and scans the shredded label. 'No idea. I don't have any prescriptions at the moment. Why's it got my name on?'

'I was hoping you could answer that.'

Nadia looks up to me, though her bemusement seems genuine. 'Where did you find it?'

'At my house,' I say, answering the question this time.

She looks from the tub to me and back again, then scratches a finger across the label. 'Why was it at yours?'

'I have no idea.'

Nadia frowns and then sits up abruptly. She mutters 'hang on' and then disappears out to the hallway. There's the sound of footsteps on stairs, first going up; then down. A moment later and she's back with two tubs. She passes both across to me: one with the label scratched away, the other with it intact.

It's not Nadia's name on the label. It's Craig's.

'It's Adderall for his ADHD,' Nadia says. 'It was prescribed after he'd been to the psychologist. It's supposed to calm him down.'

The tub I found in Katie's drawer has around a half a dozen tablets in the bottom – but the one with Craig's name has twice that.

Nadia stares at me and I look back to her. She holds out her hand and I pass her back the two tubs.

'I'll get Craig,' she says.

She heaves herself up and I follow her through the house out to the front.

Craig has been using the hose attached to a tap at the side of the house, as well as the sudsy bucket. If nothing else, he's given himself a good clean. His football kit is drenched and there are blobs of foam on both his shoulders and his head. The area surrounding my car is like a pond and there is a stream of water running down a slope towards the drain.

Craig switches off the hose and then looks between me and the car, which is unquestionably cleaner.

'I'm almost done,' he says.

Nadia holds up the two tubs of pills and the reaction is instant. Craig looks down to the floor, avoiding eye contact with both of us. His mum moves closer, showing him the nearly empty tub with the scratched-off label.

'What's going on with this?' she asks.

'What?'

'Why were these at Aunty Jen's place?'

He shuffles on the spot. 'Dunno…'

'You must have some idea. They don't just appear from nowhere.'

'I dunno…'

Nadia turns between me and her son. 'You can go to your room,' she says.

'But—'

'No buts. You can come out when you've got something better to say.'

Craig bobs on the spot and then looks pleadingly towards me.

I open my bag and find him the second five-pound note he's due, then hand it over. He mutters a 'thanks' and then drips a trail along the path into the house.

'Sorry about that,' Nadia says. 'I don't know what I'm going to do with him.'

I shake my head. 'Don't be sorry. I've got a feeling there's someone else to blame.'

THIRTY-SIX

When I get home, Katie is sitting at the kitchen table with a glass of water and a crumb-filled plate in front of her. She's thumbing something into her phone and greets me with a brief glance over the top.

'How's Nadia?' she asks.

'She's good… Craig not so much.'

That gets a briefly raised eyebrow, although it doesn't take Katie's attention away from the phone screen. She's still in her pyjamas with fluffy, oversized tiger slippers. The pimple close to her temple is larger and redder than when I first noticed it. She scratches at it, before catching herself and stopping.

When Craig was born, Katie was only five herself. She was obsessed with him to the point that she went through a stage of pretending he was her younger brother. Their bond was so strong that Bryan and I even talked about trying to give her a brother or sister but we decided that neither of us wanted more than one child. Craig and her probably saw each other most days up until Katie reached the age of about ten or eleven. A five- and a ten-year-old might well be able to play together – but it becomes a big difference in maturities when those ages turn into eight and thirteen.

'What time did you get in last night?' I ask.

Katie bites away a yawn and then puts her phone down on the table to stretch high. 'About half one, I think. Leona gave me a lift home.'

'Did you have fun?'

The answer is a shrugged 'it was okay' that could mean anything from she had the greatest night of her life – or that she's never going to leave the house again.

I reach into my bag and take out the empty tub with the scratched-off label. The pills that were inside are now back at Nadia's, added to the ones in Craig's other tub. I place it on the table next to the plate, where Katie stares at it.

'Where did you get that?'

Sharon's words run through me: *It's not like Katie's perfect.* Did she know?

'There's a funny thing with Craig,' I say. 'He's been prescribed Adderall to help calm him. It doesn't seem to be having much effect, though. He's still running around all the time. He's been having problems at school because of it.'

Katie says nothing but the room feels colder, as if the back door is open.

'He bought himself some new trainers last week. His dad's away – so the money didn't come from him. He's been cleaning a few cars – but not enough to buy expensive trainers. Nadia can't figure out how he paid for them…'

There's no movement from Katie, who is still staring at the tub.

'I looked up the Adderall side effects,' I continue. 'They include nervousness, trouble sleeping, a loss of appetite, weight loss and headaches. I also read an article from America about how there's a black market because it's supposed to help a person concentrate—'

'They *do* help me concentrate.'

Her response shuts me up, if nothing else. I was fairly certain I knew what had gone on – but now I know for sure.

When I don't reply, Katie takes the opportunity to continue. She's quieter this time: 'I wouldn't get my coursework done without it, let alone be able to take exams.'

'How much do you pay him?'

Katie turns away, facing the window and crossing her arms.

She doesn't reply, so I try again: 'How much?'

'Does it matter?'

'Of course it does.'

'A pound a pill.'

Katie hasn't moved and I slump back in my chair, rubbing my temples, wanting this all to go away.

'How many have you bought from him?'

'A few.'

'How many is that?'

She shakes her head. 'I don't know. Thirty?'

'His trainers cost more than thirty pounds.'

I wait until it's clear I'm not going to get a better answer.

'This is why you've not been eating and sleeping,' I say. 'It's probably why you were sick the other night. It's got to stop.'

She turns and stares at me defiantly, her teeth clenched together. 'If it stops, then how am I supposed to get through my exams?'

'We'll get you an appointment at the doctor. You can tell him everything about your coursework and exams – and we'll see what he says. He can prescribe you whatever he thinks works.'

'*These* work.'

She snatches the tub from the table and clamps her fingers around it, holding on as if she's clinging to the edge of a cliff.

'Where are the pills?' she asks.

'Back where they belong with Craig.'

Katie slams the tub into the table, which sends her glass spinning onto the floor. There's a crash and I look under the table to see three or four large shards of glass, with a pool of water dribbling towards the back door.

Katie says nothing at first – but then grabs the tea towel from the counter and uses it to pick up the larger pieces of glass. She drops each of them into the bin and then grabs the dustpan and brush to sweep away the smaller pieces. After everything is in the bin, she uses a cloth to mop away the water, before hanging the cloth over the sink divider. When that's all done, she settles back in her chair. It's the best and worst of her, all within a three-minute spell.

'You've turned a twelve-year-old boy into a drug dealer,' I say.

'He's not a drug dealer. He…' Katie's sentence drifts away to nothing as I hope her actions start to sink in.

Neither of us speak for a minute or so. This is not the type of conversation I ever thought I'd have to have with my daughter.

'This is serious,' I say, quieter this time. I want her to understand. 'I'm going to have to tell Nadia everything that's been going on. She thinks Craig's struggling *despite* the medicine – but it's because he hasn't been taking it. He's been selling it to you.'

Katie stares longingly at the empty tub, like it's a pool of water in a barren desert.

'We'll go to the doctor,' I say again.

'I've been.'

I watch her, expecting some sort of follow-up. This is the first I've heard of her going to the doctor by herself.

'When?'

'About a year ago. Before my AS-levels. When Richard was struggling. When I couldn't get in the football team.'

'What did he say?'

'*She* said that it was normal for someone to be nervous before exams. That I should drink lots of water and have a regular bedtime.'

There's quiet fury in Katie's tone – and a part of me understands it all too well. That's the sort of advice given to a child. Even if it's correct, I can see why she feels that she wasn't listened to.

'We'll go to the doctor together,' I say. 'Your regular one this time. Doctor Shivrabata. I'll call on Monday morning and get it booked.'

'I'm not going.'

'But—'

'I'm *not* going.' She glares at me with such ferocity that I shrink away. 'You keep saying that you don't want me to end up like Richard – then you're doing everything you can to make sure I get stuck here with you.'

Her words sting, as they're meant to.

'That's not true,' I reply.

'So you *do* want me to leave?'

'Don't be like that. I want you to go to university and I obviously want you to be happy with whatever you choose to do. That doesn't mean I won't miss you when you go.'

'You sabotaged Richard and now you're trying to sabotage me.'

I almost take the bait but take a breath and manage to hold onto anything angry.

'Do you really believe that?'

Katie turns towards the window again and her lack of reply is a better answer than it could have been.

'Are there any more?' I ask.

'Any more what?'

'Pills. You know what I'm asking you.'

'No.'

She sounds so firm and assured – but that makes it worse.

'Nadia says there's at least another tub missing…'

Katie doesn't move for a moment – but when she does it's as if she's on fast forward. She shoots up from her seat, strides past me and then bounds up the stairs.

I follow but she's moving too quickly. By the time I get to her door, she's already hunched and burrowing underneath her mattress. She ends up flipping it backwards off the bed, sending everything tumbling onto the floor and exposing the slats and the frame. She grabs another tub from the exposed space and then fires across the room and slams the identical tub into my hand. The pills left inside rattle around like a salt shaker.

'Have you got any more?' I ask.

Katie turns over her shoulder to take in the tornado trail she's created. 'No.'

I almost ask her a second time – but the thunderous look in her eyes is more than an answer.

She reaches for the door and I step back as she attempts to slam it in my face. It's hard to do because of the carpet underneath and she ends up pushing it closed. The message is clear, even if the method is not the best.

She immediately opens the door again, rages a 'stay out of my room', and then closes it a second time.

I wait for a moment, anticipating another encore, but the only sounds from Katie's room are of her rearranging the furniture.

Back downstairs, I empty the pills onto the kitchen table and count the nine discs back into the tub. My daughter has turned my best friend's twelve-year-old son into a drug dealer. If there's ever anything to be angry about, then it's this. I should be raging but, instead, there's only exhaustion. I can hardly claim the moral high ground over Katie given that I drove a car into two people, fled the scene and have said nothing about it for four days. If anyone asks where Katie gets it from, then the answer is clear.

It's from me.

THIRTY-SEVEN

Perhaps the only good thing to come from the morning's events is that my own misdeeds have more or less fallen from my mind. I force myself to eat, then spend three-quarters of an hour trying to figure out the best way to tell Nadia about what's happened. I draft a couple of texts but know I'm never going to send them. It's more for thinking about the type of apology I can make. I'm going to have to tell Nadia in person.

It's the sound of the doorbell that makes me put down my phone. When I get to the door, Bryan is outside, leaning against the door frame. He lived here for long enough but since we split, he has never turned up without messaging me beforehand. It's the unspoken agreement we made.

'Hello…?' I say.

'Where's Katie?'

'Huh…?'

'She called me and…'

There's a sound of footsteps on the stairs behind me and then Katie appears with a duffel bag in her hand. She stands on the bottom step, watching and waiting for me to move out of the way of the door.

'What's happening?' I ask.

'Are you going to let me through?' Katie replies.

'Where are you going?'

'To stay with Dad for a bit.'

I stumble to say something, before stepping away from the door.

Katie stops on the precipice: her father on one side, me on the other. 'You don't respect my privacy, so I don't want to be here anymore.'

'You don't have to do this,' I reply.

She turns and doesn't look at me as she replies with a disdainful 'Leave me alone, Mum.'

Bryan shifts to the side and Katie passes him, moving along the path until she gets to his car. She opens the back door, tosses her bag inside and then gets into the passenger seat. She doesn't look back once.

'I didn't ask for this,' Bryan says. 'She called me and asked if I'd pick her up.'

I stare past him towards the car, barely able to believe the speed of this escalation. I knew she was upset with me but I didn't expect this. When Bryan and I separated, there was never any question that Katie wanted to stay with me. Since then, there hasn't been a single occasion where she's mentioned not wanting to be here.

'How long is she going to stay with you?' I ask.

Bryan turns towards the car and then back to me. 'I have no idea. She didn't actually ask to stay. I thought she wanted to see me.'

'You could tell her she has to stay here.'

Bryan presses his lips together, keeping it polite. 'Do you think that's a good idea?'

I don't reply because I know it's the opposite of a good idea.

'She's doing drugs, Bryan…'

He does a double take, his eyes narrowing. 'What? Are you joking?'

'ADHD pills. She's been buying them off Craig.'

'Oh…' He sighs with something close to relief. 'Nadia's boy?' A pause and then: 'What are ADHD pills?'

'They calm a person down and help them concentrate. It's supposed to help with Craig's hyperactivity – but Katie's been buying them to help her focus on her coursework.'

Bryan looks at me sideways and it's like I can read his thoughts.

'Don't look at me like that,' I say.

'Like what?'

'I'm *not* putting too much pressure on her.'

'I didn't say you were.'

'You were thinking it, though.'

He says nothing to that and it's like the old days of guessing and second-guessing one another. Having arguments about thoughts instead of actual words or actions.

'I think you're making too big a deal of this,' he says.

I glare lightning bolts at him. 'You don't think it's a big deal that our teenage daughter is buying drugs off a twelve-year-old?'

'It's not like they're *real* drugs.'

'What do you mean?'

'It's not heroin, or coke, is it? She's not some sort of addict.'

He has that air of cocky assuredness about him, as if this is the only opinion that can be correct.

'Adderall *is* addictive,' I say. 'That's why it's on prescription. It's an amphetamine.'

Bryan crinkles up his face as if to say he doubts this clear fact. If he's never heard of something, then it can't possibly be as big an issue as I'm making of it. It's this type of thing that, at times, made parenting one of the worst experiences of my life. I would want to be the disciplinarian, trying to see the bigger picture. Bryan would shrug and say things were fine.

He half turns, conversation over.

'Are you going to tell me?' I ask.

He twists back: 'Tell you what?'

'Dawn's selling the café and you want your money from the house. What's actually happening with you two?'

'I told you: we're getting married.'

'What *else* is happening with you two?'

He takes a step towards the car and I can see that he's thinking about walking away. If he wants this conversation at all, then he doesn't want it now.

'Honeymoon,' he says.

'Where are you going? The moon?'

'We've booked a round-the-world trip. It's a mix of flying and cruising. We'll be gone for about a year, maybe longer.'

I've lost count of the times I've been speechless in recent days but, of everything, perhaps it is this that hits me hardest.

'But you *hate* travelling,' I say. 'I begged you for years because I wanted to visit the US. You said it was too far, that the time zone was too difficult. You kept saying you didn't want to waste money on foreign trips.'

Bryan shrugs, without a proper answer. 'I guess I changed my mind.'

It's hard to not explode at the sense of betrayal. Harder still to push away the feelings of pure anger. It's not as if I wanted to take extravagant holidays every year – it would have been the odd big holiday every few years. Something unforgettable that we could have enjoyed with Katie. It would have been saved for and budgeted because I'm not the sort of person that leaves a trail of debt in my wake. Instead, we made do with weeks at the seaside, weekend trips to London, and a one-time long weekend at Center Parcs. It was never anything to do with keeping up appearances, it was about quality of life.

I accepted his point of view for all those years and then, now we're apart and he is remarrying, he has changed his mind.

And he thinks *I* was the boring one.

The audacity of it all. The cheek. The disrespect.

I can barely get the words out. 'Have you told Katie you're going?'

I know the answer before asking the question.

'Don't you think you should?' I say. 'You left it for me to tell her you were getting married. You're going to have to act like a father sooner or later.'

He glances towards the car and then slips into the half grin he wears a fraction of a second before he says something cruel. When you live with someone for a long time, their tics and tells become so familiar that you know what they're going to do before they do it.

'I'm not sure you're in any position to be giving parenting lessons…'

Perhaps I deserve it – but his words still leave me gasping.

'Don't talk to me like that.'

His smile widens. 'I'm going home with *our* daughter. I'm sure she'll let you know if she wants to talk to you any time soon.'

'She can't leave.'

There's pity in Bryan's eyes. I open my mouth, wanting to tell him about the photo I was sent of Katie on the doorstep. It could be nothing but it could be everything. I'm so close but the words don't come. It would mean admitting to everything else. Bryan doesn't see it like that. He sees a broken woman not wanting to let her daughter go.

'It's her choice,' he says.

'I know… just… will you look after her?'

'Of course. Who do you think I am?' He seems more confused than angry at this. Hard to blame him.

He moves away from the house, throws a 'See y'around' back towards me – and then heads for the car.

THIRTY-EIGHT

Things should be looking up.

The blackmailer has stopped texting me for now. Perhaps that's because it seems like Sharon and Frank will both be okay.

But then there's Katie. We have had arguments before – though nothing to the degree that she has walked out. At some point, I know she will talk to me again. I would guess some of her anger is aimed at herself. She must know that what she did is wrong. There's obviously plenty aimed at me, because I've taken away the thing that she was using to get through her work.

Time will heal this... but it feels as if something has broken that can't be fixed. One of the hardest things in life is that there's no undo button. No reset. It's not like a video game, where a player can go back to the start of a level and try again.

I try to bury myself in my work. What else is there?

There are tutoring sessions to plan for the next week but when I try to go through the guidance pages and my own notes, everything might as well be written in another language because none of it goes in.

I take out my phone and check my last messages back and forth with Katie. There is me telling her I've gone to Nadia's, then the chat about whether I'd take her to church last night. Before that, she's asking for lifts, or I'm wondering what time she might be home. I think about messaging her to say I'm sorry and ask if she'll come home. If not that, then checking in to see whether she's okay. I don't know what any spare room might be like at Dawn's house, nor what her sleeping situation will be. A part of me hopes it's terrible so that she will want to return here faster.

Ninety minutes have passed since Bryan knocked on the door and I have achieved nothing. With books and papers scattered across the living room, I head into the kitchen and pour myself a glass of water. I want something stronger but it's early and I at least have enough self-awareness to know that it's not a good route to go.

When I turn, a brown tub remains on the table. It's the one Katie handed over after pulling apart her room. The label has been scratched away and, even though I've already read the link a couple of times, I google 'Adderall side effects'. Of the main ones, I already have nervousness, trouble sleeping, a loss of appetite and a headache. That leaves only 'weight loss' as a supposed downside – and I could definitely do with a bit of that.

I'd already made the decision as soon as I picked up the tub. Katie had hoarded nine pills – although Nadia didn't specifically say she was missing a set amount. She only mentioned a tub – and we know Katie has taken some of the tablets anyway…

The website notes say that the positive benefits of the drug can take up to two hours to kick in – although it's often quicker. I don't rush things, instead pottering around the kitchen and cleaning a few things away until there's nothing left to do.

When I return to my work, the change is frightening. The words that made no sense have swirled into cohesive sentences. It's like a jigsaw coming together. I start to make notes and they quickly become firm plans for every student I'm seeing in the next week.

When I check the clock, I expect ten minutes to have passed – but it's been almost forty-five that I've been concentrating. When I next look, I've been working for almost two hours. I've been putting off work all week but, in my new heightened state, it takes a little over three hours to get everything into a workable form. Even before everything happened with Sharon and later Katie, I would usually set aside an entire day to achieve everything I've managed to do across a long lunch. It's barely believable.

I pack all my work back into the cupboard and then, with my new-found free afternoon, I feel confident enough to drive back to Nadia's place.

Her front door is locked for the first time I can remember and my first thought is that she's probably out and that I should have messaged her to ask if she was in. I ring the bell anyway and, a few moments later, Nadia opens the door. She's out of her dressing gown, though it isn't a great change considering she's now in a loose, plush tracksuit.

'I didn't know you were coming back,' she says, as she holds open the door.

I head inside and wait for her to close it behind me.

She makes a point of locking it and then nods upstairs. 'Craig's grounded – and I don't want him sneaking out while I'm in the back.'

'I don't think much of it is his fault,' I reply.

Nadia frowns and tries to read me, before leading the way back through the house into the conservatory. The romance novel from the other day is again splayed on the table next to her lounger – but it's been joined by a second paperback that's also open. The sound of Smooth FM or something equally inoffensive drifts from the back of the area, and there's a mini manicure kit on the armrest of the chair.

She presses into her seat and I take the one on the other side of the table.

'I'm still not sure what's happened…?' Nadia says. 'Craig won't say anything – which is why he's grounded. I caught him going outside with his ball anyway and when I stopped him and locked the door, he tried to kick it through. I had to tell him I'd call the police to get him to go upstairs.'

She glances up, even though there's silence from above.

'I wasn't *really* going to call the police…'

I knew that – but it must have been bad if she had to threaten such a thing.

'Katie's been buying his medication from him,' I say.

That gets a long, confused frown and then: '*Katie…?*'

'Adderall helps people focus. That's why it works for kids with ADHD, like Craig – but it works on anyone. Katie was using the pills to help her concentrate on her coursework and exams. I didn't know anything about it.'

Nadia stares and I can see her putting the pieces together.

'I should've kept a closer eye on him,' she says, 'Made sure he was taking them.'

'It's not your fault. Katie is well aware that she's the one to blame for this.'

Nadia is still open-mouthed: 'This is why he's been playing up…'

'I know. I'm sorry.'

'Did she have any other of his pills you didn't know about…?'

I hold eye contact with my best friend and then answer with a clear and concise: 'No.'

Nadia nods the acceptance. 'They were always so good together when they were young. When was the last time she babysat him?'

It's only at this that things start to make sense. Since Katie turned sixteen, Nadia has sometimes asked her to stay at their house to look after Craig when she and Tony were going out for an evening. For Katie, it was an easy twenty quid and an evening in front of the television, or on her phone. I'm not sure how much 'looking after' went on, considering she was largely there after Craig had already gone to bed.

'I think it was the end of the summer,' I reply.

'I guess so.'

It's easy to see how Katie might have noticed the medicine Craig was on. After reading the articles about the black market in Adderall, I wouldn't be surprised if some of Katie's classmates were also 'borrowing' tablets from siblings, or wherever else they could find them. I suspect she knew all about what they did before she ever set eyes on Craig's stash.

'I think he's sleeping,' Nadia says, nodding upwards again. 'He tired himself out with all the door-kicking and crying.'

I picture the eight tablets I still have at home.

'Will you be able to get more?' I ask.

'I don't know. Probably. I'll say he dropped an open tub in the toilet – and I'm sure they will give him another prescription. I'll watch him take each one from now on. I did it with the first few he took – but he's twelve years old. You can't watch their every move…' She pauses and then adds: 'He's still grounded. I guess that answers how he bought those shoes.'

'I'll make sure Katie comes and apologises to you personally.'

Nadia bats this away. 'We did worse when we were kids.'

'Did we?'

She pauses and stares off into nothing, mulling it over. 'I guess not. Either way, don't worry about it. No harm done. People do silly things when they're young.'

We sit quietly for a while, neither of us needing to say anything. Bryan could never understand why we were friends.

You have nothing in common, he'd say. *She's so… dim.*

What he never understood is that it's things like this which is why we're friends. With other people, this would have led to a huge falling-out. The argument could have raged back and forth over years, else we simply would have never spoken again. With Nadia, it's all dealt with by a massive shrug. Things could be worse. Life goes on. She's not perfect but neither am I. I'm lucky to have her in my life.

'Katie's left home,' I say.

I'm staring through the glass towards the shed at the back of the garden. A bird is on the roof, pecking away at the attached table, on which there sits an assortment of nuts and seeds.

'What do you mean?'

'She's gone to live with Bryan and Dawn for a while.'

'Because of this?'

'I had to go through her room to find the pills. She said I invaded her privacy, so she left.'

'That's a bit extreme…'

'I hated my mum going through my room.'

'You never walked out, though.'

'My parents never separated…'

Nadia leaves it for a moment – the perfect amount – and then she adds: 'I'm sure she'll be back.'

We sit quietly again as I watch a couple more birds join the first. Word has obviously gone out that there's free snacks over at the Bayliss house. The silence is bliss – and it's only broken by the buzz of my phone. I would ignore it if it wasn't for the fact that I'm hoping it's Katie and that she's changed her mind.

It's not Katie.

Anon: *I have one more job for you. I promise this is the last thing*

It's another 'last thing' – the third already. There will be another and another. I've got to think of a way to stop it. I wonder if ignoring the person really *is* an option. If they have anything that the police don't, then they haven't shared it with me. I've got away with this for four days now.

Then there's Katie – and that photo of her on the doorstep in her slippers. Is she safe with Bryan? How long can someone hold her safety over me – and, more to the point, do I believe the threat is anything other than empty? Am I willing to gamble with Katie's welfare?

Me: *What?*

Of all the replies I might have expected, the one I get is the last thing I could have predicted.

Anon: *Kill Josh Tanner*

THIRTY-NINE

Until now, there was still a part of me thinking that the person messaging me *was* Josh. In terms of location and opportunity to have seen me, he was top of the list. The text is confirmation that it's not him and, I suppose, it never could have been. I ignored the obvious stuff, such as the way he was talking to the police – and our argument in the car park. I went for the person who'd likely be the most angry at me. The obvious choice, not the real one.

And somebody wants him dead.

'Something wrong?'

I'd almost forgotten I was in Nadia's conservatory and it's only the sound of her voice that brings me back.

I blink up from my phone and tell her it's fine but that I have to go. We say goodbye and then I hurry out to my car. I sit in the driver's seat and send my reply.

Me: Is this a joke? I can't do that. Stop texting me.

The person doesn't stop.

Anon: You almost killed 2 ppl, incl a baby – and you didn't worry about that

I don't know how to reply to this. It's not true that I didn't worry about what I'd done – but it's certainly the case that I've avoided all responsibility for my actions. What I did to Sharon and Frank was an accident. What this person is asking me to do is something planned and deliberate. It's not the same.

Perhaps I should have done it when I received that first text – but I'm sure it's the right thing to do now.

I ignore the message and turn on the engine.

It's a short drive across town and my phone is silent the entire time. This message is different to the others. Every other request was within my means, which is why they felt so irresistible. This is completely beyond something I would ever do.

When I get home, I almost call up to see if Katie is home. Habit is a hard thing to switch off. The house is quiet and I find myself checking the back door and windows to make sure everything is secure.

I'm not going to do anything to Josh – but if I can find out who might want him harmed, then perhaps I can figure out who's been messaging me.

I start with Facebook – but the Josh Tanner who lives in Prowley is either not on it or he's hidden his profile. There's no sign of him anywhere online – or certainly nowhere that I know of. When I asked Katie about Josh, she said that everyone knows someone who's been bullied by him – and that even his teachers were scared of him. It feels like there might be a long list of people who hold a grudge.

I don't know what to do. My head says to do nothing… but what if something does end up happening to Josh? Is there a way I could tip him off that someone wants him dead? If I were to tell him in person, he'd likely laugh, so it would have to be something different to that. A note, or… an anonymous text.

Whoever wants him dead is also a person that knows my movements – and *that* can't be a long list. That person knew that I had coffee at Bread And Butter on Wednesday morning and that I took a bike to the scene of the accident. The only person

I saw in both places was Gary. He's also the person that left an online review of AD Investments because they cost him money. I can't think of anyone else who links those three things – plus it would have been easy enough for him to find the spare key that was hidden underneath Gnomey.

Not only that, Leah was reluctant to go to the church because Josh was going to be there. She said it wasn't to do with her – and that she didn't think her dad knew about whatever it is – but perhaps he does? Leah also said her father had an idea of who was driving and that this would all be over soon.

If it *is* Gary then I can hardly go to the police with the text messages. It would implicate me and there's nothing that proves it is one hundred per cent him.

Except I could ask.

Sometimes the craziest ideas are the best, aren't they? I could simply ask him if he's been texting me, without letting on about me being the driver. If he already knows, then there's not much I can do.

I cross the road and knock on Gary's front door, already planning what to say. I won't bother with niceties, I'll ask him outright if he's been texting me anonymously.

There's no answer – but there is a loud bump from inside, as if someone has closed a door. I wait and listen, then knock again. This time, there is silence.

The prickling, knowing sense of being watched is impossible to ignore. I turn and look across the road, although there's nobody in any of the windows of my neighbours' houses.

The only thing blocking the side of Gary's house from the street is a small gate that has no lock. I unlatch it and move around to the side door, which opens into the kitchen. I'm about to knock on the glass when I spot Leah pressed into the corner, peeping around the wall towards the front of the house. She doesn't see me at first and it's only when I tap on the glass that she jumps in shock. Her gaze swivels from the front door, which I guess gives an indication that she heard me the first time. When I was a home-alone teenager, I used to hide from whoever was at the door, too. One thing was always certain – it was never anybody for me.

I motion towards the back door and mouth 'can you open it?'.

Leah crosses the kitchen with a foot-scuffing reluctance but she does as she's asked.

'Is your dad in?' I ask.

'No, he's, um—'

She's interrupted by a booming crash from deeper inside the house. Leah jumps even higher this time and then turns and dashes inside. She doesn't close the door, so I follow her through the house.

I hear her before I catch up to her.

'What have you done?! Dad will go mad.'

By the time I reach the living room, a large photo frame is on the floor – and the glass that should have been in it has shattered across the carpet. Standing on the other side of the frame, like a rabbit in the headlights, is a boy. Thomas.

He boggles at the sight of me. The last time I saw him was outside the corner shop when I asked him why Josh had slapped him in the car park. It feels like a lifetime ago.

Thomas turns from me back to Leah.

'What did you do?' she says.

'Nothing! I was walking past and it fell over.'

'My dad's going to go mental.'

'It's not my fault.'

They look to one another, neither with any idea of what to do.

'Are there oven gloves in the kitchen?' I ask.

Leah has seemingly forgotten I'm here. 'In the drawer,' she says.

'Go and get them and we'll pick up the bigger bits of glass. The smaller ones are going to have to be vacuumed.'

'What about Dad?'

'It's going to have to be picked up whether he's here or not.'

She pauses for a moment and then disappears past me towards the kitchen. All the while, Thomas stares between me and the shattered glass, not knowing which of the two is more horrifying.

Leah is soon back with the gloves and a roll of black bin liners. She also gets some paper flyers from the recycling bin and, as I use the gloves to pick up the glass, she wraps them in paper and discards them into the black bag. When we've cleared as much as we can, she drags the vacuum out from the cupboard underneath the stairs – and then rolls it back and forth across the carpet as the small shreds of glass clink their way up the spout.

Thomas watches all of this silently. It's only when we're almost done that he levers the glass-free frame up from the carpet and leans it back on top of the counter from which, if he is to be believed, it levitated through the air with no interference.

The photo is of Leah and her dad. Gary is standing tall and proud in his police uniform, while she's in a black dress. It looks like they're at some sort of official function, possibly a dinner. When Leah returns from the kitchen, she must notice me eyeing the photo.

'He won an award last year,' she says.

'What for?'

'I don't know. Something with the police.' She turns to Thomas and then nods at me. 'This is Ms Hughes, my maths tutor.'

Thomas nods along, although he must still be confused as to why some random woman has walked into the house when he's got other plans about what he and Leah could be getting up to.

Leah must see something in his expression that I don't, because she suddenly sounds emboldened. 'You're the one that could do with a tutor,' she says. 'You're the one that got held back a year.'

'You're not complaining. You don't *have* to sit next to me.'

I look between them and see my fourteen-year-old-self from times that are oh so distant. Those years of pining for the plainest of boys, of agonising with my friends about the smallest things. I even miss the arguments and resentment sometimes. There's something about that youthful naivety that's wistfully appealing.

'I'll go,' I say, talking to Leah. 'I was only here to see if your dad was around.'

I take a step towards the kitchen but the angst in Leah's voice stops me. 'You won't tell Dad, will you?'

'About the picture frame? I think he'll notice.'

'No…'

Leah angles towards Thomas and doesn't need to say anything else. A lot of things suddenly make sense. He's a year older than her and has been kept back a year. Not exactly the type of person of whom a father would approve. Thomas is watching me, too, and I can almost feel the pleading.

'It's none of my business,' I say. It feels as if both Thomas and Leah breathe out together.

I take another step towards the kitchen and then stop and turn back to Thomas.

'What happened with you and Josh in the car park that day…?'

He glances to Leah and something passes invisibly between them. He shrinks away, as if he's trying to hide himself within the walls. Any lightness of mood has now gone.

It's Leah who answers. 'Josh picks on people with two parents.' She glances across to Thomas, who has crossed his arms. 'You know it's true… we worked it out.'

'No *we* didn't.'

Thomas sounds annoyed but Leah continues as if he hasn't interrupted: 'Someone in our year said that they were in his class at primary school. He wasn't very big then and the kids used to pick on him because he didn't have a dad. Now he picks on people who have both.'

Thomas huffs a loud breath: 'That's what *you* think. You don't know.'

'So why does he pick on you, then?'

Thomas has no answer for this and instead turns to the side, so that his back is towards me. I suspect he's embarrassed at being a victim, especially in front of his girlfriend and a strange woman that he doesn't know.

The awkwardness hangs for a few seconds until I break it. 'I'll catch up with your dad another time,' I say.

'Do you need me to tell him you came by?'

I deliberately let my gaze fall upon Thomas. 'Best not.'

It's not subtle – but it's enough for Leah to understand that I won't say anything if she doesn't say anything.

I let myself out the back door and trail around to the front. In the time I've been inside the sky has turned a dark grey. The temperature has dropped and night feels close.

I wonder if that moment of Josh's vulnerability outside my house – *how do you live with it?* – was him asking himself how the bullied became the bully.

That doesn't answer who might want him dead. Josh has been bullying Thomas – but Gary seemingly doesn't know his daughter is in a relationship with Thomas, so why would he care? All I can think is that there's something else going on that I don't know about.

I'm back in my hallway when my phone buzzes.

Anon: *I hope Katie is all right*

It's cold again. I scroll through my contacts list until I find Katie's name. I press to call her and can feel my heart beating as each ring goes unanswered. I try a second time, though the outcome is the same. After everything that happened today, she could simply be ignoring me. No need to panic yet.

I call Bryan instead and find myself gasping with relief as he answers.

'Are you calling already? I thought it would be at least a day.'

'Is Katie there?'

He sighs. 'Leave her be, Jennifer. She needs time and space before she wants to talk to you.'

I want to shout at him. This isn't about me and him.

'Where is she?' I demand.

Another sigh. 'Jen—'

'Tell me!'

'She went out almost as soon as she got in and told me not to wait up. I don't know where she is. She's seventeen. She'll be fine.'

The hairs stand up on the back of my neck and, even though I don't say anything, Bryan must pick up on something.

'Is something wrong?' he adds.

'I—'

I'm so close to telling him everything that I have to bite the tip of my tongue to stop the words coming out.

'Will you tell her to call me?' I say.

'That's not—'

'Please, just ask her. At least let me know when she's home.'

He sighs one more time. 'Fine. Is that everything?'

I tell him that it is and then hang up.

I try calling Katie one more time but it rings through to her voicemail. I leave a short message, although I'm not sure what I say. Something about calling me when she gets it, I think.

With little other option, I send a message back.

Me: *What do you mean?*

The reply is instant – and the stuff of my nightmares. The photo comes through first: a close-up of Katie on her side, lips slightly apart, eyes closed. I can imagine her breathing deeply, with a pillow clutched to her chest. Moments after the photo, another message arrives.

Anon: *Do as you're told and she'll be fine. You have until midnight*

FORTY

I scroll up to the previous message – *Kill Josh Tanner* – and it doesn't feel real. It's a few minutes past four p.m. Eight hours to go.

Me: *How?*

Anon: *I don't care. You pick. Run him over if you want. It wouldn't be the first time*

I try calling Katie again but the outcome is the same as on the first three occasions. I don't leave a message this time. I shouldn't have underestimated the person that's been messaging me. I shouldn't have stopped responding. Whoever it is has Katie.

What do I do?

The obvious answer is to tell the police? I could – but by the time I've finished explaining that it was me who hit Sharon – plus gone into detail about all the texts since, how much time would be left to find Katie?

I stare at the photo of her unconscious, fearing she's been drugged and looking for any sort of clue as to where she could be. All I can see is the pimple close to her temple that matches the one I saw on her this morning. There's no chance this is a trick, or an old photograph. This is now.

If I can't go to the police, and I don't know where she is, then what options are left?

Josh is a bully who has seemingly made life worse for a lot of people – but can I really kill him to save my daughter? Can I kill any person? *Really?*

Even if I wanted to, then *how?* This isn't America, where everyone seemingly has a gun under their pillow and two more lying around the living room. The only thing this plan has going for it is that Josh is likely to be at his home at some point this evening. Sharon and Frank are both apparently still in hospital.

I head upstairs and change into my dark jeans with a black top then go to the kitchen and take the biggest knife from the rack. It's the one I use to chop vegetables and is pointy and sharp at the tip, with a thick, solid blade near the handle. It's light in my hand, though not particularly easy to conceal. I return it to the rack, then immediately pick it up again.

I have no other ideas.

After grabbing the gloves from the pockets of my jacket, I put on the black anorak that I haven't worn since Bryan and I got into the habit of weekend walks a few years ago. As soon as the damp weather hit, we – or, more specifically, *I* – quickly got out of the habit. It's not warm but it is dark and, for now, that will do. I put on the hiking boots I've not worn in over a year and take a look at myself in the mirror. It's not vanity, not really. I stare into my own eyes, looking for any hint of the person I'm supposed to be.

I'm definitely different. There's something in my eyes that goes so far beyond tiredness. So much has happened in the last four days that I fear that person I used to be is long gone.

I get into the car and reverse out of the garage onto the road. Aside from skipping onto the alley at the back of the corner shop to avoid the camera, I take the same route as I did four days ago when I was off to collect Katie. Saturday evenings might be buzzing in other areas of the country – but not in Prowley. The locals will be tucked up in their cosy living rooms, with the heating cranked up, waiting for *Strictly*, or whatever else is on TV tonight. There is barely a car on the road and, as soon as I pass the town limits and get onto the country lanes, it's deserted.

The moon shines white across the overhanging trees and the verges are damp with dew. The sky is clear and the constellations blink so brightly that they are impossible to miss.

I slow to a stop and then turn off the engine as I reach the entrance to Dawn's house. The driveway winds up a slope and leads to a wide stone bungalow. Even though it's only one storey, I would guess it's big enough to hold at least three bedrooms. There is a chimney at either end and I flashback to my fantasies of opening presents in front of a roaring Christmas morning fire. It was only ever a fiction. When I first found out that Bryan had moved into Dawn's house, I would park on the other side of the road – like now – and yearn for a life that would never be mine. It took me a long time to admit that I'm jealous of her – but I am. I'm envious of him, too.

Katie should be in there. I should have told Bryan to keep her inside and make sure she was safe.

It's too late now.

I call Katie again but it doesn't ring this time. There's a pause and then a message to say the phone is out of service.

It was about a year ago when I asked her why she never answered her phone. She looked at me crookedly, as if I was some sort of alien, and then said that *nobody* answers their phones. 'Just text me,' she said. 'That's what *normal* people do.'

I do just that, asking Katie to contact me when she reads the message. I get the little 'sent' indicator underneath but Katie turned off the 'read' notifications that used to let me know she'd seen my messages. She did that because I'd always ask why she hadn't got back to me.

There's a light on inside Dawn and Bryan's house and I can imagine them inside, enjoying that Saturday evening in front of

Strictly. Aside from blaming me, what would Bryan do if he knew Katie was in danger? He already said he didn't know where she was.

It's as I'm thinking of Bryan that I realise the one other option I have. I scroll through the contacts in my phone until I find the name 'Helen'. Richard's mother and I swapped numbers when we first met. Aside from brief hellos and the meeting in the garage, we've had no interaction since.

I call her and hold my breath as it rings once… twice.

'Hello…?'

'Is that Helen?'

'Who's this?'

'This is Jennifer, Katie's mum. I was wondering if Katie's at your house…?'

There's a pause that feels like it lasts an age. She's going to say yes and this will all be revealed to be a misunderstanding…

'I've not seen her since last weekend.'

My stomach lurches. She's gone.

'Is Richard in?'

'No…'

'I don't suppose you could give me his phone number, could you?'

There's another pause, though I can sense the confused reluctance from the other end of the line. If it had been the other way around and Helen had called me for the first time ever and asked for Katie's contact details, I doubt I'd have passed them on.

'Is something wrong?'

'No… just that I've not been able to get hold of her.' I take a breath and then try to laugh it off with: 'You know what they're like.'

Helen doesn't laugh – but she does tell me to hang on a minute. The line goes silent and I sit waiting and watching as my breath spirals ahead of me. It's probably only a few seconds – but it feels like an age. Helen returns with no build-up.

'—It's oh-seven-five-four…'

I have to tell her to wait and then put her on speakerphone as I write the numbers into the condensation on the inside of my window. There's probably a cleverer way of using the phone *and* entering a number into contacts – but I don't know it.

When Helen is done, I thank her and then hang up before typing Richard's number into my phone and pressing dial.

It rings.

And rings.

Then he answers with a crisp: 'Hello…?'

'Is that Richard?'

'Yes…'

'It's Jennifer… I was wondering if you've seen Katie today?'

There's a muffled cough as I presume he holds the phone away from his mouth – and then he's back. 'I saw her a few hours ago,' he says.

'Is she with you now?'

'No…'

The cramps are back in my stomach.

'When did you see her?'

'Near the green. We were going to do something together but she said she needed to be alone for a bit. We're going to meet up tomorrow instead.'

'Do you know anyone else who might know where she is?'

'I don't think so. I assumed she was at home.' There's a pause and then: 'Is she okay…?'

There's no good way to answer this.

'She'll be fine,' I say. 'But if you hear from her, can you ask her to call me? *Actually* call.'

There's a brief silence and I know this sounds erratic and anything but convincing.

'I'll ask…'

Neither of us know what to say next, so I mumble a 'thanks' and then hang up.

She's gone.

I check the photo and take in the curves of her face, the shape of her nose. Even the spot near her temple. Where could she have been taken? It must be someone she knows, else why would she have gone with them? Unless she didn't – and she scratched and fought instead?

It's almost half past five and I've wasted more than an hour. I switch on the engine and continue for a few hundred metres or so along Green Road until there's a turn-off. It's a gravelly path that would be used by a farmer to get a tractor onto the adjacent field. At this time of night, especially in December, the chances of anyone using it are zero.

I park underneath the trees and, after walking back to the road, it's so dark that I can't see the vehicle, even though I know it's there.

The knife hangs heavy from where it is buried in the inner pocket of my anorak. I grip the handle through the material of the jacket and tell myself I know what I'm doing. Tell myself that whatever happens next is for Katie. It always has been, all along.

The irony isn't missed as I walk along the edge of the road towards Sharon's house. Given the speed I was doing, it would have been around this spot when my phone pinged with that text which started it all. It feels so different now that the rain has stopped. There's something beautiful about the crisp wintry white that now grips the edges of the roads.

It's not long until I'm standing at the entrance to Sharon's house. There are more flowers spread throughout the verge, plus a selection of small cards scattered among the colour. Someone has tied a soft bear to the gatepost.

I've already caused so much needless harm to this family.

The car with no wheels is still propped up on the driveway – but as I take a step onto the gravel, I spot the other vehicle parked next to it.

Josh isn't alone.

There are lights inside the house, though no sign of anyone moving around. I creep through the shadows until I'm at the back of the rusting car, where I hunch onto a pair of breeze blocks that have been tossed to the side. The ground crunches underneath my feet from a smattering of broken glass and scraps of rubble that are strewn across the ground.

The knife feels heavier now.

Light from my phone pierces the night as I hastily shield it with my hand. I try calling Katie once more but it doesn't ring. There have been no more texts – and certainly nothing from her. It's almost six o'clock.

The blocks are angled and uncomfortable underneath me and I watch my breath swirl into the night as the cold bristles through my jacket.

I don't know what to do.

There are no winners from any of this.

The front door of the house opens in a blink, sending a corridor of light across the drive. I remain swallowed by the shadows, still like a statue, as two figures emerge from the doorway. The height makes Josh's silhouette unmistakable – and there's a smaller, hunched figure hanging onto his arm once more. It's the same woman that I saw him with at the church; likely his grandmother.

They stop to say something to one another on the front porch – but, even though they're not that far away, the burn of cold on my ears makes everything sound as if it's underwater.

Josh guides her away from the house and along the drive until they get to the car that has wheels. The woman fumbles with her bag and then some keys before the car's indicator lights flash in unison. It takes her a while to get into the driver's seat as she goes down in stages. Knees first, hand on seat, back arched, knees bent a bit more, head dipped, knees bent a bit more… and in.

The headlights flare against the house as the engine rumbles. It feels as if the earth itself is trembling as she reverses in a crescent before surging forward. The lights flail across the propped-up car, momentarily dousing me in brightness before dipping away again. I don't move. I barely breathe. Seconds later and the car has gone.

Josh stands impassively on the driveway, clouded by the night. I can't see his face but the moon sends his shadow trailing back towards the house. He doesn't move, though I can see his breath dancing into the dark as he stares towards the abandoned car. Towards me. I can feel his piercing gaze boring through the black and have to fight the urge to shiver. And then, as if it was never there, it's gone. He spins and heads back to the house, closing the door behind him.

He shouldn't be alone but he is. I tell myself that he's still a boy, even though he looks like a man. Perhaps I should be trying to convince myself of the opposite.

I try calling Katie again but it doesn't ring. There are no more text messages and there is no more hope. Tick tock.

The knife slides out from my pocket and instantly catches the light of the moon. It's so heavy that my arm aches as I clutch it. I will go to the door, knock, wait for Josh to answer, and then stab him there and then.

Despite hiding the car, plus the dark outfit and the gloves, there is no chance of me escaping this. I will leave DNA and hair particles. There will be blood: definitely his and maybe mine. Even by sitting on this cold, crusty breeze block, there will be fibres from clothes left behind. If we were complete strangers, there might be no trace back to me – but that's far from the truth.

It's over for me – and that's if I manage it. Josh is bigger than me. Stronger. All I have is surprise and hope.

I'm doing this for Katie. It's me for her.

I edge across the crunchy gravel towards the front door, then, with the knife clutched tightly in one hand, I ring the doorbell with the other.

FORTY-ONE

There's a bored-looking woman at the police station counter. Hard to blame her considering there's a little over a week until Christmas and it's a Saturday evening. The bigger surprise is that this station is still open at the weekends.

A tall window separates us and she takes me in with the air of someone who is used to nutters wandering in at this time of the weekend.

'Can I help you?' she asks.

I step closer to the window. 'My name is Jennifer Hughes,' I say. 'I'm the person who drove into Sharon and Frank Tanner last week.'

She stands up straighter, eyes widening. Not what she was expecting.

'Sorry… you…?'

I point towards the poster at the front of the station that has the picture of the silver car. 'That was me,' I say. 'I was driving. Someone has been blackmailing me ever since. They have my daughter. You can do whatever you want to me – but please go find her first.'

The white of the woman's eyes flare and she seems momentarily frozen before she springs up. 'Give me one moment,' she says – and then she bounds off through a side door.

The reception area of the station is silent and empty. There's something old-fashioned about the browny-cream walls and the tiled floor, combined with the slightly off-white lights.

I should have come here three hours ago. I should have come here four days ago.

There's a bump from beyond the doors but nobody emerges. It's then that my phone starts to ring. I pluck it from my pocket and stare at the screen. RICHARD.

I press to answer.

'Hello…?' I say.

I'm expecting a male voice – but it isn't. It's Katie.

'Mum…?'

There's such relief that I can barely get the words out. My knees crumple and I have to lean on the counter to hold myself up.

'Are you safe?' I ask.

'Of course I am.'

'Where have you been?'

'What do you mean?'

'I've been trying to call you.'

'I lost my phone, Mum.' There's a short silence and I have no idea how to process what's going on. 'Is this about me coming home, because—'

My attention is drawn by the dual doors opening. The woman emerges back behind the glass, while a man in a police uniform enters through a second door on my side of the counter. I don't recognise him and he looks me up and down, his face stony and grim.

'Ms Hughes…? I gather you have something you want to tell me…?'

FORTY-TWO

DAYS LATER

My back creaks as I ease down onto the plastic chair in the white-washed interview room. The officer says this is a favour to me and that they don't have to do this. After the time I've been here, I'm grateful for anything. My solicitor says I'll be in court in a few hours and I don't think many favours will be forthcoming after that.

There's a clink from the door and then Katie edges inside. I can tell from the way she sidesteps inside with her hands behind her back that she's nervous. Hard to blame her for that. The police station is hardly a welcoming place – but it's still better than the cells downstairs.

I tell myself that she's safe and that's what really matters. It's true but it isn't. Everything else is ruined.

Katie presses further into the room and Richard follows a little behind. His black clothes are sharpened against the white of the room. Behind them, a uniformed officer eyes me, gives a short nod and then closes the door, leaving the three of us inside.

I stand but everything aches, from my neck, all the way along my back and through my legs. Katie moves to the side of the table and we hug – although all the pressure comes from me. She pats my back gently and then moves away to take one of the two seats on the other side of the table from me. Richard slots in next to her and then I sit, too. It feels like they're about to interview me and I suppose, in some ways, they are.

'You look tired,' Katie says.

'It's hard to sleep. The bed is so stiff.'

Katie nods though doesn't respond. I suppose the talking is mine to do.

'I've confessed,' I say.

'To what?'

She will already be aware of what I did – but I know she'll want to hear the words from me. I would if things were reversed.

'I was driving the car that hit Sharon and Frank.'

The words float around the room and settle, leaving an odd sort of relief that they're finally out there. Since I confessed the first time on Saturday evening, I've not been able to stop admitting to everything. It's cathartic.

'It was an accident,' I add. 'I glanced away from the road for a second or two and then…'

'You hit a child,' she says.

'I didn't know that.'

'You drove away.'

I nod to concede the point. I definitely did that. 'I wish I hadn't,' I say.

Katie looks to Richard and something silent passes between them. He takes her hand and squeezes. I've drastically misjudged him. While I'm in here, having done everything I've done, he's been supporting her. She's going to need him more than ever in the next few months. She has exams to do.

She's talking to him when she next speaks. 'I don't think I can listen to any more.'

'Please don't go,' I say.

When she spins back to me, she's angled forward with fury. 'You should have said it was you! You took us to that service at the church and you *knew* the whole time.'

'I know…'

She's worked up and breathing heavily. 'People are saying you were blackmailed…?'

I can't meet her eyes because the betrayal in them is too much. 'Someone knew what I did,' I say.

'Who?'

'I don't know.'

'Do the police know?'

I shake my head. 'I don't think so. They have my phone and all the messages but my solicitor says there's probably no way to trace who sent them. It was done anonymously on the internet.'

'What did they want you to do?'

I take a breath. It feels so silly when I say it out loud – and I've been doing that a lot recently. The regret has almost overwhelmed me – but there's embarrassment, too.

'Small things,' I say. 'At first, anyway. They wanted money.'

I can't bring myself to bring up the stupid drive to McDonald's, or the broken window. It doesn't feel real any longer.

'Is that it?'

'They said you were in danger…'

'Me…?'

It's this that I've not been able to explain in the days since I stood on the driveway of Sharon's house and watched Josh with his grandmother. I was so sure that Katie had been taken.

I don't answer quickly enough and Katie continues, demanding answers. *'When?'*

'Saturday.'

'I wasn't in danger. I just lost my phone.'

'I didn't know that then.'

'But why did you think I was in danger?'

'They sent me a photo of you sleeping.'

Katie's chair grinds against the floor as she shunts herself away from the table. Assuming the police didn't tell her, this is the first time she's heard this.

'…Of me… *sleeping?'*

She shudders.

'I talked to your dad but he said you were out. Richard said he wasn't with you – and I couldn't get hold of you. I got that picture and thought you were…'

I can't finish the sentence.

'I fell asleep on the bus twice this week,' Katie says. 'I fell asleep at the library as well. I've not been sleeping well at night. I keep dropping off…'

She tails off and then looks to Richard at her side.

I wait for Katie to look back to me. This is the question I've been wanting to ask her since my phone rang when I was standing in the reception of the police station. The police themselves probably already know.

'Where were you?' I ask.

'I had to clear my head after what happened.'

She bows her head slightly and that argument over the Adderall pills seems such a long time ago – not to mention inconsequential.

'I didn't go anywhere,' she adds. 'I was in Prowley. I met Richard and we were going to get something to eat – but I wanted to be by myself. He left me and I ended up in the church. It was warm in there – and quiet. Easier to think.'

It's bad of me but when I think of my daughter, it's not in these terms. I see her on her phone, or dressed for football practice. She's grumpy in the morning, or spending hours in her room. There's never this sort of contemplation and it breaks my heart at how I've underestimated the person she is.

'I lost my phone at some point,' she says. 'The man in the church helped me look but I couldn't find it. I still haven't. I have no idea where it went.'

'What did you do then?'

'I used the church phone to call Richard to ask if his mum would pick me up. I couldn't remember anyone else's number. When she got there, his mum said you'd called, so I borrowed Richard's phone to call you back.'

We sit in silence for a moment. All that time I thought Katie was in danger and she was in the church, thinking about our argument.

I stretch my hand across the table, hoping Katie will take it. She stares at my hand for a moment and then slowly, reluctantly, she grips it. She winces slightly and I'm not surprised given how cold my skin is.

There was a time when I thought they might leave me hand-cuffed in here. I suppose being as honest with them as possible – even if it was days too late – has counted for something.

'They wanted me to kill Josh,' I say quietly.

Katie's fingers twitch against mine. She laughs humourlessly, more in disbelief than anything else. 'Who did?'

'Whoever was texting me.'

'Why?'

'I don't know. I guess someone has a grudge.'

'But why would anyone think you'd do that…?'

'Because I thought *you* were in danger. I thought it was you or him.'

Katie catches my eye and, perhaps for the first time since everything unfolded, she realises what a mess this has all become.

'I don't understand,' she says.

'I'm not sure I do, either.'

There's an impasse and I suspect both of us feel bewildered. It's not only the hard bed that's kept me awake these past nights – it is these irreconcilable thoughts.

Katie takes her hand away from me and crosses her arms. 'But Josh is fine…? You'd never do that.'

I nod. Of course he is. Of course I wouldn't.

I stood on his doorstep and rang the bell, before scuttling away into the shadows and praying he didn't see me. He stood on the step for a few seconds and shouted 'I know you're there' into the night before returning inside. When he was gone, I hurried back along the lane to my car – and then drove to the police station.

I should have done that in the first place.

Katie moves on, not realising how close I was to doing as I'd been asked. Or at least attempting. That's one secret I have kept to myself. Nobody needs to know.

'They must have some idea who was messaging you…?'

'I think…' The sentence sticks and I have to try again. It doesn't feel real. 'I think they're trying to say that I sent them to myself…'

Katie's eyes narrow. '*Why?*'

'My solicitor said they think it's because I was trying to get sympathy for what I did in the car.'

I didn't understand it until he explained. There's no proof I left any money in the library. They would know a window was smashed at AD Investments – but that doesn't mean somebody ordered me to do it. Katie was seemingly never in any sort of peril. All I have is a photo of her sleeping that, of everyone, I had the best opportunity to take. The messages were sent via the internet, something which I could have conceivably done.

My solicitor said that, given the time that had passed between the collision and me going to the police station, it looked bad regardless of whether I confessed. Because of the way the texts were sent anonymously, the police might be working under the assumption that I set up the idea of a blackmailer myself. With the story of my week of terror, it might help garner some sympathy.

I couldn't believe it at first. Those texts *happened*. They were sent to me. I lived it.

But then there's the question that I can't answer and never could. The interviewing officer has asked me it at least three times.

How did someone know what I did?

I can't answer it because I don't know. My solicitor says that the police have no CCTV footage of me driving anywhere near the area and no firm witnesses have come forward. Even the description of the silver vehicle was based on a sighting from the vague area that likely wasn't me. If it wasn't for my confession, they wouldn't know what happened. Whatever Leah told me about her dad being close to arresting someone was either a misunderstanding, wrong, or youthful exaggeration.

Because that question can't be answered, it's easier for them to assume I made up the blackmailer in an attempt to gain sympathy.

'Did you…?' Katie cuts herself off but she's already half asked the question, as she wonders whether I sent the messages to myself.

'Of course not.'

'I didn't mean…'

She trails off but I know what she meant. This is what happens when someone you trust does something awful, like plough into someone and then drive off. Nothing they say can then be trusted.

Katie pushes her chair away from the table and starts to stand. 'I think I should go…'

'Please don't.'

She's already turned to the door. 'I'll come back another time, just… not today.'

'I'm not going to be here for long. I'm in court later and then…'

Katie doesn't stop. She mutters 'Dad's outside' – and then she slips through the door. It's happened so quickly that it's left me breathless. Richard hasn't moved from his chair and I suppose the speed of Katie's determination to get away has surprised him too.

'I shouldn't be here,' he says quietly.

'No,' I say, reaching for him. He looks at my hand but doesn't touch it. 'Thank you for supporting Katie,' I add. 'She's going to need you.'

He stands and shakes his head a little. His voice is steady and only a little above a whisper. 'I meant I shouldn't be *here*. I shouldn't be in Prowley. I should be in London.'

'Oh…' I blink at him and can't understand why he's bringing this up. 'I did say I'd help you reapply. I guess not now, but…'

He rocks back on his heels, then angles forward again. 'Do you know why I didn't get in?'

'I thought it was the grades…?'

'No.' I'm still sitting but he leans in further, lowering himself so that our eyes are almost level. 'It's because you didn't want me to. You were supposed to help with tutoring – but where did that get me?'

I stare at him, unsure what to say. I open my mouth to reply but he cuts me off.

'Don't blame me again,' he says. 'Not like every other time. I did my bit.'

'I did my best, too,' I say.

'*Did you?* You were scared Katie would come with me to London, so made sure I had no chance of passing. Now I'm stuck here.'

It isn't only anger in his eyes; there's hatred.

And, suddenly, I know.

'The iPad…' I say.

Richard steps away from the table and doesn't say a word.

'I searched for something like, "What to do if you hit someone while driving". I looked at all those pages about failure-to-stop offences and causing death by dangerous driving…'

He doesn't move but I can see it in him. Nobody saw me on Green Road. I was found out because Richard saw my search history on the iPad. Katie asked to borrow it, saying she wanted it for her coursework. There was something about it being easier to type on her laptop while searching for things on the iPad. It shouldn't have made sense – but I was so distracted by what I'd done that I didn't question her. She said Richard was job-hunting and when she got upstairs, I'm now sure she handed him the iPad. It wasn't Katie who left it on the dresser next to the bathroom: it was Richard.

'Where was your job interview?'

Richard's eye twitches. 'What interview?'

'Katie said you had an interview last week. Was it at AD Investments?'

There's no answer but I know. I was wrong about Gary and that negative review. If he's 'G Porter', then it's a coincidence – because now I *know* what happened.

'You didn't get the job, did you?' I say. 'That's why she hadn't heard from you. That's why you had a grudge against them. You wanted to get away from working with your uncle but they wouldn't hire you.'

Nothing.

He wanted money, because who wouldn't. He wanted me to go to McDonald's not for some stupid picture – but because it left him alone in the house with Katie. What teenage boy wouldn't want that?

Then there was Katie's photo. Aside from me, who else had a better chance to take a picture of her sleeping? She hadn't been drugged, or kidnapped. There was the spot on her temple, showing the photo had been taken that week. He might have even done it after sending me out to the McDonald's. Then Katie told me in not so many words that Josh had been bullying Richard. Leah worked out that Josh only picks on people with two parents, so it even fits into that.

'How long has Josh been bullying you?'

This gets a smirk. 'Who?'

'You stole Katie's phone. Then you texted me to make me think she was in danger. There was always a risk I would find out where she was – but it wouldn't matter. The blackmail would have been over but you hadn't lost anything. You were trying it on. If I did something stupid, then all the better. You didn't know she'd end up back at yours and your mum would say I'd called. When she asked for your phone, you would've thought the fun was over – but you had no idea I was already confessing.'

He opens his mouth and, just for a second, I think he's going to confirm it. He got so lucky. If I'd waited ten minutes longer before going to the police, then Katie would have called me and I would have known she was in no danger. Not even ten minutes.

Richard does speak – but it's not what I want to hear. 'You did this,' he says.

He's calm and measured. Utterly unemotional, as if telling someone the time. He holds my gaze for a moment, wanting me to know that he's beaten me. It might never be proven what he did but I know and so does he. In this moment, that's all that counts. I was still the person who hit Sharon and Frank – and now everybody knows.

He turns to the door.

I try to call him back but my throat is dry and the words are stuck. He's right: I did this to myself. The door clinks open and Richard disappears through, leaving me momentarily alone.

All this time, I've made everything about me. When people were in hospital, I thought of myself. I wondered how *I* could get away with it all, not about the impact on others.

And now, as the door bumps closed, Richard is leaving me here alone to head back to my daughter. The girl of whom he took creepy photos. He's a blackmailer, a manipulator and a liar. He wanted Josh dead. I have no idea whether he's capable of being a murderer, too.

That is who I've left Katie with.

This *is* my fault.

It's not getting to the police station a few minutes before Katie called that cost me everything, it's those two seconds where I turned away from the road.

Two seconds.

Richard has my daughter to himself and there's nothing I can do to save her.

All because of two seconds…

The Perfect Daughter publishing team

Editorial
Ellen Gleeson

Line edits and copyeditor
Jade Craddock

Proofreader
Liz Hatherell

Production
Alexandra Holmes
Hamzah Hussain
Ramesh Kumar Pitchai

Design
Lisa Horton

Marketing
Alex Crow
Hannah Deuce

Publicity
Noelle Holten
Kim Nash
Sarah Hardy

Distribution
Chris Lucraft
Marina Valles

Audio
Nina Winters
Rhianna Louise
Alba Proko
Arran Dutton & Dave
 Perry – Audio Factory
Alison Campbell

Rights and contracts
Peta Nightingale
Saidah Graham
Richard King

Printed in Great Britain
by Amazon